Penguin Books
The Sum of Things

Olivia Manning was born in Portsmouth, Hampshire, spent
much of her youth in Ireland and, as she put it, had 'the
usual Anglo-Irish sense of belonging nowhere'. She married
just before the war and went abroad with her husband,
R. D. Smith, a British Council lecturer in Bucharest. Her
experiences there formed the basis of the work which
makes up *The Balkan Trilogy*. As the Germans approached
Athens, she and her husband evacuated to Egypt and ended
up in Jerusalem, where her husband was put in charge of
the Palestine Broadcasting Station. They returned to
London in 1946 and lived there until her death in 1980.

Olivia Manning's publications include the novels *Artist
Among the Missing* (1949); *School for Love* (1951); *A
Different Face* (1953); *The Doves of Venus* (1955); *The
Balkan Trilogy* (1960–65), which consists of *The Great
Fortune* (1960), *The Spoilt City* (1962) and *Friends and
Heroes* (1965); *The Play Room* (1969); *The Rain Forest*
(1974); and *The Levant Trilogy* (1977–80), which consists of
The Danger Tree (1977, *Yorkshire Post* Book of the Year
award), *The Battle Lost and Won* (1978) and *The Sum of
Things* (1980). She also wrote two volumes of short stories,
Growing Up (1948) and *A Romantic Hero* (1967). She spent
a year on the film script of *The Play Room* and contributed
to many periodicals, including the *Spectator*, *Punch*, *Vogue*
and the *Sunday Times*. Olivia Manning was awarded the
CBE in 1976.

The Balkagle
narrative e rgess
described i ecord
of the war f
personages thos
controlled, gle
certainly is characters in modern fiction.'

Olivia Manning

The Sum of Things

Penguin Books

Penguin Books Ltd, Harmondsworth, Middlesex, England
Penguin Books, 625 Madison Avenue, New York, New York 10022, U.S.A.
Penguin Books Australia Ltd, Ringwood, Victoria, Australia
Penguin Books Canada Ltd, 2801 John Street, Markham, Ontario, Canada L3R 1B4
Penguin Books (N.Z.) Ltd, 182–190 Wairau Road, Auckland 10, New Zealand

First published in Great Britain by Weidenfeld & Nicolson 1980.
Published in Penguin Books 1982
Reprinted 1982

Printed and bound in Great Britain by
Cox & Wyman Ltd, Reading
Filmset in Linotron 202 Plantin

TO THE MEMORY OF JIM FARRELL
TAKEN BY THE SEA AUGUST 1979

The Sum of Things concludes 'The Levant Trilogy' which follows 'The Balkan Trilogy'.

The six volumes comprise one narrative which is called 'Fortunes of War'.

One

In December, when the others, the lucky ones, were advancing on Tripoli, Simon Boulderstone was sent to the hospital at Helwan. Before that he had been held in a field dressing-station then moved to a makeshift first-aid station at Burg el Arab. The desert fighting had so crowded the regular hospitals that no bed could be found for him until the walking wounded were moved on to convalescent homes. While he waited, he was attended by orderlies who gave him what treatment they could. He did not expect much. His condition, he felt, was in abeyance until he reached a proper hospital where, of course, he would be put right in no time.

The Helwan hospital, a collection of huts on the sand, was intended for New Zealanders but after the carnage of Alamein anyone might be sent anywhere. Simon was carried from the ambulance into a long ward formed by placing two huts end to end. Because he was an officer, even though a very junior one, he was given a curtained-off area to himself. This long hut was known as 'The Plegics' because few of the men there could hope to walk again.

Simon did not know that but if he had known, he would have seen in it no reference to his own state. At that time, he exulted in the fact he was alive, when he might so easily have been dead.

He and his driver, Crosbie, had run into a booby trap and, like an incident from a dissolving dream, he could still see Crosbie sailing into the air to land and lie, a loose straggle of limbs, motionless on the ground. In his mind Crosbie would lie there for ever while he, Simon, had been picked up by a Bren and taken back to the living world. And here he was, none the worse for the curious illusion that his body ended half-way down his spine.

The wonder of his escape kept him, during those first days, in a state of euphoria. He wanted to talk to people, not to be shut away at the end of the ward. He asked for the curtains to be opened and when he looked down the long hutment, its walls bare in the harsh Egyptian sunlight, he was surprised to see men in wheel-chairs propelling themselves up and down the aisle. He pitied them, but for himself – he'd simply suffered a blow in the back. It was a stunning blow that had anaesthetized him, so, for a while, he thought more about Crosbie than about himself. It was not until he reached Burg el Arab that he realized part of his body was missing. It seemed he had been cut in half and wondered if his lower limbs were still there. Sliding his hand down from his waist, he could feel his thighs but could not raise himself to reach farther. Speaking quite calmly, he told the man on the next stretcher that he had lost his legs below the knees. He was not surprised. The same thing had happened to his brother Hugo and accidents of this sort ran in families. He had dreaded it but now it had happened, he found he did not mind much. Instead, for some odd reason, he was rather elated. He talked for a long time to the man on the next stretcher before he saw that the man was dead.

The male nurse who dressed his wound asked him if he needed a shot of morphine. Cheerfully, he replied, 'No thanks, I'm all right. I'm fine.'

'No pain?'

'None at all.'

The nurse frowned as though Simon had given the wrong answer.

Brens were arriving every few minutes with wounded from the front lines. Simon was at the first-aid station a couple of days before a doctor was free to examine him. When the blanket was pulled down and he saw his legs were there intact, he felt an amazed pride in them.

'Nothing wrong with me, doc, is there?'

The doctor was not committing himself. He said he suspected a crushed vertebra but only an X-ray could confirm that.

'It'll mend, won't it, doc?'

'It's a question of time,' the doctor said and Simon, taking that to mean his paralysis was temporary, burst out laughing. When the doctor raised his brows, Simon said, 'I was thinking of my driver, Crosbie. He looked so funny going up into the air.'

At Helwan, he was still laughing. Everything about his condition made him laugh. After the early days of no sensation at all, he became subject to the most ridiculous delusions. At times it seemed that his knees were rising of their own accord. He would look down, expecting to see the blanket move. Or he would imagine that someone was pulling at his feet. Once or twice this impression was so strong, he uncovered his legs to make sure he was not slipping off the end of the bed.

And then there was his treatment. His buttocks were always being lifted and rubbed with methylated spirits: 'To prevent bedsores,' the nurse told him. Every two hours he was tilted first on one side and then on the other, a bolster being pushed into his waist to keep him there. The first time this happened, he asked, 'What's this in aid of?'

The nurse giggled and said, 'You'd better ask the physio.'

The physio, a young New Zealander called Ross, did not giggle but soberly told him that the repeated movements helped to keep his bowels active. Not that they were active. The first time a young woman had given him an enema, he had been filled with shame.

She had said, 'We don't want to get all bogged up, do we?' Soon enough the enemas were stopped and suppositories were pushed into him. He became used to being handled and ceased to feel ashamed. He had to accept that his motions were not his to control but after a while, he recognized the symptoms that told him his bladder was full. His heart would thump, or he would feel a pain in his chest, and he must ask to be relieved by catheter.

Ross came in three times a day to move his knees and hip joints, performing the exercises carefully, with grave gentleness.

Everything they did to him enhanced for him the absurdity of his dependence. 'You treat me like a baby,' he said to Ross who merely nodded and tapped his knee.

The tap produced an exaggerated jerk of the leg and Simon, interested and entertained, asked, 'Why does it do that?'

'Just lack of control, sir. Your system's confused – in a manner of speaking, that is.'

Once when his left leg gave a sudden move, he called for Ross, saying, 'I must be getting better.'

11

Ross shook his head: 'That happens, sometimes, sir. It means nothing.'

Even then, Simon's laughter went on, becoming, at times, so near hysteria that the doctor said, 'If we don't calm you down, young man, your return to life will be the death of you.'

He was given sedatives and entered an enchanted half-world, losing all inhibitions. Seeing everything as possible, he asked the staff nurse to telephone Miss Edwina Little at the British Embassy and tell her to visit him.

'Your girlfriend, is she?'

'I'd like to think so. She was my brother's girlfriend. I don't know whose girlfriend she is now but she's the most gorgeous popsie in Cairo. You wait till you see her. D'you think I'll be out of here soon? I'd like to take her for a spin, go out to dinner, go to a night club . . .'

'Better leave all that till you're on your feet again.'

'Which won't be long now, will it, nurse?'

'I can't say. We'll have to wait and see.'

'You mean it's just a matter of time?'

The nurse, making no promises, said vaguely: 'I suppose you could say that,' and Simon was satisfied. So long as he felt certain he would eventually recover, he could wait for time to pass.

Two

Now that 8th Army had left Egypt, a slumberous calm had come down on the capital: Cairo was no longer a base town. The soldiers that had crowded the pavements, wandering aimlessly, disgruntled and idle for lack of arms, had all been given guns and sent into the fight.

The British advance after Alamein had been impressive but no one thought it would last. Everyone expected a counter-attack that would bring the Afrika Korps back over the frontier. But this time the counter-attack failed and by January, the Germans had retreated so far away, they seemed to be lost in the desert sand.

The few British officers who still took tea in Groppi's garden had an apologetic air, feeling they had been cast aside by the runaway military machine.

It was a pleasant time of the year. Winter in Egypt was no more than a temperate interval between one summer and the next. It did not last long and there was no spring though a few deciduous trees that dropped their leaves from habit were now breaking into bud again. They went unnoticed in Garden City, lost as they were among the evergreens and palms and the dense, glossy foliage of the mango trees. The evenings were limpid and in the mornings a little mist hung like a delicate veil over the riverside walks.

The mid-days were warm enough to carry the threat of heat to come. In the flat that Edwina Little shared with Dobson and Guy Pringle, the rooms that looked on to the next-door garden were already scented by the drying grass.

Dobson, who held an embassy lease, had a room in the cool centre of the flat. The others, in the corridor under the roof, were let to friends. Now only two friends remained. Guy Pringle's wife, Harriet, had left Cairo to board an evacuation ship at Suez.

This ship, the *Queen of Sparta*, was bound for England by way of the Cape. It had sailed a few days after Christmas and now, in January, there was a rumour that she had been sunk in the Indian Ocean with the loss of all on board. Guy, when he heard it, refused to credit it. Rumours were the life of Cairo and usually proved to be wrong. Dobson and Edwina, also suspicious of rumours, agreed behind Guy's back that, until the sinking was confirmed, they would not speak of it or commiserate with him.

He was glad of their silence that seemed to prove the whole thing was a canard. He began to feel it was directed at him because his wife had not wanted to be evacuated. He half suspected his friend Jake Jackman, a noted source of rumours, who had been fond of Harriet and may have resented her going.

Sitting with Jake at the Anglo-Egyptian Union, he said as though to justify himself: 'You know, this climate was killing Harriet. I doubt whether she would have survived another summer here.'

'Yep, she looked like a puff of wind,' Jake agreed then, unable to resist his own malice, he sniggered and pulled at his thin, aquiline nose: 'You know what they say: if you want to know a man's true nature, look at the health of his wife.'

Guy was indignant: 'Who said that? I never heard a more ridiculous statement.'

Jake, having delivered his shaft, was ready to be conciliatory: 'You don't believe these rumours, do you? Leave them be and they'll die of their own accord.'

But they did not die. People who had friends or relatives on board the ship approached Guy and asked if he had any information. Dobson received a letter from a diplomat in Iraq whose wife, Marion Dixon, had sailed on the ship. He appealed to Dobson for news and at last the matter was brought up at the breakfast table, the one place at which the three inmates of the flat met and conversed.

Guy was the first to speak of it. He, too, appealed to Dobson: 'You must have heard this about the *Queen of Sparta* being lost! If it's true, surely you would have had official confirmation by now?'

'Yes, in normal times, but the times aren't normal. The ship had passed out of our sphere of influence so we might not hear for months.'

Edwina, eager to reassure Guy, said: 'Oh, Dobbie, you would have heard by now. Of course you would!'

'Well, we *should* have heard by now, I agree.'

Dobson's tone suggested they might still hear and Guy, disturbed, left the table and went to the Institute where, by keeping himself employed, he could put his anxiety behind him.

After he had gone, Edwina said: 'You know, Dobbie, Guy's not a bit like himself. You can see he's terribly worried but trying to hide it. If Harriet is dead – of course I'm sure she isn't – I know she'd want me to console him. I feel I should, don't you?'

Dobson, regarding her with an ironical smile, asked: 'And how do you propose to do it?'

'Oh, there are ways. I could ask him to take me out. He once took me to the Extase when he found me crying because Peter hadn't turned up. He was really sweet.'

'And what did Harriet say about that?'

'I don't think she said anything. You know we were great friends. I was thinking we might go to a dinner-dance at the Continental-Savoy. I suppose Guy does dance?'

'I don't know. I've never heard of his dancing.'

'I'm sure he can. He's very clever, you know. I sang in his troops' concert and he was wonderful. He said I sang like an angel.'

'I hope, in the midst of this mutual admiration, you won't forget he's married to Harriet.'

'Dobbie, how could you say that? I'll never forget Harriet. But when you're doing a show together, a special relationship grows up. That's what Guy and I have: a special relationship.'

Dobson laughed indulgently and Edwina remembered another special relationship. 'You remember that nice boy Boulderstone who was killed, the one I liked so much? What was he called?'

'I can't remember.'

'Well, now his brother's been wounded. He's in hospital at Helwan and I've promised to go and see him. It's quite a journey, so if I'm late this evening at the office, you'll understand, won't you, Dobbie dear?'

Dobson laughed again and said: 'Don't worry. We'll forgive you, as we always do, my dear.'

Edwina's appearance in Plegics caused a wondering silence to come down on the men. Anyone who could move his neck, followed her as she walked the length of the long ward to find Simon at the farther end. She was wearing a suit of fine white wool and the heels of her white kid shoes tapped on the wooden floor. The whiteness of her clothing enhanced the gold of her hair and skin. Becoming aware of the intent gaze of the men, she shook her hair back from her right eye and smiled, kindly but vaguely, from side to side.

Simon, as she approached, shared the wonder of the ward. When she reached him and sat beside him, saying: 'How are you, Simon dear?', he sank back against his pillows, benumbed, without power to reply.

She put some white carnations on the table then leant towards him so he was enveloped both by the scent of the flowers and the heavy scent she was wearing. He remembered that Hugo had ordered him to buy perfume for her at an expensive little West-End shop: *Gardenia* perfume. For some moments its aroma was more real than her presence. Though he had been expecting her, he could only marvel that a creature so beautiful, so elegant, so far removed from the desert suburb of Nissen huts and sand, should come to visit him.

Misunderstanding his silence, she asked in a tone of concern: 'You haven't forgotten me, have you?'

'Forgotten you?' He gave a laugh that was nearly a sob: 'How could I forget you? I've thought of no one else since I first saw you.'

'Oh, Simon, really!' His vehemence disconcerted her. That he was infatuated with her, did not surprise her, but she was not quite the girl she had been at their last meeting. She, too, had been infatuated, not with this poor boy but with a man, an Irish peer, who, having pursued their affair in a carefree, generous manner, had ended it by telling her he was already married. He had returned to the desert and she had lost not only him, but some inner confidence. And all the time she had been yearning for Peter Lisdoonvarna, this young lieutenant had been yearning for her! At the thought, she smiled sadly and he asked anxiously:

'What's the matter, Edwina? You aren't cross with me for saying that?'

'Cross? No, not a bit cross, but do you remember that colonel, Lord Lisdoonvarna? He was in the flat when you came to tell us about your brother's death.'

'You bet I do. Because of him, I got a liaison job. He put my name up for it. Jolly decent of him, wasn't it?'

'I didn't know about that.'

Now, knowing, this act of kindness made her loss seem the greater. Tears blurred her eyes and she said in a breaking voice: 'Oh, Simon, you've no idea how he treated me. It was dreadful. I haven't got over it.' She paused, shaking her head to control herself: 'He deserted me. Yes, deserted. For months we went everywhere together. He simply appropriated me, so I never had a chance to see anyone else. Then, would you believe it, he felt he'd had enough and he wangled his return to his unit.'

'That's monstrous!' Simon stretched out his hand and she put her hand into it. He had been outraged when he believed she had rejected Hugo, and he was outraged now because Lisdoonvarna had rejected her. He could only say, 'I am sorry,' but it was such heartfelt sorrow that Edwina squeezed his hand.

'Dear Simon, what a comfort you are!' She looked into his face that was so like his brother's face and, seeing in it the same youth and sensitivity and absolute niceness, she was moved to something like love for him. She said: 'Let's forget Peter. There are other men in the world, aren't there? You're so sweet, you restore my faith in myself. I'd begun to think no one would ever find me attractive again.'

'Good lord! Why, my brother Hugo said . . .'

'Yes, Hugo,' Edwina seized on the name that had been evading her: 'Hugo was wonderful. You know, he was the one for me. I was just dazzled by Peter, that was all. He was a lord and a colonel and . . . well, I was silly, wasn't I?'

Simon felt there was some confusion in this protest but said: 'So you were Hugo's girl, after all?'

'Oh, yes, I was. Of course I was. And you know, Simon, you're so like him. Your face, the way you speak, everything about you. Just like Hugo.' She smiled encouragingly at him.

Though good-looking officers did not offer much of a future, they were a lot of fun while they lasted.

Smiling back at her, Simon said: 'We used to be mistaken for twins. My mother said that sometimes she couldn't tell us apart.'

'But how are you, Simon. You seem quite well. There can't be much wrong with you. You weren't badly wounded, were you?'

'No, it's nothing much. I was hit by a piece of flak. I'll soon be out and about, and I wonder! If I got hold of a car, would you let me take you for a drive?'

'I'd love it.'

The word 'love' spoken by Edwina quite overthrew him. He flushed as a thought came into his head, probably the most daring thought of his whole life. If he seemed to her so like Hugo, might she not feel for him as she had felt for his brother? After all, he was the survivor and the survivor was, by right, the inheritor. As his blush deepened, he had to explain that he was still running a temperature. Because it was winter, it did not worry him much but in summer it would be tiresome.

Edwina, not taken in, responded to his hopeful, aspiring gaze as she had responded to many other young men. She smiled a smile that was enticing and slightly mischievous, and seemed to Simon full of promise. He remembered that like Peter Lisdoon-varna, he was already married, but what did that matter? He had been married for only a week before he was sent to join the draft. Now that week had sunk so far out of sight, it might never have existed.

They were still holding hands but Edwina felt she could now loosen her fingers. As she did so, Simon gripped them tighter and said, 'Don't leave me yet.'

'I'm afraid I must.' Laughing, she slid from his grasp and picked up her gloves and handbag: 'I'm a working girl, you know. I have to go back to the Embassy.'

'But you'll come again?'

'Of course I will.' She touched his cheek with her finger-tips: 'Again and again and again. So, just for now: goodbye.'

Choked with gratitude for this promise, he could scarcely say, 'Goodbye.'

Watching her as she walked away down the ward, his mood changed. His exaltation had reached its apogee during her visit and as she departed, his excitement went with her. He saw the men in wheel-chairs shift to let her pass and for the first time, he identified himself with them. He realized what sort of ward it was and why he was in it. Terror formed like a knot in his chest and he moved restlessly against his pillows, in acute need of reassurance.

For some time the only person who came near was the orderly with his tea. Simon caught at his arm and tried to question him, but the orderly only said: 'Don't ask me, sir. Afore I come to this kip, all I'd ever done was shovel coal.'

'Where's the doctor? Why hasn't he come round? I must see him.'

The orderly, a big, red-haired fellow, looked pityingly at him and said: 'Don't you get upset, sir. It'll be all right. The physio'll be here in a minute.'

Simon let the man go then lay, impatient for Ross to arrive. He realized that all his laughter, all his high spirits, had been a screen to divide him from the poor devils in the wheel-chairs.

He heard them singing an old troops' song that they had adopted as their theme song. He had taken it to be, 'Beautiful Dreamer, Queen of my song/I've been out in Shiba too fucking long . . .'

Now, hearing it again, he realized it was something different:

> Beautiful Dreamer, Queen of my Song,
> I've been here in Plegics too fucking long . . .

and this ward was Plegics – paraplegics, quadraplegics! They sang mournfully, going on to the next lines:

> Send out the *Rodney*, send the *Renown*,
> You can't send the *Hood* for the bleeder's gone down.

How long, he wondered, had some of them been in Plegics? How long was he likely to be there?

When Ross came to his bedside, Simon could appreciate his solemnity.

Ross, seeing his distraught face, made a noise in his throat as though acknowledging the change in him, but said nothing. With his usual gentle efficiency, he uncovered Simon's legs and began to manipulate them.

Looking down at them, Simon could now see how strange they were. Not his legs at all. Having lost their sunburn, they looked to him unnaturally white; marble legs, too heavy to move; lifeless, the legs of a corpse.

The exercises finished, Ross pulled a pencil along Simon's right sole, from heel to toe: 'Feel that?'

'No.'

As the blanket was pulled back over them, Simon imagined his legs disappearing into the darkness of death. He said: 'Wait a moment, Ross. I want you to tell me the truth.' He nodded towards the chairbound men who seemed in the sunset light to be moving in a limbo of infinite patience: 'Am I going to be like them?'

Ross regarded him gravely: 'How long since you copped it, sir?'

Simon had lost count of time since he had been picked up at Gazala but he said: 'About a month.'

'You begin worrying when it's five weeks.'

Ross went to his other patients and Simon, with nothing to do but worry, realized it must be all of four weeks since he and Crosbie ran into the booby trap. The Gazala dogfight had been in the middle of December and he had followed the advance not much later. Now it was January. Early January, but still January. Facing up to the passage of time, his desolation became despair.

The sister, paying her evening visit, came in cheerfully: 'And how are we today?' Meeting with silence, she asked: 'What's the matter? Girlfriend not turn up?'

He did not reply till her ministrations were ended, then he said: 'Sister, if that young lady comes again, I don't want to see her.'

'You'd better tell her that yourself.'

'Please close the curtains.'

The sister, who understood the change in him, pulled the curtains round three sides of his bed and left without saying anything more. On his fourth side there was a window without shutters. He had to tolerate the light but if he could, he would have blotted it out and closed himself into wretchedness as in a tomb.

Three

The *Egyptian Mail* confirmed the sinking of the *Queen of Sparta* but in its report there was reason for hope. A correspondent in Dar-es-Salaam had informed the paper that one life-boat, crowded with women and children, had got away. Its steering was faulty and it drifted for ten days before being sighted by fishermen who towed it into Delagoa Bay. By that time the children and some of the adults had died of thirst and exposure.

But not all. Not all. There had been survivors.

Edwina said earnestly to Guy: 'I'm sure, I'm *absolutely* sure, that Harriet is alive.'

Guy became as sure as she was and his natural good-humour returned. His nagging fears and anxiety were displaced by the certainty that any day now Harriet would cable him from Dar-es-Salaam.

He said: 'She's a born survivor. After all she's been through since war began, ten days in an open boat would mean nothing to her.'

Dobson agreed: 'She looked frail but these frail girls are as tough as they come.'

Guy said, 'Yes,' before being caught in an accusing memory of why she had been persuaded on to the boat in the first place. But all that was past. When she returned to Cairo, neither he nor anyone else would talk her into going if she did not want to go.

Seeing Guy himself again, Edwina said: 'Oh, Guy darling, do let's have an evening out together!'

'Perhaps, when I have some free time.'

'Let's go to the dinner-dance at the Continental-Savoy.'

'Heavens, no.' Guy was aghast at the suggestion. He said he would celebrate Harriet's return, preferably when Harriet was safely back, but nothing would get him to the Continental-Savoy.

'Oh!' Edwina sighed sadly: 'Didn't you ever go dancing with Harriet?'

'No, never.'

'Poor Harriet!'

Not liking that, Guy left her and she set out for Helwan where she expected more cordial entertainment.

Certain of her welcome, she did not enquire for Simon at the office but went straight down the ward to where he lay, hidden behind curtains. Parting the curtains, she said, 'Hello,' but there was no reply. Simon gave her one glance, filled with a suffering that disturbed her, then turning away, pulled the cover over his face. She was perplexed by the change in him. He was no longer her ardent admirer but a shrunken figure that seemed to be sinking into a hole in the bed.

'What is it, Simon?' She bent over him, trying to rouse him: 'Don't you want to see me?'

His silence was answer enough. It occurred to him that his legs were not the only part of him that might never function again. He not only hid under his blanket but turned his face into the pillow. Standing beside him, she said several times: 'Simon dear, do talk to me. Tell me what's the matter.'

He at last mumbled, 'Go away,' and unable to bear the misery that hung over the gloomy little cubicle, she left him. At the other end of the ward, she went to the sister's office and asked what had caused this dramatic change in Mr Boulderstone.

The sister said, 'He'll get over it. It happens to all of them. First, they're up in the air, thankful to be alive, then they realize what being alive probably means. It's not easy to accept that one may never walk again. Still, if he's worth his salt, he'll meet the challenge. Next time you come, I expect he'll be trying to cheer *you* up.'

'Cheer me up? But he told me he'd be out of here in no time.'

'Even if he recovers – and I don't say there isn't still a chance – it'll be a long haul before we get him on his feet again.'

The sister, a homely, vigorous, outspoken woman, gave Edwina a critical stare, weighing her ability to face up to this information, and Edwina could only say, 'Poor Simon, I didn't know. I thought . . .' but she did not say what she thought. She was dismayed to learn of Simon's condition and dismayed, too, that the sister had summed her up correctly. They both knew she would not come to Helwan again.

Returning to Cairo, she told herself the visit had been too painful and what could she do for a man so lost in misery, he would only say, 'Go away'? Yet she was hurt by the sister's judgement and wondered how to discount it. By the time the train reached the station, she had found a way out of her discomposure. She could not go to Helwan again but someone could go in her place. She decided that Guy, so warm, so magnanimous, was the one to take Simon in hand.

When this was put to him next morning, Guy agreed at once. He was always ready to visit people in hospital. Of course he would see the poor boy.

'I'll go on my day off.'

Guy's day off was often a day of work but the following Saturday would be given up to Simon Boulderstone. He was leaving the flat to catch the Helwan train when Dobson came in the front door. Dobson had gone to the office and, for some reason, had come back again.

He said, 'Guy!' The unusual solemnity of his tone stopped Guy with a premonition of evil tidings. Dobson put an arm round his shoulder.

'Guy, I didn't telephone – I had to come and tell you myself. We've had official confirmation that the evacuation ship was sunk by enemy action. Only three people survived in the life-boat. We had their names this morning. Harriet was not among them.'

Guy stared at him: 'I see, Harriet was not among them,' then shifting his shoulder from under Dobson's arm, he hurried from the flat.

Four

On the day before Edwina's second visit, Simon had come of age. He had once thought of his twenty-first birthday as the summit of maturity, a day that would change him from a youth to a man. Having climbed up to it through the muddle of adolescence, he would find himself on a proper footing with the world. His parents would give him a party and someone important, like his Uncle Harry who was a town councillor, would make a speech and hand him a golden key, saying it was not only the key of the door but the key to life.

As it was, the day passed like any other day. He did not mention it even to Ross. Here in Plegics it had no meaning, but that night he had a dream. He dreamt he was running through the English countryside, running and leaping over miles of green grass. When he came to a hedge, he took a very high leap, a pre-ternatural leap. It lifted him so high into the air, he felt he was flying and when he came down he said as he woke: 'That was to celebrate.' The elation of the dream remained with him for several seconds then faded, and he knew there was nothing to celebrate.

After Edwina's second visit, he began to think of suicide. Death would solve everything, but how to achieve it? Nothing lethal – no sleeping pills, no poisonous substances, not even the meths bottle – was ever left within his reach. They saw to that. He was like a child in their hands and he had begun to feel like a child, dependent, obedient, resentful.

He was wondering if he could smother himself, or refuse to eat till he died of starvation, when someone came fumbling through the curtains. He expected a nurse but the newcomer was not a nurse. He was a padre.

'Thought you'd like to see one of us,' the padre said. 'I'd've come sooner but we're in demand these days. Was talking to your quack and he said you were in high old heart. Glad to be alive and all that. Expect you'd like to give thanks, eh?' Getting no reply, the padre explained himself: 'Give thanks to the One Above I meant, of course. Eh?'

Still no reply. The padre's red-skinned face, like a badly shaped potato, remained amiable but he was puzzled by Simon's silence. 'C of E aren't you?'

Simon nodded. He knew he had made a mistake in putting down 'C of E'. He had been warned often enough by his old sergeant in the desert: 'Don't never admit to nothing, sir. Whatever they ask you, you say, "Don't know," then they can't get at you, see!' But 'don't know' had not seemed the right answer when one was asked to state one's religion. Anyway, it was too late to retract now. The padre, satisfied by the nod, took out his pipe and gained time by stuffing the bowl.

'Can't get round much, can you?'

Simon shook his head.

'That's all right. We've got a special arrangement for chaps like you. We bring the Eucharist right here to your bedside. Chaps find it a great comfort. Now, how about after Sunday service?'

Simon shook his head again.

'You mean you're not a regular communicant?'

'I mean, I want to be left alone.'

The padre, undefeated, put his pipe in his mouth and began to deal with the situation: 'Depressed, are you? What's the quack been saying?'

'Nothing. He didn't need to. My legs are useless.'

'But it's not permanent.'

'It probably is. They've been like it a bit too long.'

'Oh, cheer up, old chap. Keep your pecker up. Even if it comes to the worst, you're only one chap among a lot of chaps who've been unlucky. You must remember Him. Think of His sacrifice. Think of the sparrow's fall. Think of His love.'

Simon began to feel sorry for the padre. It could not be easy preaching the love of God to young men whose future had been ended before it began.

The padre went on: 'You're down now, but it won't last. You'll jump out of it, see if you don't. And if the old legs don't shape up, well, it's not the end of the world. You can be thankful you're a para and not a tetra. There's still plenty you can do. You can earn a living, you can swim, you can play games . . .'

'*Games!*'

'Yes, you'd be surprised. They'll teach you all sorts of larks. And everywhere there'll be people to help you.'

What people? Simon asked himself when the padre had gone. Who would have time for a legless man? – a legless, impotent man? He had an appalled picture of Edwina, driven by pity, pushing him round in a chair like a baby in a perambulator. Everyone using the soothing, patronising, simplified speech reserved for infants and invalids.

'Not for me,' he told himself, but what was to become of him? His brother had bled to death in No-man's-land when his legs were blown off. Had he lived, he could have been fitted with two artificial legs but what happened to a man whose legs were in place but no use to him? He was simply the prisoner of their existence. No doubt people would help him. Some girl might even offer to marry him but no, one life wasted was enough.

He wondered why the ward looked so bare. When he had been with men on the troopship and in the desert, each had kept, like a private reredos, his pictures of women. But there were no pictures in the ward. It occurred to him that this fact was a symptom of the loss of manhood. When the sister next came round, he said to her: 'No pin-ups.'

'No what?'

'Bare walls. No pin-ups.'

'I should think not, indeed! We don't want our nice, clean walls cluttered with that sort of rubbish.'

So that was it! Perhaps, after all, some spark would remain to torment him.

That day another visitor came fumbling through the curtains. He was afraid the padre had returned, or perhaps it was one of those welfare workers who imposed themselves on the other ranks. But the newcomer was not the padre and did not look like a welfare worker. Peering short-sightedly into the shadowed cubicle, he did not seem sufficiently purposeful or righteous of manner, and there was a largeness about him, not only of the flesh but of the spirit, that did not suggest to Simon any sort of organized mission. The pockets of his creased linen jacket were stuffed with books and papers, and he held under his arm some bags of fruit and a bunch of flowers, all badly crushed.

His appearance startled Simon into sitting up and saying: 'Hello.'

'Hello. I'm Edwina's deputy. I live in the same flat. My name's Guy Pringle. She asked me to come because she could not come herself.' Guy dropped the flowers and bags of fruit on to the table and sat down: 'I've brought you these things. If there's anything else you need, let me know.' He began to pull books from his pockets: 'I thought these might interest you. I can get more from the Institute library.'

'Thanks, but I'm not much of a reader.' Then, feeling he must acknowledge Guy's gifts, he picked up a book: 'Still, I'd like to look at them.'

While Guy talked about the books, Simon's dejection lifted a little. Here, he supposed, was one of those who would help him but more important than that, one from whom he was not unwilling to accept help. He wondered how this large man fitted into the Garden City flat. When he went there, just after Hugo's death, the inmates had all been women. There was Edwina, of course, and a strange woman called Angela Hooper, and there was the dark girl Harriet.

He said: 'You're called Pringle? Then you must be the husband of Harriet Pringle?'

Guy's head jerked up. He caught his breath before he said: 'You knew her?'

'Yes, we went together on a trip into the desert. And we climbed the Great Pyramid and sat at the top talking about Hugo. He was alive then. She said you met in Alex and had supper with him. He was killed a month later.'

'Yes, I heard. I was very sorry. Harriet is dead, too.'

'Harriet! Your wife?'

'Yes, she was lost at sea. She went on an evacuation ship that was torpedoed and only three people were saved. But not Harriet. Not poor Harriet.' Then, to Simon's consternation, Guy choked and put his face into his hands, giving way to such an anguish of grief that Simon stared at him, forgetting his own misery. He had seen men weep before. He himself had wept bitterly over Hugo's death, but the sight of this man so violently over-thrown by sorrow shocked him deeply.

Guy gasped: 'Forgive me. I've only just heard . . .'

'But if three were saved, there might be more somewhere . . .'

'No.' Guy tried to dry his face with a handkerchief but his tears welled out afresh: 'No, only one boat got away. The steer-ing was broken and it drifted until it was taken into Dar-es-Salaam. By then there were only three people left alive.'

'There could have been other boats that went to different places.'

'I would have heard by now. Wherever she was, she would have cabled me. She wouldn't leave me in suspense.'

Simon, not knowing what other comfort he could offer, shook his head despondently: 'People are dying all the time now. Young people. I mean not people you might expect to die. People with their lives before them.'

'Yes, this accursed war.'

They were silent, contemplating the calamity of their time, while Guy scrubbed his handkerchief over his face and looked, red-eyed, at Simon. Simon looked back in sympathy but as he did so, he felt – not quite a sensation, rather a presentiment of sensation to come, then there was a stirring in his left upper leg as though an insect were crawling under his skin. He put his hand down and touched the spot but the skin was smooth. No insect there. He tried to disregard it, knowing Ross would say, 'It means nothing.'

'I suppose it will end one day,' Guy was saying, 'but that won't bring them back . . .'

Simon was about to say that grief did fade in time; that it be-came no more than a sadness at the back of the mind, but he was distracted as the insect movement repeated itself in his thigh. Then a trickle, slow and steady, rather sticky, like blood, ran down to his knee and he again touched the spot. He looked at his fingers. There was no blood. He was afraid to hope that the trick-le was a trickle of life. Guy was speaking but he could not listen. His whole consciousness was gathered on the area of the sensa-tion. A pause, then the insect moved in his other leg and the same sticky trickle went down to his knee. Cautiously, he tried to

28

press his thighs together and for the first time since his injury, he felt his legs touch each other. He held his breath before letting it out in his excitement, and he knew this was the sign he had longed for, the sign that one day he would walk again.

In his relief, he wanted to shout to Guy, expecting him to rejoice with him, but he was checked by the sight of the other man wiping tears from his face.

Simon repressed, or tried to repress his joy, but his joy transcended his sense of decorum and he could not hide his laughter.

Guy was too absorbed by his own emotion to notice Simon's and Simon bit his lip to control himself. Guy said it was time for him to go. He dried his eyes and gathering up the books Simon did not want, put out his hand. Taking it, Simon said, 'You'll come again, won't you?'

The invitation was vivaciously given but Guy felt no surprise. Most people, having met him once, were eager to see him again.

Five

Unaware that she was mourned for dead, Harriet was alive in the Levant. She had not boarded the evacuation ship. Instead, she had begged a lift on an army lorry that would take her to Damascus. The two women with whom she absconded, members of a para-military service, made regular trips to Iraq, taking ammunition and other supplies.

They would admit only to surnames. For the duration they were Mortimer and Phillips, or rather Mort and Phil, two strongly-built young females, their faces burnt by the sun and wind and worn down to a ruddy-brown similarity. Sitting together in the cabin of the lorry, they took it in turns to drive or sleep so they could keep going all day and all night.

Harriet, in the back among cases of ammunition, hardly slept at all. The road over the desert was little more than a track and full of pot-holes. Each time she drifted into sleep, she was jolted awake as the lorry bumped or skidded or swayed into the sandy verge. In the end, she sat up and stared into darkness, seeing waterfalls tumbling black through the black air, huge birds sweeping to and fro across the night, enormous animals that paused to stare back at her before lumbering away out of sight. When the dawn came, she saw none of these things, only the empty road stretching from her, away into the desert hills.

Soon after daybreak, they stopped at a frontier barrier, then the lorry moved on to tarmac and Harriet, exhausted by the uneasy night, fell into a heavy slumber. When she woke again, the lorry was standing on a rocky shoulder that overlooked the sea. There was no sign of Mort and Phil.

She had left Egypt and was in another country. In Egypt the sun shone every day in a cloudless sky. Here the sky was blotted over with patches of cloud and the wind had an unfamiliar smell, the smell of rain. Because of the rain, grass was coming up, a thin shadow of green over the pinkish hills. In Egypt there had been rain only once during her time there: a freak storm that hit Cairo like a portent and turned the roads to rivers. Winter in Egypt was like a fine English summer but here it was really winter, wet and cold. Revived by the freshness of the air, she stood up, stretched her stiff muscles, then jumped down to the road. She had been ill but now she felt well, and free in a new world.

The rocks hid the foreshore but she could see, rising above them, the bastion of a castle that breasted the water of a bay. The water, glassy smooth, reflected every stone and crevice in the wall so there seemed to be two castles, one inverted below the other.

Climbing up the rocks, she saw Mort and Phil barefoot by the edge of the sea. She was about to call out to them but was checked by the sense of intimacy between them. She realized how little she knew about them. Of Phil she knew nothing at all. Mortimer she had met only twice but each time there had come from her such a sense of warmth, that, seeing her on the quay at Suez, she had run to her, calling out: 'Mortimer! Mortimer! God has sent you to save me.'

She walked away from them towards the other side of the bay. The sand was firm and brown, like baked clay, and her feet sank into it, leaving behind her a string of footprints. She took off her shoes and waded into the torpid water and walked until she came on a half-buried piece of fluted pilaster. Sitting down, she could observe Mort and Phil from a safe distance. They were standing close together, looking into each other's faces and she began to suspect that they would have preferred to be alone. When she asked Mortimer to save her from the evacuation ship, she had not considered Phil as an obstacle. She had not considered Phil at all. That was a mistake. Turning away from them, she wondered what she would do if they decided to drive off without her. Some time passed, then she glanced back at them. As the sun came and went among clouds, the figures merged and wavered against the dazzle of the sea. They remained locked together for several minutes then began to walk back towards the lorry.

As she watched them go, she realized how precarious her position was. She had fifty pounds that was to have been her spending money on board the ship. Now she would have to live on it while she found herself a job of some sort. She had one friend in

Syria, Aidan Pratt, who was a captain in the Pay Corps and might find her work. He was, in a way, responsible for her escapade because he had suggested she visit him in Damascus. He had hoped Guy would come with her. Now she would have to explain why she was alone and why she had to earn her own living.

She kept her face turned to the sea, giving Mort and Phil the chance to go without her, and was startled by Mortimer's lively, baritone voice speaking behind her: 'How do you feel after that bumpy ride?'

Harriet rose, again caught up in Mortimer's friendly warmth: 'It wasn't too bad.'

'Come on, then.' Contrite perhaps at having left her alone so long, Mortimer linked her arm and walked her back to the lorry: 'I expect you're hungry? We brought food with us. We'll have a picnic.'

There were packets of sandwiches in the cabin and two flasks of canteen tea. They sat on the rocks to eat their meal. The sandwiches, slabs of corned beef between slabs of bread, were dry and roughly cut but Mort and Phil devoured them with the appetite of old campaigners. Harriet, who was recovering from amoebic dysentery, envied their vigour and wondered if she would ever feel well again.

After eating, they sat for a while, made sleepy by the food and sea air, until Phil started up: 'Holy Mary, what's that?'

A grunting and rustling was coming from behind the slopes on the other side of the road, then a large, dark, dirty pig swaggered towards them, followed pell-mell by a dozen other pigs and a swine-herd equally dirty and dark. Midges clouded about them and a strong smell of the sty filled the air.

The man's eyes shone out from behind a fringe of black curls. Bold and curious, he stared at the three women. He was naked to the waist, his broad shoulders and chest burnt to a purple-red, his bare feet grey with dust.

Mort shouted: 'Hello there. How are you and all the pigs?'

Hearing a strange language, the man grunted and hurried his herd down to the sea.

'I say!' Mort's eyes opened in admiration: 'What a splendid figure! He might be Ulysses on the island of the Phaeacians.'

32

Phil asked in her wondering Irish voice: 'Did Ulysses keep pigs?'

'Not exactly, but his followers were turned into pigs somewhere along the line. This is an heroic shore, isn't it? I bet that castle was built by the Crusaders.'

Harriet said: 'Have you ever been inside?'

'Yes, but there's not much to see. The Bedu have taken it over. They've burrowed into it like rabbits and live in holes in the wall, but there's a café. Phil and I had coffee there once. We might go in again.'

They entered through a gateway. Large hinges showed where the gates had hung but the gates had gone and as Mortimer said, there was not much to see. A lane followed the outer wall, pitted with dark cells that served as dwelling places. At the sight of the strangers, children ran out to clamour for baksheesh and followed the women wherever they went. They came to a cavern that was no more than a hole in the original fabric. This was the café. Inside men in grimy galabiahs sat at grimy tables. The place depended for light on a break in the wall through which gleamed the motionless silver of the sea.

Mortimer led Harriet and Phil inside and ordered coffee. The men stared in silence, obviously confounded by this female presumption and Harriet felt proud of Mort and Phil and their confidence in the world.

On their way back to the lorry, a sharp burst of rain sent them running and Mortimer, climbing up among the cases of ammunition, pulled out a tarpaulin to shelter Harriet who was wearing only the blouse, skirt and cardigan that had been her winter wear in Egypt. Sitting with the tarpaulin over her hair, she looked out on wild and empty hill country patched light and dark by the sun and cloud. On one side the sea, disturbed by the wind, rolled in on a deserted shore. On the other were hills, rocky and bare except for the fur of grass. Black clouds and white clouds wound and unwound, sometimes revealing a stretch of clear blue sky. The rain slanted this way and that, cutting through broad rays of light, one moment pouring down, the next coming abruptly to a stop.

It was evening when they reached the Haifa headland and

skirting the town by the coast road, drove up on to the downs before the Lebanon frontier. The officials, who saw Mort and Phil once a week, waved them on.

As the wet sunset faded into twilight, the lorry was stopped on the verge of the road and driver and co-driver, without a word to Harriet, jumped down and walked away among the shadowed hills. Some twenty minutes later they returned and, looking up at Harriet, Mortimer said: 'How about some supper?'

Descending, Harriet took the tarpaulin with her, intending to spread it out for the three of them but Mort and Phil, whose slacks were already soaked by the wet ground, laughed at her precaution.

There was a tinkle of bells in the distance and Phil said: 'More pigs?' But this time the visitants were camels laden with bundles and decked out with fringes and tassels and camel bells. One after the other, tall and stately, they came swaying out of the twi-light to cross the road. As their feet touched the tarmac, they grumbled and grunted then, catching sight of the women, they shied away and the drovers, shouting, pulled at the lofty heads. The men made a show of ignoring the women but came to a stop nearby. The camels, forced to kneel, gave indignant snorts as though even rest was a form of servitude.

While they ate corned-beef sandwiches and drank the second flask of tea, the three women watched the camp's braziers being lit and skewers of meat being laid across the charcoal.

Phil said: 'How about Arab hospitality? D'you think we'll get an invite to supper?'

'Heaven forbid,' said Mortimer, 'I've heard pretty hair-raising stories about these chaps. Some British officials stopped their car to watch a Bedu wedding party and were invited to join in. They said they were in a hurry and after they'd driven off, the Bedu got together and decided the refusal was an insult. They galloped after them, and slaughtered the lot.'

'Women as well?' Harriet asked.

'There weren't any women but if there had been they would have escaped.'

'Why, I wonder?'

'Apparently Lady Hester Stanhope so impressed the Arab world, English women have been treated as special ever since.'

Harriet laughed: 'That's a comfort. I'll feel safer now.'

But alone in the back of the lorry, she did not feel very safe. The countryside was silent, the sky heavily clouded and there was no light but their own head-lights. There were few houses and those were in darkness. The villages seemed to be deserted yet twice, passing through a village street, there were conflagrations, produced by lighted petrol poured into the gutters of some main building. If these displays marked an occasion, there were no witnesses, no one to rejoice. Each time, after the raw brilliance of the flames, they returned to dense and silent darkness. Harriet became nervous at the thought of leaving Mort and Phil, and wished she could keep the comfort of their company.

Perhaps they, too, were unnerved by the black, endless road to Damascus for they began to sing together, loudly and aggressively:

> Sing high, sing low,
> Wherever we go,
> We're Artillery ladies,
> We never say 'No'.

There was another verse that ended:

> At night on the boat deck
> We always say 'Yes'.

They sang the two verses over and over again, their blended voices conveying to Harriet a union she could never hope to share.

Damascus appeared at last, a map of lights spread high on the darkness. As the road rose up among gardens and orchards, a scent of foliage came to her and her fears faded. Here she was in the oldest of the world's inhabited cities. The oasis on which it was built was said to be the Garden of Eden. Adam and Eve were created here and here Cain killed Abel. Damascus had been a city before Abraham was born and had been one of the wonders of the Ancient world. Who knew what pleasures awaited her in such a magical place?

A sound of rifle fire came to them. As they drove into the main square, they saw through the yellowish haze of the street lights that men were rushing about, screaming and firing pistols into the air. The large buildings on either side looked ominous and unwelcoming.

The lorry stopped at the kerb. Harriet could go no farther and perhaps Mort and Phil would not want her to go farther. Whether she liked it or not, she had arrived.

They were outside a shabby, flat-fronted building that had the word 'Hotel' above the door. Mortimer jumped down and lifted Harriet's suitcase to the pavement. She said: 'I know it doesn't look very encouraging, but it's the only hotel I know. I expect it will do till you find something better.'

Harriet nervously asked: 'Is there revolution here?'

'Oh no, this usually goes on at night. It's a demonstration against the Free French but it's harmless.'

Harriet was not so sure. She remembered Aidan Pratt telling her that his friend had been killed by a stray bullet during one of these demonstrations. She appealed to Mortimer: 'Couldn't you stay here just for one night?'

Mort and Phil shook their heads. Standing together, smiling their farewells, they said they must press on to Aleppo where they planned to stay at the Armenian hospital. For a moment she thought of asking them to take her with them, but wherever she went she had to leave them sometime. Here at least she had Aidan Pratt.

Seeing her trying to lift her heavy case, Mortimer took it from her and carried it easily into the hotel hallway. There was a small night-light on the desk but no one behind the desk.

Mortimer said: 'The clerk will come when you ring. You'll be all right here, won't you?'

Eager to be back on the road, she took a quick step forward and kissed Harriet's cheek: 'You're not staying here long, are you? We'll meet again back in Cairo. Take care of yourself.'

Harriet watched through the glass of the door till the lorry was out of sight, then she struck the bell on the desk. There was a long interval before the clerk appeared, looking aggrieved as though the bell were not there for use. He seemed disconcerted by the sight of a solitary young woman with a suitcase and he shook his head: 'You wan' hotel? This not hotel.' He pointed to a notice in French that said the building had been requisitioned by the occupying force. It was now a hostel for French officers.

Dismayed, Harriet asked: 'But where can I go? It's late. Where else is there?'

The clerk looked sympathetic but unhelpful: 'Things very bad. Army take everything.'

Having nothing to offer, he waited for her to go and she, having nowhere to go, went out and stood on the pavement. There must be someone, somewhere, who could direct her to an hotel. Eventually a British soldier sauntered by with the appearance of abstracted boredom she had seen often enough in Cairo. She stopped him and asked if he knew where she could stay. He gave a laugh, as though he could scarcely believe his luck, and lifting her bag, said, 'You a service woman?'

'More or less.'

'That's all right then. There's a hostel over here.'

He led her across the square and into a side street. There was more rifle fire and she asked what the trouble was.

'Just the wogs. They're always ticking.'

'What's it like here in Damascus?'

'Same as everywhere else. Lot of bloody foreigners.'

They came to another shabby, flat-fronted building, this one distinguished by a Union Jack hanging over the main door.

When Harriet thanked him, the soldier said: 'Don't thank me. It's a treat seeing an English bint.'

Harriet thought she had found a refuge until she was stopped in the hall by an Englishwoman with scrappy red hair and foxy red eyes. She looked Harriet up and down before she said accusingly: 'This hostel's for ORs.'

'Does it matter? I've come a long way and I'm very tired.'

'I don't know. Suppose it doesn't matter if you aren't staying long. I've got to keep my beds for them as they're meant for.'

Harriet followed the woman through a canteen, a stark place shut for the night, to a large dormitory with some thirty narrow, iron bedsteads.

'Which can I have?'

'Any one you like. There's a shower in there if you care to use it.'

The beds had no sheets but a thin army blanket was folded on each. The shower was cold, but at least she had the place to herself; or so it seemed until the early hours of the morning when

37

she was wakened by a party of ATS, all drunk, who kept up a ribald criticism of the men who had taken them out. They finally subsided into sleep but at six a.m. a loudspeaker was switched on in the canteen.

Raucous music bellowed through the dormitory. Harriet, giving up hope of sleep, rose and went to the shower. As she passed the ATS, one of them lifted a bleared, blood-shot eye over the edge of the blanket, and observed her reproachfully.

The person in the canteen was a half-Negro sweeper who seemed as baleful as the red-haired woman. When Harriet asked about breakfast, he mumbled, 'Blekfest eight o'clock,' and went on sweeping.

With an hour and a half in which to do nothing, Harriet set out to look at Damascus. Independence had not begun well for her and she was inclined to blame herself. If she had taken the woman into her confidence, charmed her, flattered her, she might have been set up as the hostel's favourite inmate. But she had no gift for ingratiating herself with strangers. And she was sure that if she tried it, it would not work.

The square, ill-lit and sinister the previous night, was at peace now in the early sunlight. The ominous buildings were no longer ominous. There were towers and domes and minarets, sights to be seen, a new city to be explored. She could imagine Aidan escorting her round and helping her to find employment and lodgings. She would warn him to keep her presence a secret. She could not have Guy coming here out of pity to rescue her and take her back to Cairo. Later, perhaps, she would contact him but while the evacuation ship was at sea – the voyage around the Cape would take at least two months – no one would expect to hear from her.

She sat for a while in a garden beside a mosque, watching the traffic increase and the day's work beginning. The city was set among hills as in the hollow of a crown. The highest range, to the west, was covered in snow and a cold wind blew towards her. She was not dressed for this climate. Shivering, she rose and found a café where she could drink coffee at a counter among businessmen to whom she was an object of curiosity. Cairo had become conditioned to the self-sufficiency of western women but she was now in Syria, a country dominated by Moslem prejudice. In spite of the bold gaze of the men, she remained on her café stool until the military offices were likely to start work.

Seeing nothing that resembled the Cairo HQ, she took a taxi and was driven to the British Pay Office. This was a requisitioned hotel where the walls had become scuffed and the furniture replaced by trestle tables. Here, among her own countrymen, she felt at ease. The worst was over. She had only to find Aidan Pratt and he would take care of her.

When she asked for him, a corporal said: 'Sorry, miss. He's been transferred.'

'Can you tell me where he's gone?'

'Sorry, miss, can't help you. Not allowed to reveal movements of army personnel.'

'But I'm a friend. Surely, under the circumstances . . . At least, tell me, is he in Syria?'

The corporal conceded that he was not in Syria but beyond that would disclose nothing. He said apologetically: 'Security, you know, miss.'

She said: 'Do you know anywhere I can stay? A hotel or guest-house?'

The corporal shook his head: 'Haven't heard of one. Sorry.'

Harriet returned to sunlight that was beginning to fade. Clouds were drifting over the snow-covered mountains and fog dimmed the towers and minarets. She said aloud: 'So you really are on your own!' and as the first drops of rain hit her face, she started back to the hostel, hoping for breakfast in the canteen.

Six

Guy was going through a period of stress unlike anything he had known in his life before. There had been only one death in his family and that was in his childhood. When told his grannie had gone to a much nicer place, he had said, 'She'll come back, won't she?' She did not come back and he had forgotten her. But after his outburst in Simon's ward, he could not forget Harriet. He was haunted by her loss and the haunting bewildered him. He was like a man who, taking for granted his right to perfect health, is struck down by disease. But the loss was only one aspect of his perplexity. He had to consider the fact that going, she had gone unwillingly. He refused to blame himself for that. He had suggested she go for her own good. He told himself it had been a sensible suggestion to which she had sensibly agreed. In fact, in the end, she had *chosen* to go.

But however much he argued against it, he knew he had instigated her departure. He could not cope with her physical malaise and air of discontent. There were too many other demands upon him. He simply hadn't the time to deal with her. So he had persuaded her to return to her native air where, sooner or later, she would regain her health. No one could blame him either for her illness or her deep-seated discontent. She needed employment and in England she would find it. He had expected, when he eventually joined her at home, that once again she would be the quick-witted, capable, lively young woman he had married.

Her going, too, was to have been a prelude to their post-war life. She was to be the advance guard of their return. With her particular gift for doing such things, she was to find them a house or flat and settle all those problems of everyday life which he found baffling and tedious.

Now it was not simply that Harriet would not be there when he returned, she would never be there.

Faced with the finality of death, he could not accept it. In the past, he had had many an easy laugh at those gravestone wishes: 'She shall not come to me but I shall go to her,' 'Not lost but gone before . . .' and so on. As a materialist, he still had to see the absurdity of belief in an after-life. He could not tell himself that Harriet had gone to a 'much nicer place' but, in his confusion of grief and guilt, he almost convinced himself she had not gone at all. Perhaps, at the last, she had decided against the journey to England and had come back to Cairo. She had hidden herself from him but when he turned the next corner, he would find her coming towards him. Then, not finding her there, he went on expectantly to the next corner, and the next.

If he had no extra classes, he would spend his afternoon walking about the streets of Cairo in search of someone who was not there. When people stopped to condole with him, he listened impatiently, imagining they had been misinformed, and that she was somewhere, in some distant street, if only he could find her.

One day, coming into the lecture hall, he was shocked to see an immense wreath of flowers and laurel propped up against the lectern. Refusing to acknowledge it, he took his place as though it were not there. But, of course, his students could not let him escape like that. They all rose and their elected spokesman stepped to the front of the class.

'Professor Pringle, sir, it is our wish that I express our sorrow. Our sorrow and our deep regret that Mrs Pringle is no more.'

He said briefly, 'Thank you,' angry that they had blundered in to confirm a fear he had rejected. The student spokesman, respecting his reticence, retired and nothing more was said, but in the library he found the librarian, Miss Pedler, waiting for him.

'I'm so sorry, Mr Pringle. I've only just heard.'

Guy nodded and turned away but she followed him to an alcove where the poetry was stacked: 'I wanted to say, Mr Pringle, I know how you feel. I lost my fiancé soon after the war started. He contracted T B. If he could've got home, he would have been cured, but there was no transport. It was the war killed him just as it killed your wife. I know it's terrible but in the end you get over it. The first three years are the worst.'

Aghast, he murmured, 'Three years!' and hurried away from

her. Back in the lecture hall, he found the wreath still propped against the lectern. What was he supposed to do with it? He thought of Gamal Sarwar, one of his students, who had been killed in a car accident and buried in the City of the Dead. He could take the wreath up for Gamal, but he knew he would never find the Sarwar mausoleum among all the other mausoleums. And the cemetery, though at night it took on a certain macabre beauty, was in daytime a desolate, cinderous place he could not visit alone. The thought of it reminded him of the afternoon when he and Harriet had attended Gamal's *arba'in* and the Sarwar men had made much of him. Harriet had waited for him, and then, as the moon rose, she had asked him to go with her to see the Khalifa tombs. It had meant only a short drive in a gharry but he had refused. When he said she could go with someone else, she had pleaded: 'But I want to go with you.'

Angry again, he said to himself: 'I hate death and everything to do with death,' and picking up the wreath, he threw it into the stationery cupboard and shut the door on it.

Guy felt betrayed by life. His good nature, his readiness to respond to others and his appreciation of them had gained him friends and made life easy for him. Now, suddenly and cruelly, he had become the victim of reality. He had not deserved it but there it was: his wife, who might have lived another fifty or sixty years, had gone down with the evacuation ship and he would not see her again.

Edwina, thinking that Guy was becoming resigned to Harriet's death, said to Dobson: 'He can't go moping around for ever. I think I should try and take his mind off it.'

'If I were you, I'd leave it a bit longer.'

'Really, Dobbie, anyone would think I had designs on him. I only want to help him.'

That was true but Edwina, too, felt betrayed by life. She had had a lingering hope that she would see Peter Lisdoonvarna when he came on leave but the British army was now so far away, the men no longer took their leave in Cairo. Guy was a prize that had come to hand just when she had begun to fear her first youth was passing. Before she became obsessed with Peter, she had taken life lightly, receiving the rewards of beauty. But what good had they done her? She had been offered only futureless young men like Hugo and Simon Boulderstone, or men like Peter who would not leave their wives. Now, just when she needed him most, here was Guy bereft and available and much too young to remain unmarried.

'You know, Dobbie dear, I was very fond of Harriet, but she's dead and the rest of us have to go on living.'

'I still think you'd be wise to leave it for a bit.'

'And have some Levantine floosie snap him up?'

Dobson laughed: 'I agree, that could happen. They're great at getting their hooks into a man, especially when he's feeling low.'

'There you are, then! I'm not risking it.'

On Saturday, Guy's free day, Edwina said in a small, seductive voice: 'Don't forget, Guy dear, you promised to take me out.'

'Did I promise?'

'Oh, darling, you know you did! I'm not doing anything tonight so wouldn't it be nice if we had a little supper?'

Guy, who would have refused Harriet without a thought, felt it would be discourteous to refuse Edwina. Edwina, unlike Harriet, was the outside world that called for consideration.

He said: 'All right. I'll be back for you about seven.'

Edwina's voice rose in joyful anticipation: 'Oh, darling, darling! Where shall we go?'

'I'll think of somewhere. See you later, then.'

Returning at a time nearer eight o'clock than seven, Guy found Edwina waiting for him in the living-room. She was wearing one of her white evening dresses and a fur jacket against the winter chill. Both seemed to him unsuitable for a simple dinner but worse was the jewel on her breast: a large, heart-shaped brooch set with diamonds. He frowned at it.

'You can't wear that thing. It's ridiculous.'

'You gave it to me.'

He was puzzled then, looking more closely at it, he remembered he had indeed given it to her to wear at his troops' entertainment. He had no idea where it came from.

He said: 'It's vulgar. It's just a theatrical prop.'

'It's not a theatrical prop. They're real diamonds. It's a valuable piece of jewellery.'

This protest recalled for him another protest and he realized the brooch had belonged to Harriet. She had said: 'It's mine. It was given to me,' but that had meant nothing to him. He had taken the brooch from her because it was exactly right for the show. He recalled, too, her expression of disbelief when he pocketed the absurd object. And soon after that she told him she would go on the evacuation ship.

He said to Edwina: 'Please take it off.'

'Oh, very well!' She unpinned it with an expression of wry resignation and offered it to him: 'I suppose you want it back?'

'It belonged to Harriet.'

Deciding that nothing must spoil their evening, she smiled a forgiving smile: 'Then, of course, you must have it back.'

He did not want the thing yet did not want Edwina to have it. He wished it would disappear off the face of the earth. Edwina, still smiling, slipped it into his pocket and not knowing what else to do with it, he let it remain there.

A taxi took them to Bulacq Bridge and Edwina supposed they were going to the Extase night club. Instead, they stopped at one of the broken-down houses on the other side of the road.

'What is this?'

'The fish restaurant,' Guy said as though she ought to know.

They went down into a damp, dimly-lit basement where there were long deal tables and benches in place of chairs. The other diners, minor clerks and students, stared at Edwina's white dress and white fur jacket, and she asked nervously: 'Do Europeans come here?'

'My friends do. The food is good.'

'Is it? It's very interesting of course. Quite a change for me.' Edwina, trying to suffer it all with a good grace, looked about her: 'I didn't even know there was a fish restaurant.'

Before she could say more, Guy's friends began to appear. The first was Jake Jackman. When he came to the table, Edwina thought he only wanted a word with Guy but he sat down, intending to eat with them. She had not expected anything like this. Her evening with Guy was to be an intimate exchange of sympathy that would lead to   well, there was no knowing!

Still, Jackman being there and meaning to stay, she would have to put up with him. She had never liked him. She supposed he was, in his thin-faced fashion, attractive, but her instinct was against him. She knew that in a sexual relationship, the only sort that interested her, he would be unscrupulous. But there he was: a challenge! She acknowledged his presence with a sidelong, provocative smile that had no effect upon him. He was intent on Guy to whom he at once confided his discovery of a 'bloody scandal'. The western Allies were uniting themselves against Russia and he had inside information to prove it.

'What sort of information?'

Sniffing and pulling at his nose, Jake leant towards Guy, lifting his shoulder to exclude Edwina: 'This "Aid to Russia" frolic – it's all my eye. The stuff they're sending is obsolete and most of it's useless. They don't want the Russkies to advance on that front. They want them wiped out. They want the Panzers to paralyse the whole damn Soviet fighting force.'

'I can't believe that. It would mean German troops pouring down through the Ukraine and taking our oil.'

'Don't be daft. We'd have made peace long before that. Or the Hun would've exhausted himself. It's the old policy of killing two birds with one stone. It was the policy before Hitler invaded Russia and it's still the policy...' Jake dropped his voice so Edwina could not hear what he said and she felt not only excluded but despised.

Guy had forgotten they were there to eat and the waiter, leaning against the kitchen door, was quite content to let the men talk. Hungry and neglected on her comfortless wooden seat, Edwina sighed so loudly that Guy was reminded of her presence. He turned but at that moment there was another arrival at the table. This was Major Cookson, a thin little man without income, growing more shabby every day, who followed after anyone who might buy him a drink.

He said to Jackman: 'I've been looking for you everywhere.'

Since his friend Castlebar had disappeared from Cairo, Jackman had admitted Cookson as a minor member of his entourage. He looked at him now without enthusiasm and said: 'Sit down. Sit down.'

Hearing him called 'major', Edwina gave him a second glance, but he did not relate to the free-spending young officers she had known in the past. As he sat beside her, he enveloped her in a stench of ancient sweat and she felt more affronted by him than by Jackman.

Giving up his revelations of Allied intrigues, Jake said: 'I suppose we're going to eat some time?' imposing on Guy the position of host.

'Good heavens, yes.' Guy, becoming alert, called the waiter and gave Edwina the menu.

It was a dirty, handwritten menu that listed three kinds of river fish. Guy recommended them all but advised Edwina to choose the *mahseer* which, he said, was a speciality of the house. Edwina did not like fish but concurred from a habit of concurring with the male sex.

Jackman had now become the joker. Giving Edwina a smile full of malice, he said: 'Something funny happened today. Was passing Abdin Palace and saw a squaddie, drunk as arseholes, his cock sticking out of his flies. He'd got hold of an old pair of steel-rimmed specs and having perched them on the said cock, was saying, "Look around, cocky boy, and if you see anything you like, I'll buy it for you."'

Knowing he meant to offend her, Edwina ignored Jackman's laughter and gave her attention to the plate in front of her. The fish, if it tasted of anything, tasted of mud.

'Which,' Jackman went on, 'reminds me of lover-boy Castlebar. But he's not bought anything, has he? He's been bought.'

Guy shrugged: 'If they're happy, why worry?'

'Happy? You think Bill's happy acting the gigolo? I bet he's sick to his stomach.' Jackman turned to Cookson for agreement and Cookson, giggling weakly, said:

'Live and let live.'

'What a bloody amoral lot you are!' Jackman sulked for a while then began another story but was interrupted by yet another arrival at the table.

The newcomer was a dark, gloomy-eyed man who incongruously wore the uniform of an army captain. Guy introduced him as, 'Aidan Sheridan, the actor. He's now in the Pay Corps and calls himself Pratt.'

Edwina caught her breath: 'Oh, Aidan Sheridan!' she said, and widened her eyes at him.

Aidan viewed her with distaste then turned accusingly on Guy: 'Where's Harriet?'

There was dismay at the table. Edwina and Jackman glanced at Guy who did not speak.

'What's the matter? You haven't split up, have you?'

Guy shook his head and said: 'I would have written but I didn't know where you were.'

'I've been transferred to Jerusalem. But where is she?'

'I should have told everyone who knew her. I didn't think . . .'

'Whatever it is, tell me now. Where is she?'

'She's dead. She was on an evacuation ship that was sunk . . . She's dead. Drowned.' Unable to say more, Guy shook his head again.

Aidan sank down to the bench and after a moment said: 'You're sure? There are so many false reports going round.'

Guy could only shake his head and Edwina, speaking for him, said: 'I'm afraid it was confirmed. I'm at the Embassy and I saw the report. The ship was torpedoed off the coast of Africa. Poor Harriet, it was terrible, wasn't it? Three people were saved but she . . .'

Guy broke in, frowning: 'What's the good of going over it again! She's lost. Nothing will bring her back, so let's talk of something else.' He looked at Aidan who stared down at the table as though not hearing what was being said: 'You'll have something to eat?'

The others were trying to talk of something else but for Aidan the news was too sudden to be put aside: 'No, I can't eat. I'll go . . . I'll walk to the station.'

'You're going back tonight?'

'Yes, I've a berth booked . . .'

'Then I'll walk with you.' As he rose, Guy remembered he was Edwina's escort and he said: 'Sorry, I must go. I want to talk to Aidan. Jake will see you home.'

'Look here,' Jake put in quickly: 'I've come out without cash. I'll need something for a taxi.'

Guy paid the bill and handed Jackman a pound note then went off with Aidan.

'A disastrous evening,' Jake said.

For Edwina, too, it had been a disastrous evening. Hiding her

47

resentment, she said: 'Yes, poor Harriet!' but her mind was on the treatment she had received. She added: 'And poor Guy! I suppose that actor not knowing brought it all back.' At the same time she was telling herself that Guy and the company he kept would not do for her.

Seven

Guy was surprised by Aidan's reaction to Harriet's death and at the same time felt grateful to him. That others grieved for her in some way lightened his own burden and the debt he owed her. Out in the street, he said: 'I didn't realize you felt any special affection for her.'

'We had become friends.'

That also surprised Guy. Though he rewarded him by going with him to the station, Guy was bored by Aidan and could not imagine he would have had much attraction for Harriet.

'She used to tease me,' Aidan said: 'I deserved it, of course. I know I'm a bit of a stick. You remember, I came on her in Luxor and we saw some of the sights together.'

Guy said, 'Yes,' though he had forgotten Harriet's trip to Luxor. Thinking about it and about her association with Aidan, he began to imagine her with a whole world of interests about which he knew nothing. He did not begrudge them but had a disquieting sense of things having happened behind his back. Not that anything much could have happened. He had taken her away from her friends in England and, abroad, she had had few opportunities to make more. For the first time, it occurred to him that while he had kept himself occupied morning, noon and night, she had been often alone.

He said: 'She was on that boat the *Queen of Sparta*. I thought she ought to go – this climate was killing her.'

'When we were in Luxor, she didn't look well, but she didn't look happy, either. I would say the unhappiness was more destructive than the climate.'

'Unhappiness? Did she say she was unhappy?'

'No. There was no mention of such a thing, but she seemed lonely down there. I wondered why you didn't go with her.'

'Go with her?' Guy disliked this hint of criticism: 'She did not

49

suggest it. The whole thing was fixed up by that woman Angela Hooper. She took Harriet to Luxor then went off and left her there. It was typical of the woman. She's unbalanced. I couldn't have gone, anyway. I had much too much to do.'

'You do too much, you know.' Aidan spoke gently but his tone expressed more censure than sympathy and Guy felt annoyed. He was not used to criticism and he said:

'I suppose you are blaming me because she's gone. Well, there's no point in it. Anyway, the past is past. We have to manage the present, even if it is unmanageable. We can't stay becalmed in memories.'

'No, I suppose not.'

Aidan's agreement was not wholehearted and Guy walked in silence until they reached the station then, saying a curt, 'Goodbye,' he swung round and walked back to Garden City. Aidan, he told himself, was not only a stick but a prig. He put him out of his mind but for all that, he felt the need to make some amends to Harriet. He began to look about him for an image to adopt in her place. The only one that presented itself at that time was the young lieutenant, Simon Boulderstone. Harriet was beyond his help but the injured youth had to remake his whole life.

Now that he showed signs of recovery, Simon ceased to be the helpless object of everyone's devotion. He was expected to contribute towards his own progress but the progress seemed to him depressingly slow.

As soon as he could flex the muscles of his hips and lift his knees a few inches off the mattress, parallel bars were brought to his bedside and Ross said: 'Come on now, sir, we've got to get you out of bed.'

Ross and the orderly lifted him into place between the bars and told him to grip them with his hands. He was expected to hold himself upright and swing his body between them. This was agony. His arm muscles were so wasted, he could scarcely support his torso but, encouraged by Ross, he found he could move himself by swinging his pelvis from side to side.

Ross said: 'You're doing fine, sir. Keep it up. A bit more effort and you'll get to the end of the bars.'

Simon laughed and struggled on, but in all these exercises

there was a sense of fantasy. Without ability to walk, he seemed to be acting the part of a man who could walk. It was a hopeless attempt. He was troubled by the illusion that he had only half a body and was holding it suspended in air. Yet he had legs. He could see them hanging there, and he lost patience with them, and shouted: 'When on earth will they start moving themselves?'

'Don't you worry, sir. They'll come all right in time.'

His feet, from lack of use, had become absurdly white and delicate. 'Look at them,' he said to Ross: 'They're like a girl's feet. I don't believe I'll ever stand on them again.'

Ross laughed and running his pencil along Simon's left sole, asked: 'Feel that?'

'Nope.' He was disgusted with himself; with his legs, his knees, his feet, every insensate part of himself.

Guy, who visited him two or three times a week, decided that he needed mental stimulation and told him that to recover, he had only to decide to recover. Guy believed in the mind's power over the body. He said he had been ill only once in his life and that was the result of Harriet's interference. His father, an admirer of George Bernard Shaw, had refused to have his children vaccinated in infancy. Coming to the Middle East where smallpox was endemic, Harriet had insisted that Guy must be vaccinated. He had reacted violently to the serum. He had spent two days in bed with a high temperature and a swollen, aching arm, whimpering that he, who had never known a day's illness before, had had illness forced upon him. He had been injected with a foreign substance and would lose his arm. He was amazed when he woke up next morning with his temperature down and his arm intact.

'You see, I was a fool. I allowed Harriet to influence me against my better judgement and, as a result, became ill.'

Simon protested: 'But I'm not ill. I was injured when we ran into a booby trap – that was something different.'

'Not so very different. There are no such things as accidents. We are responsible for everything that happens to us.'

Simon was puzzled yet, reflecting on all Guy said, he remembered how he had been attracted to the palm tree where the trap was laid. The tree had seemed to him a familiar and loved object and he had said to Crosbie: 'A good place to eat our grub.' Guy

could be right; perhaps, somehow or other, one did bring catas-
trophe upon oneself.

'What should I do?'

'Make up your mind that having got yourself into this fix,
you're going to get yourself out of it.'

Whether because of this conversation or not, he became aware
of his feet in a curious, almost supernatural, way. They had
entered his consciousness. He could almost feel them. When he
spoke of this to the sister, she said: 'Oh? What do they feel like?'

'Not exactly pleasant. Funny, rather!'

She threw back the blanket and put her hand on them: 'Cold,
eh?'

'No, I don't think it's cold.'

'Yes, it is. You've forgotten what cold feels like.'

Simon waited for Ross, intending to say nothing of this
development until Ross said: 'Feel that, sir?' then he would
say: 'Yes, my feet feel cold.'

But it did not happen like that. That day, when Ross ran the
pencil along his sole, an electrical thrill flashed up the inside of
his leg into his sexual organs and he felt his penis become erect.
He turned his buttocks to hide himself and pressing his cheek into
the pillow, did not know whether he was relieved or ashamed.

Ross, seeing him flush, threw the blanket over him, saying:
'You're going to be all right, sir.' He laughed and Simon laughed
back at him, and from that time a new intimacy grew up between
them. Ross, losing his restraint, ceased to look upon Simon as a
dependant and began to treat him as a young man like himself.
He took to lingering at the end of each session and talking about
small events in the hospital. This gossip led him on to a subject
near to his heart: his disapproval of the 'Aussies'. He felt the
need to impress Simon with the respectability of New Zealanders
that contrasted with the wild goings-on of the Australians.

'A rough lot, sir,' he said. 'Some of 'em never seen a town till
they were taken through Sydney to the troopship. And take that
Crete job? The Aussies blamed us and the Brits for lack of air-
cover. Well, you can't have air-cover if you haven't got aircraft,
now can you, sir? They just couldn't see it. They weren't reasonable. When they got back, they took to throwing things out of
windows. In Clot Bey they threw a piano out. And they threw

out a British airman and told him: "Now fly, you bastard!" From a top floor window, that was. Not nice behaviour, sir.'

'No, indeed. What happened to the airman?'

'I never heard.' Ross shook his head in disgust at his own story.

Simon sympathized with Ross but, secretly, he envied the Aussies their uninhibited 'goings-on'. They had frequently to be confined to barracks for the sake of public safety. And at Tobruk, ordered to advance in total silence, they had wrecked a surprise attack by bursting out of the slitties bawling, 'We're going to see the wizard, the wonderful wizard of Oz'. He had to put in a word for such lawless men.

'After all, Ross, they needn't have fought at all. We started the war and they could have told us to get on with it.'

'Oh, no. With respect, you're wrong there, sir. It's our war as much as yours.'

To the sister, Simon said: 'You know that young lady who came here, the one I said I didn't want to see? Did she come back?'

The sister answered coldly: 'How do I know? I'm not on duty every day and all day, am I?'

'Sister, if she does come, you won't stop her, will you? I want to see her.'

'*If* she does come, I'll bring her along myself.'

A few days later, having had no visitor but Guy, Simon appealed to him: 'Could you ask Edwina to come and see me?'

'Of course,' Guy cheerfully agreed: 'I'll speak to her. I expect she'll come tomorrow or the day after.'

But Edwina, when he spoke to her, blinked her one visible eye at him and seemed on the point of tears: 'Oh, Guy, I really can't go to Helwan again. It's so embarrassing. Simon's got it into his head that I was his brother's girlfriend and I find it such a strain, playing up to him.'

'Why play up? Just tell him the truth.'

'Oh, that would be unkind. Besides, the place upsets me. When I went last time, I had a migraine next day. I do so hate hospitals.' Edwina gave a little sob and Guy, afraid of upsetting her further, said no more but he decided there would be a meeting somewhere other than the hospital.

He arranged to hire a car and asked the sister for permission to take Simon for a drive. They would go to the Gezira gardens. He asked Edwina to meet him there, telling her that he would see there was no distressing talk about Simon's brother. Edwina said: 'Of course, I'll come, Guy dear. How sweet you are to everyone.'

Much satisfied, Guy put his plan to Simon who was upset by it. Closeted in his cubicle, he had become like a forest-bred creature that is afraid to venture out on to the plain. Even Edwina's promise to join them in the gardens had its element of disappointment.

'So she won't come here?'

'She says hospitals have an unfortunate effect on her.'

'I'd rather not go to the gardens, Guy. I don't think she wants to see me.'

'Oh, yes, she agreed at once,' Guy persuaded Simon as he had persuaded Edwina and a day was fixed. By the time the car was outside the Plegics, Simon had worked himself into a state of restless anticipation. He several times asked Guy: 'Do you really think she'll be there?'

'She's probably there already. So, come along!'

Simon's chair, brake-locked, stood beside his bed and Guy and Ross watched while he manoeuvred himself into it. He shifted to the edge of the bed and pushed his legs over the side then, gripping the chair's farther arm, he swung himself into the seat. Comfortably settled, he looked at his audience and grinned: 'How's that?'

Both watchers said together: 'Splendid.'

Ross came to the car where Simon, depending on the strength of his arms, lifted himself into the back seat. His movements were ungainly and Guy and Ross were pained by the effort involved but they smiled their satisfaction. Simon was progressing well.

Heat was returning to the Cairo noonday. The drive over the desert was pleasant and Simon, looking out of one window or the other, said: 'Funny to be out again. Makes me feel I'm getting better.'

The gardens, that curved round the north-eastern end of the island, were narrow, a fringe of sandy ground planted with trees.

Constantly hosed down with river water, the trees had grown immensely tall but their branches were sparse and their leaves few. They were hung with creepers that here and there let down a thread-fine stem that held a single pale flower, upright like an alabaster vase. Nothing much grew in the sandy soil but it was sprayed to keep down the dust and the air was filled with a heavy, earthy smell.

Simon moved his chair noiselessly along the path with Guy beside him. They were both watching for a sight of Edwina but they reached the end of the gardens without meeting anyone.

Simon said in a strained voice: 'She hasn't come.'

'She will. She will.' Guy was confident she would. They turned back and mid-way between the garden gates found a seat where Guy could sit. He said it was four o'clock so she would probably come in on her way to the office. She would have to make a detour and cross by the bridge, all of which would take some time. An hour passed. The afternoon was changing to evening and Simon's expectations began to fail. He could not respond to Guy's talk and soon enough Guy, too, fell silent. They faced the opposite bank of the river where Kasr el Nil barracks stood, its red colour changing as the light changed until it was as dark as dried blood. The long, low building, so bug-ridden that only fire could disinfest it, was hazed by river mist and looked remote, a Victorian relic, a symbol of past glory.

Gazing across at it, Simon remembered his first days in Egypt, when Tobruk had fallen. Ordered to join his convoy at dawn, he had taken a taxi to the barracks, fearing that the other men would laugh at him for his extravagance. He soon realized that no one knew or cared how he got there. Hugo had been alive then. Now, with Hugo dead and Edwina uncaring, he looked back on those early days as a time of youth and innocence he would never know again.

He sighed and glanced at Guy who also seemed lost in some vision of the past. He said, perhaps unwisely: 'You loved her very much, didn't you?'

Surprised and startled by the question, Guy said: 'You mean Harriet? I suppose I did. Not that I've ever thought much about love. I've always had so many friends.' He stood up to end this sort of talk: 'You ought to be back at the hospital by now.'

When they reached the main gate, two people were descending from a taxi: Edwina and an army officer.

Looking round, seeing Simon in his chair, Edwina ran in through the gates, holding out her hands: 'Oh, Simon! Simon darling, I was so afraid we'd be too late.' She seized his hands and gazing warmly into his face, asked: 'How are you? Dear Simon, you're looking so much better!'

Simon, glancing over her shoulder, could see her companion was a major, an old fellow, thirty-five or more; much too old for Edwina. But the major had two good legs and he came strolling after her with a possessive smile, conveying to the world the fact that he and Edwina had spent the afternoon in intimate enjoyment.

He was introduced as Tony Brody, recently appointed to GHQ, Cairo – a tall, narrow-shouldered man with a regular face that was too fine to seem effectual. Edwina, her eyes brilliant, her voice halted by a slight gasp, seemed elated by her new conquest.

She kept saying: 'Oh dear, I'm sorry I'm late,' and even Simon could guess why she was late. He wanted to get away from her. Guy, meeting his appealing glance, said they had no time to talk. Simon was due back at Helwan. Cutting short Edwina's excited chatter, he helped Simon back into the waiting car and took him away from her.

Eight

Harriet had settled into a pension recommended by the waiter behind the café bar. It was called the Anemonie, a large, draughty building, dark inside and, in wet weather, very dark. It had a garden where a mulberry tree spread its crinoline of branches over a long table and half-a-dozen rickety chairs. The rain lay in pools on the table-top but Harriet could imagine the tourists sitting out to dine in the long, indolent twilights of peace-time summers.

The war had ended all that. The pension proprietors, Monsieur and Madame Vigo, were surprised when Harriet arrived at the door but they admitted her. They lived in an out-building and kept themselves to themselves, so Harriet had the whole pension to herself. Madame Vigo, who served her meals, spoke French and Arabic but she could make nothing of Harriet's anglicized French or her Egyptian Arabic.

Harriet knew the Vigos were curious about her and wondered what she was doing there, alone in Syria. Now that her escapade had lost impetus, she wondered herself.

The dining-room, where she ate alone, could have accommodated fifty or sixty guests. At night a single bulb was lit behind her seat and the large room stretched from her into total darkness. She would have been glad to have her meals with the Vigos but they maintained their privacy and were not relenting for Harriet's sake. The food, that was cooked by Monsieur Vigo, was served in a businesslike way by Madame Vigo who put the plates on the table and immediately made off.

After supper, Harriet would sit on at the table, afraid to go up to the bedroom floor where thirty or more empty rooms led off from a maze of corridors. Wherever she went, there was silence except for the creak of the boards beneath her feet.

She wondered how long she could bear to stay there? How

long, indeed, could she afford to stay there? And when she went, where would she go?

During the day, she walked about the streets or sheltered in doorways from the rain. The shopping area was much like that of any English town except for the Arabic signs. The real life of the place was in the covered souks. When the sun shone, she could see the Anti-Lebanon with its sheen of snow, but this was not often. It was winter, the rainy season, and most days a foggy greyness overhung the town. Harriet's suitcase was filled with light clothing intended to see her across the equator. Her winter clothing had been forwarded to the ship and she could imagine it going to England and lying unclaimed at Liverpool docks. She could not waste what money she had to buy more and so, conditioned to the heat of Egypt, she shivered like an indoor cat turned out in bad weather.

Wandering aimlessly beneath the sodden sky, she felt persecuted by the Abana, a river in flood, that would scatter out of sight into a drain only to reappear round the next corner, its rushing, splashing water enhancing the air's cold. She began to forget that she had been ill most of her time in Egypt and she longed for the sumptuous sunsets, the dazzling night sky, the moonlight that lay over the buildings like liquid silver. She remembered how the glare of Cairo produced mirages in the mind, so vivid they replaced reality, and she forgot the petrol fumes and the smell of the Cairo waste lots.

There were no mirages in Damascus. Instead, there was rain and she could escape that only by returning to the pension or by pushing her way through the crowds in the big main souk, the Souk el Tawill, the Street called Straight where Paul had lodged in his blindness. Here there were tribesmen, hillmen, businessmen in dark, western suits, peasants, donkey drovers and noise. She was astonished by the energy of the crowds and after a while, she realized her own energy was returning. The Syrian climate was restoring her to health. She felt she could walk for miles but wherever she went, she was on the outside of things, a female in a city where women were expected to stay indoors.

One morning she found the souk in a state of uproar. Something was about to happen. The roadway had been cleared and the crowd pressed back against the shops. The shopkeepers had pulled down their shutters and become spectators, straining their necks and bawling with the rest of them. Harriet, at the back of the crowd, stood on a piece of stone, remnant of a Roman arcade, and looked over the heads in front of her, eager to see what was to be seen. While she waited, she became aware that one man in the crowd was not looking expectantly down the souk but looking up at her. He wore a dark suit, like the businessmen, and was holding a flat, black case under one arm. He was a thin man with a thin, sallow face and a way of holding himself that denoted a self-conscious dignity. Catching her eye, he bowed slightly and she, tired of her own company, smiled and asked him: 'What are they all waiting for?'

'Ah!' He pushed his way towards her, speaking in a serious tone to make clear the honesty of his intentions: 'They are waiting for a political leader who is to drive this way.' He paused, bowed again and said: 'May I offer you my protection?'

'Good heavens, no,' she was amused: 'I don't need protection. I'm an Englishwoman.' Then, the noise becoming a hubbub, she looked for the political leader and saw him being driven slowly between the two rows of excited onlookers. He was standing up in the back of an old, open Ford, and, as the enthusiasm became frantic, he waved to right and left, grinning all over his fat, jolly face, seeming to love everyone and being loved in return. His followers screamed and applauded and, drawing revolvers from waistbands, fired up at the tin roof of the souk. There was a frenzy of gunfire and pinging metal and Harriet felt she had been unwise in refusing any protection she could get. She looked to where the sallow man had stood, holding his black case, but he was no longer there and she feared her answer had driven him away.

As the Ford passed, the crowd pressed after it and Harriet could safely get down from the stone and walk back to her solitary meal in the pension. If she had replied to the man in a more encouraging fashion, she might have made a friend. But did she want a friend who looked like that? She liked large, comfortable men. She wanted a large, comfortable man as friend and companion, like Guy but without his intolerable gregariousness. If Guy were with her, he would not be a companion. Nothing would get him into the Ummayad Mosque or the El Azem Palace. She had spent too much time bored by left-wing casuists; she thought marriage with Guy had been hopeless from the start. They had never enjoyed the same things.

But without Guy, she was not enjoying herself very much. And her money would not last long. Having paid for her first week at the pension, she realized she would soon be in need of help. And where could she find it? The only person to whom she could turn was the British consul and he would advise her to go back to her husband. She thought: 'What a fool I've been! If I'd gone on the evacuation ship, my whole life would have changed. In England, I would have been among my own people. I would have found work. I would have had all the friends I wanted.'

A few evenings later, coming down to supper, she heard voices in the dining-room. Several more lights had been switched on and three people – a man and two women – were sitting at the table next to hers. The man was talking as she took her seat and went on talking, though he gave her a covert stare, then broke in on himself to say: 'You were wrong. We aren't alone here. There's this young lady: black hair, oval face, clear, pale skin – Persian, I'd guess!'

Harriet did not blink. His words having no effect on her, he returned his attention to his two companions and talked on in an accent that at times was Irish and at other times American. He was large but Harriet would not have called him comfortable. The women seemed insignificant beside him. His milky colouring and heavy features produced the impression of a Roman bust placed on top of a modern suit. It was a talking bust. Served with pilaff, he forked the food into his mouth and gulped it as though it were an impediment to be got out of the way. The pilaff finished, he threw aside his fork and gestured, shooting his big, white hands out of his sleeves and waving them about as he discoursed on the origins and cultures of the people of the eastern Mediterranean. The two women gave him so little attention they might have been deaf but Harriet, having been cut off from conversation for a week, listened intently.

'Now, take the Turks and Tartars of the Dobrudja,' he said. 'And the Gagaoules – Mohammedans coverted to Christianity and then converted back to Mohammedanism! They speak a language unknown anywhere else in the world.'

At this statement, Harriet could not help catching her breath and the man instantly swung round. Pointing his fork at her, he said: 'Our Persian lady is asking herself what on earth we're talking about.'

Harriet laughed: 'No, I'm not. I know what you're talking about. I used to live in Rumania.'

'Hey, d'ya hear that?' he gawped at the women: 'The Persian lady speaks English.'

'I am English.'

'Well, what d'ya know!' He stared at Harriet then told the two women: 'She's not Persian after all.' Quite unaffected by this revelation, the women went on with their meal.

Harriet said: 'May I ask what you are? Irish or American?'

'I'm neither. I'm both. I'm an Italian who's lived both in Dublin and in the States. I acquired an Eire passport because I thought it was the answer to life in these troubled times, but it's been a goddam bother to us. No one in the occupied countries will believe that Eire isn't part of England and as much at war as you are. To tell you the truth, we've stopped trying to stay in Europe. It's too much trouble. So we've shaken the dust and here we are monkeying around the Levant gathering material for my book. You've probably heard of me: Beltado, Dr Beltado, authority on ancient cultures. And this here's m'wife, Dr Maryann Jolly, another authority, and this is our assistant, Miss Dora O'Day.'

Dr Beltado looked at Dr Jolly and Miss Dora as though expecting them to carry on from there, but neither showed any interest in Harriet.

Dr Beltado spoke to cover their silence: 'You are called . . .?'

Harriet said: 'Harriet.' Dr Beltado again referred to his wife but she remained unmoved. She was a small, withered woman and, Harriet now saw, not to be disregarded, and Miss Dora, physically like her, was her handmaiden. Together they owned the large, flamboyant Dr Beltado. They might ignore him, they might even despise him, but no one else was going to get him. Harriet need not try to enter the group.

Having no wish to compete for Dr Beltado's attention, Harriet looked away from him and pretended not to hear when he directed remarks towards her. Their meal finished, Dr Beltado asked Madame Vigo for Turkish coffee and he and Dr Jolly lit Turkish cigarettes. The warm, biscuity smell of the smoke drifted towards Harriet like an enticement and Dr Beltado said: 'How about coffee for the Persian lady?' Harriet did not reply. She would remain apart but in her mind was the thought: 'In one minute, Guy would have had them eating out of his hand.'

The dining-room door opened a crack and someone looked in. Beltado said under his breath: 'Here's that guy Halal.' There was no welcome in his tone but lifting his voice, he shouted: 'Hi, there, Halal, nice to see ya. Come right in.'

Glancing up through her eyelashes, Harriet saw that Halal was the man who had offered his protection in the souk. He gave her a swift look and she suspected she was the reason for his visit, but he went directly to Beltado's table and, bowing, said: 'Good evening, Dr Jolly and Miss Dora. Good evening, Dr Beltado. Jamil has asked me to deliver an invitation. This evening he has a party and would ask you to his house.'

'Is that so?' Dr Beltado beamed and was about to accept when Dr Jolly's thin, dry voice stopped him: 'No, Beltado, we are all too tired.' She lifted her eyes to Halal: 'No. We have spent the day driving from Alexandretta.'

Dr Beltado began: 'Perhaps if we just looked in to say "hello" . . .' but Dr Jolly interrupted more firmly: 'No, Beltado.'

Beltado shrugged his acquiescence then, as though not wishing to waste the occasion, pointed to Harriet: 'Why not take Mrs Harriet! Believe it or not, she's English.'

'I am aware of that.' Halal looked towards Harriet and bowed. A slight smile came on his face as he remembered her avowal in the souk: 'If she would care to come, she would be made most welcome.'

'Thank you, but I'm just going to bed.'

'Bed! At nine o'clock, a young thing like you!' Beltado waved her away: 'Go and enjoy yourself. See one of the big Arab houses. It will be an experience.'

Yes, an experience! Knowing it would be faint-hearted to refuse, Harriet smiled on Halal and said: 'Thank you, I will come.'

'That's right,' said Beltado approvingly and as she passed him, he patted her just above the buttocks as though encouraging her towards an assignation.

A large car stood outside the pension gate. 'I suppose this is Dr Beltado's?'

'Certainly, yes. Few own such cars in Syria.'

'Do you know him well?'

'No, I cannot say well. He has been here twice before, working on his book.'

'The book about comparative cultures? He seems to have been working on it a long time.'

'Yes, a long time.' Halal spoke respectfully and there was an interval of silence before he next said: 'Mrs Harriet, you were displeased, were you not, when I offered my protection. I meant no discourtesy. I am myself a Christian and I know that among Moslems one must be circumspect.'

'Was I not circumspect? You mean my standing up on the stone? I'm sorry if I sounded ungrateful.'

'No, not much ungrateful. It is only, I would not wish to be misunderstood. Now, let me tell you where we are going. We are going to a khan. Do you know what a khan is? No? It is a private souk owned all by one man. This one is owned by Jamil's father who rents out the shops and is very rich. Jamil is my friend. He is very handsome because his grandmother was a Circassian. He tells me his wife, too, is very handsome but, of course, I have not seen her. They are Moslems. Yes, Jamil, a Moslem, was my great friend at Beirut. We went together to the American University so, you see, you will be with an advanced circle.'

'Is it so remarkable for a Moslem and a Christian to be friends?'

'Here, yes, it is remarkable. In the past the Christians suffered much persecution and hid their houses behind high walls. But Jamil and I are advanced. We mix together as our parents would not dream of doing.'

'I look forward to meeting him.'

'Yes, you will like him. He is a superior person. I am fortunate in knowing him.'

Halal spoke modestly but Harriet understood that, as proved by his association with Jamil, Halal, too, was a superior person.

Glancing aside at him, seeing he still carried his black leather case, Harriet asked him: 'What did you study at the university?'

'I studied law.'

'So you are a lawyer? You work in an office?'

'I am a lawyer but I do not work in an office. My father owns a silk factory and I conduct his legal affairs. That gives me more time than working in an office.'

They had reached the Souk el Tawill, deserted now and half-lit, at the end of which was the khan, walled and protected by decorated iron gates. Halal pulled a bell-rope, a shutter was opened and an ancient eye observed them before the gates were opened. Inside, a spacious quadrangle, under a domed roof, was lit by glass oil-lamps.

'See, is it not fine?' Halal pointed to the tessellated floor and the Moorish balcony that ran above the locked shops: 'If it were summer, Jamil would entertain out here, but now too cold.'

Halal was so eager for Harriet to appreciate the splendours of the khan that he kept her for several minutes in the cold before taking her to a door in the farther wall. Passing through a court-yard, they entered the family house. In the reception room, a plump young man came bounding towards them with outstretched arms: 'Ha, ha, so you found the lady, eh?'

Halal said reprovingly: 'I went as you requested to invite Dr Beltado . . .'

'Who could not come but sent this lady instead? That is good. See,' Jamil shouted joyfully to the other men in the room, 'we have a young lady.'

Jamil was a much more ebullient character than Halal. He had the rounded, rose-pink cheeks and light colouring of the Circassians and an air of genial self-indulgence. He took Harriet like a prize round the room. The guests, all men, were Moslems, Christians and Jews.

'A mixed lot, are we not?' Jamil asked, taking a particular pride in the presence of the Jews whom he introduced simply as Ephraim and Solomon. Before Harriet could speak to them, she was hurried over to a large central table where there was food enough to feed a multitude.

Jamil tried to persuade her to take some pressed meats or cakes or sweets but she had already had supper.

'Then you must drink,' he said.

There were jugs of lime juice and bottles of Cyprus brandy, Palestine vodka, wines and liqueurs.

Harriet took lime juice and Halal, under pressure, accepted a small brandy but protested: 'Why, Jamil, are you drinking nothing? You are not so abstemious when you come to visit me.'

'Shush, shush!' Jamil, giggling wildly, covered his face with his plump hands. 'Do not speak of such things. I know I can be a little devilish at times, but in my own house I consider the servants. If they saw me drink brandy, I could never lift my head among my people.'

The men crowded around Harriet, treating her with ostentatious courtesy so all might see how enlightened was their attitude towards the female sex.

Conducted to a place of honour on the main divan, she unwisely asked: 'Is your wife not coming to the party?'

Jamil, disconcerted, said: 'I think not. She is a little shy, you understand! But if you will come to meet her, she would be very much honoured.'

Harriet would have preferred to stay with her group of admiring men but Jamil, taking for granted that a woman would prefer to be with women, helped her to her feet and led her through a passage to another large room where she was left to sit while Jamil found his wife. The room was empty except for a number of small gilt chairs closely ranged round the walls.

Jamil returned. 'This is Farah,' he said and hurried back to his friends.

Farah was not, as Halal said, very handsome but she looked amiable and was very richly dressed. As she spoke little English and could not understand Harriet's Arabic, she could say nothing at first. The two women sat side by side on the gilt chairs and smiled at each other. After some minutes, Farah touched Harriet's skirt and gave a long, lilting, 'Oo-oo-oo-oo,' of admiration. Harriet, with more reason, returned admiration for Farah's kaftan of turquoise silk encrusted with gold. Even if too shy to attend the party, she seemed to be dressed for it.

A servant brought in Turkish coffee and dishes of silver-coated sugared almonds. They drank coffee, still marooned in smiling silence. Several more minutes passed, then Farah, gesturing gracefully in the direction of the Anti-Lebanon, said: 'Snow.'

Harriet nodded: 'Yes, snow.'

'In England snow every day?'

'Not every day, no.'

Farah regretfully shook her head and sighed.

When an hour, or what seemed like an hour, had passed, Harriet rose to say 'Goodbye'. Farah gave a moan of disappointment, then smiled bravely and went with Harriet to the door of the room. There she held out her hand and said slowly: 'Please come again.'

The party was over when Harriet returned to the reception room. Halal, waiting for her, stood with Jamil beside the table where the food and drink had hardly been touched.

Jamil, escorting his last guests across the khan to the gate, insisted that Harriet must return 'many times'. 'It is a great treat for my wife to talk with an English lady.'

'I'm afraid we could not talk much. We have no common guage.'

'What does that matter? Ladies do not need language. They look at each other and they understand.'

Walking back through the souk, Halal eagerly asked: 'Was she beautiful, Halal's wife?'

Harriet replied: 'She was very nice' and Halal was satisfied.

Reaching the lane that led to the pension, Halal stopped and said: 'I wish to show you something' and led her to a cul-de-sac at the side of the souk: 'Come. Look in here.'

Harriet peered into an area of darkness that might have been the interior of a great cathedral. There was light only in one corner where three Arabs sat with their camels round a charcoal brazier.

'What is it?' she asked.

'The greatest caravanserai in the world. Once, at this time of night, it would have been filled with camel trains settled in round their fires, all eating, all talking, then lying down to sleep. Here every route converged and it was called the Hub of the World. But now, you see: only the one small caravan, and soon no more. Perhaps that is the last to come here. It is sad, is it not?'

'Yes.' Harriet gazed into the vast darkness with its one corner of light and felt the sadness of things passing.

Halal said: 'Mohammed must have slept on this ground many times. His caravan went from Mecca to Aqaba and back to Mecca. When he conquered Damascus, he called it Bab Allah, the Gate of God, because from here the road runs straight to Mecca.'

'No doubt you have seen many things in Damascus?' Halal asked as they went towards the pension. When Harriet had to admit that as a woman and alone, she had been nervous of entering the Moslem sites, he said: 'If you would permit, I could be your escort. There is, I assure you, much to see.'

Harriet, not wanting to encourage Halal, said: 'Thank you,' and was glad that a distant burst of rifle fire interrupted him when he started to speak again.

'What are these demonstrations about?'

'Oh, it is just doleur. Food is scarce, prices keep rising and they blame the military, the Free French or the British. They do not harm. It is nothing to worry you. But, Mrs Harriet, you have not said "Yes" or "No". So tell me, may I call tomorrow and take you to see the Azem palace?'

'Well, not tomorrow. Perhaps another day.' Harriet knew she should be thankful for his company but leaving him, she hoped he would understand that that 'another day' was meant as a refusal.

Nine

Ross was the first to tell Simon that he would be transferred to the 15th Scottish hospital.

'But why?'

'Can't say, sir. Not exactly. I believe they've got a rehabilitation unit there where you'll get proper treatment.'

Simon, heartsick over Edwina's defection, felt this move was another blow. He was so despondent that Ross tried to coax him into a better humour: 'You wouldn't want to stay here for ever, now, would you, sir?'

'No, but I don't want to go anywhere else. I want to stay with the people I know. I thought they'd keep me here till I was back on my feet.'

Of the people he knew – the doctor, the sister, the nurses – Ross was the one who meant most to him. Ross had become a friend, more than a friend. He was like a faithful lover whom he might hope to keep about him for the foreseeable future. Now, for no reasonable reason, he would be taken from him, not by enemy action, against which there were no arguments, but on the orders of some administrator who had never seen Simon or Ross, and cared nothing for either of them.

But it was not only the separation from Ross that vexed him. Here, in his small area of Plegics, he was an important patient. The doctor, nurses and Ross were all concerned for his recovery and so closely related to his needs, emotions, fears and uncertainties, they were like members of his own family. To break with them would cause him anguish.

Simon took his appeal to the doctor: 'Surely, sir, I could stay till I'm better? It shouldn't take long.'

The doctor agreed that Simon was 'on the mend'. He could now get around on crutches. 'But when you can walk without them, I just cannot say. You need exercises and there's a proper unit at the 15th Scottish. There you'll get better faster, you wait and see.'

Simon's next appeal was to the sister who was brisker and blunter than Ross or the doctor: 'You've got to go, young man. We need your bed. This is a New Zealand hospital and we must put our own lads first. We've had a signal warning us to prepare for casualties. Our lads have taken a beating on the Mareth Line and they'll be coming in soon from the dressing-stations. So, there's nothing for it. We have to accommodate them.'

'The Mareth Line? Where is it? I've never heard of it.'

'Somewhere in Tunisia. That's where the Kiwis are now.'

Simon had to realize that while he had been lying there disabled, the fighting had moved a long way west. He felt resentful that he had been left behind and he was eager to be back in the desert. He asked Ross: 'How long before I'm fit again for active service?'

'That depends, sir. It's what the doc said. The thing you need now is exercise. If you keep at it, you'll be fit sooner than you think.'

Simon still hoped that the move, if it must come, would be delayed so he was shocked when Ross told him the ambulance was waiting for him. Sitting on the edge of the bed, he put on his clothes and fitted his few possessions into the box that held his dress uniform. Then he swung himself on to his crutches and made his way out of Plegics. The other men, though his officer status had kept him separate from them, said goodbye to him. One even said: 'Sorry to see you go, sir.'

Simon could only nod, too affected to speak.

The ambulance men helped him up the steps and sat him on a bunk. There, looking out at Ross, he said: 'You'll come and see me, won't you, Ross?'

'You bet, sir.' Ross smiled and saluted, then turned away. He did not look back as the ambulance was started up. Instinctively, Simon knew that Ross had finished with him. The physio had other work to do. New patients were due and there would be another special case in Simon's cubicle. So far as Ross was concerned, Simon had ceased to exist.

The 15th Scottish was bigger and better equipped than the New Zealand hutments but Simon disliked it from the start. The place seemed to him impersonal. The new team attendant on him had no great interest in him. They had had no part in his recovery. To them he was merely another wounded man half-way to health.

As the hospital was only a tram-ride from the Institute, Guy could visit Simon more often now. He found him peevish and resentful of his changed life. He was passing through a difficult stage of convalescence when he was expected to do more for himself and make an effort to adjust to the normal world. He longed for Ross to take responsibility for him and knowing he would never see Ross again, he turned to Guy, looking to him as to a much older man on whom he could lean. Guy could not have this. Simon had to face his own independence and his own future. He had too much time in which to feel sorry for himself and Guy urged him to spend it in study of some sort.

'What was your job before you were called up?'

'I didn't have a job. I'd just left school when the war started. My dad was keen for me to become a teacher. I was entered for a teachers' training college but I never got there.'

Guy said: 'Splendid!' He would have encouraged Simon to prepare for any profession but none seemed to him as worthy as teaching. He said with enthusiasm: 'I'll apply for the preliminary examination papers and you can begin work here and now. What were your best subjects at school?'

Simon shook his head vaguely: 'I was all right at some things, I think.' Looking back at his last days in the sixth form, he could remember only the excitement of waiting for the war to break out. He had excelled in the officers' training course and he had come to see warfare as his natural occupation.

He said: 'I was never keen on mugging up school books. I liked games. I liked the OTC.'

'Well, now's your chance to train your mind. There's a well-stocked library at the Institute and I've a collection of books on teaching methods. I'll give you all the help I can.'

'What's the point?' Simon was dismayed by Guy's plans for his further education: 'It may be years before I'm demobbed. I'd forget everything I'd learnt. It would just be a waste of time.'

'Learning is never a waste of time. Even if the war does drag on, you should keep your mind active so when you return to civilian life . . .'

'But I don't want to return to civilian life. The army's my life. All I want now is to get back into the fight. Out there no one thinks of the future because, well, there may not be any future.'

Guy argued but all Simon would say was: 'Let's leave it, Guy. Just now I've got to concentrate on getting better.'

And he was getting better, but not as fast as his new physio wished. Though he now had every sort of exercising device, his feet would not support him on the floor. The physio, Greening, had him fitted with callipers and ordered him to take his hands off the parallel bars. The result was he toppled forward and struck his chest on a bar. Greening, barely suppressing his anger, knelt down and savagely pulled Simon's feet forward, one after the other, requiring him to place them firmly on the ground.

Simon was out of sympathy with Greening who had been a sergeant drill-instructor in the regular army. Middle-aged, more experienced than Ross, he had a habit of command rather than persuasion. He was irascible, even brutal, and had little patience.

'It's up to you,' he told Simon: 'You've got to work at it.'

As Simon strained to keep himself upright, his hands would return to the bars and Greening would bawl: 'Take your hand off.' His face distorted with the effort, Simon managed at last to shift his right foot forward but the left refused to follow.

Greening, relenting, said more amicably: 'All you have to do is forget you can't do it. You can feel your feet, can't you?'

'Yes. I know they're there but they're sort of ghostly.'

'Well, you think of them as solid flesh and blood, and tell them to get on with it.'

That night he again had the dream of running across fields unbroken except for some giant trees that rose out of the ground and quivered in front of him. As he ran, he could see the flash of his feet but not the feet themselves. Suddenly fearful, he slowed down to look and seeing them there, solid flesh and blood, he sped on in sheer delight of being whole again. He shouted out and waking himself, realizing his condition, he gave a cry that brought the night nurse running to him.

Now that he was regaining energy, he was bored by the claustrophobic routine of hospital life. Details of his time in the desert came back to him and he felt an intense nostalgia for events that had once meant nothing to him: brewing-up, making a fire of scrubwood between stones, boiling the brew can and throwing tea in by the handful; the whiplash crack of bursting shells, even the sandstorms and the pre-dawn awakening.

When Guy again tried to interest him in a teaching course, he said: 'I know teaching's fine. My dad thought the same, but it's not for me. I want to be with the chaps. I'd like to join a regiment stationed somewhere like India or Cyprus. I want to see the world.'

'But you'll want to settle down later. You'll want to marry and have a home of your own.'

'Later, perhaps.' Simon had not told Guy that he was already married because that marriage did not count, but another thought came into his head and he said as lightly as he could: 'How's Edwina? Is she still seeing Major Brody?'

'I expect so but she'll soon get tired of him.'

'Really? You think so?'

'Oh, yes. Edwina aspires towards a title. She's looking for another Lord Lisdoonvarna.'

Simon laughed. He did not consider that Edwina's aspirations lessened his own chances but was happy to think that Major Brody would soon be out of the way.

Guy sometimes asked Greening about Simon's progress and discussed what could be done to hasten his recovery. Greening said he intended trying electrotherapy and thought it a pity there was no swimming-pool at the hospital. Hydrotherapy often proved useful in these cases.

Giving this some thought, Guy decided to take Simon to the Gezira pool, a place he would not visit on his own. Having grown up far from the coast, he could not swim and saw water as an unreliable element. He had first thought of taking Simon to Alexandria but realized the dangers of the open sea. He applied to the Gezira Club for temporary membership and when this was granted, he thought all difficulties were at an end.

Intending to surprise Simon, Guy did not say where they were going. The winter was petering out and the afternoons were very warm. When they reached the club garden, a sound of laughter and splashing came from the pool and Simon looked alarmed.

'We're not going in there, are we?'

'Yes. We'll probably see Edwina. She's always in the pool.'

Simon left the car unwillingly and self-conscious on his crutches, let himself be led inside the enclosure. As he feared, the pool was full of girls and able-bodied men and he would, if he could, have fled, but Guy wanted him to be there and saying nothing, he sank into the deck-chair that Guy placed for him.

Guy had imagined that the sight of Simon would arouse sympathy and there would be willing helpers to induce him into the water, but those who noticed the disabled man seemed discomforted and embarrassed by his presence. And Guy realized he had not thought the plan through. Before he could swim, Simon had to undress. Bathing trunks and towels would have to be found for him and he would need a clear stretch of water in which to try and propel himself. As it was, there were not two square feet of it free of bodies.

Sitting beside Simon, Guy said: 'Later, when they've gone into tea, there'll be more room for you . . .'

Realizing what was intended, Simon said fiercely: 'Good heavens, I'm not going in there.'

'But some of them will help you.'

'I don't want their help. I'd only be a nuisance among that crowd.'

That, Guy feared, was true. Simon, gazing with sombre fixity at the merriment in the water, twitched as though in pain. Guy, following his gaze, saw that Edwina had appeared on the diving-board. In a white bathing-dress, her hair caught up in a white cap formed of rubber petals, she stood, a tall, golden girl, poised to dive. Tony Brody was clearing a space in the water, officiously asserting his claim on her. She dived, came up, saw Guy and swam across to him: 'Hello. I haven't seen you here before.'

'I've never been before. I brought Simon for an airing.'

'*What* a good idea!' Edwina, startled to see Simon with his crutches, said: 'Oh Simon, how well you look!'

Simon knew that was not true. Thin and pallid from his days in bed, he was also exhausted by his efforts under Greening. He blushed, hung his head and did not reply.

Edwina cajoled him: 'It's great fun here, isn't it?'

Guy began to say: 'Can't you persuade him to join in?' But Edwina, whether she heard or not, pushed off from the side and went to join Brody who was waiting for her, a medicine ball held above his head. She jumped up to seize it and they scuffled together, churning the water and shrieking in their excitement.

Simon watched so intently he did not hear when Guy spoke to him.

'Shall we go?'

Simon, becoming aware of the question, shook his head. Miserable though he was, he could not leave while Edwina was there, and so they sat until the sun began its descent towards the west. Near them lay one of the young women known to officers as 'Gezira lovelies'. Plump, round-faced, not pretty but with a bloomy look, she stretched and roused herself as a safragi came to serve her with iced coffee.

To Guy, the whole idle, sensual, self-indulgent ambience of the pool was unbearably boring. Had it not been for Simon, nothing would have kept him there, and as the afternoon advanced, he felt he could tolerate no more of it.

'I'll have to take you back. I'm due at a staff meeting at five.'

In the car, fearing he had cut short Simon's pleasure, Guy said: 'We'll come again another day.'

'No, thank you. I don't want to go there again.'

'I expect you felt as I did: messing about there is just a waste of time?'

Simon was surprised: 'No, I didn't think that. I felt envious. I longed to be like them.'

Guy was surprised but said to encourage him: 'You will be, soon enough. It's only a question of time.'

'That's what they all say,' Simon said bitterly, thinking of the time he had lost, the time that had been taken from him.

Ten

A few days after the party at the khan, Halal turned up at the pension with a taxi. The inmates of the pension were still at breakfast and Beltado, seeing Halal making his shadowy, uncertain way into the room, began: 'Hi, there, Halal!' then realized the visitor was not for him. Watching Halal, his case under his arm, moving warily towards Harriet, Beltado smiled a salacious smile.

'Mrs Harriet, may I sit down?'

'Yes, but my name is not Mrs Harriet. I am a married woman. My husband is called Guy Pringle.'

'Ah, I understand – so you are Mrs Pringle. I have come to ask if you would care to make a visit to some place of interest? The big mosque, or the castle, perhaps? I can tell you about them. I would be your guide.'

Unable to think of a reason for refusing, Harriet said: 'I would like to see the mosque.' As she left the pension in Halal's company, she heard Beltado chuckling with satisfaction.

In the taxi, Halal said: 'I have made bold to hire this driver for a week in the hope we may make many excursions together.' After a pause, he added: 'So your husband is in this part of the world? Where, may I ask?'

'He is in Cairo.'

'So! I presume you are here for a short holiday only? Tell me, Mrs Pringle how long are you planning to stay in our city?'

'I suppose till my money runs out.'

Taking this for a joke, Halal made a slight, choking noise intended for a laugh: 'Then I may hope you will be here a long time.'

Harriet laughed, too, but she knew he felt there was something odd about her presence in Syria though he had not the courage to ask what it was.

The taxi stopped at the mosque and Halal announced: 'We are now outside the great mosque of the Ummayad.'

An attendant, lolling half asleep on a bench, leapt into life as he saw Harriet and, reaching into a closet, brought out a black robe which he held out to her.

Halal said: 'I fear you must wear this. He says to put the hood over your head so it hides your face.'

Disliking the robe, which was dusty and not over-clean, Harriet asked: 'Why must I wear it?'

'I'm sorry but they fear a lady will distract the men from their devotions. The men have, you understand, strong desires.'

'You mean they are frustrated. Tell him that you can't make men chaste by keeping women out of sight.'

Halal stared at her, disconcerted, then smiled, not knowing what else to do: 'You are an unusual lady, Mrs Pringle. Very unusual. You think for yourself.'

'Where I come from that's not unusual.' Harriet shook the robe and laughed: 'This is ridiculous but if I must, I must.' She adjusted it about her, trying to give it some dignity, then started to walk away. The keeper croaked a protest and pointed to her shoes. Halal said:

'Ah, I forgot. We must enter barefoot.'

'In Cairo they give you felt slippers to put over your shoes.'

'Here they are more strict.'

At last they were admitted to the spacious, sunlit courtyard where the marble flooring was cold beneath their feet. They paused under the porticos to admire the mosaics.

'See, they are very old, very beautiful,' Halal said, as though Harriet might not be aware of these facts: 'You must understand, the cities they portray are not real. The buildings, the forests, all are fanciful. You will observe that there is no human figure, no animal, no creature that could be mistaken as an object of worship.'

'Because of the ancient Egyptians, I suppose?'

'I suppose, yes. You can hit the nail very nicely, Mrs Pringle.' Halal smiled again, more warmly, beginning to approve Harriet's habit of independent thought. 'Now we enter the mosque proper.'

The vast interior hall, lit only by the glow from stained-glass windows, was in semi-darkness so Harriet had no clear view of the men whose devotions were to be protected against a female form. A few were at prayer but most of them seemed to treat the mosque as a social centre. They sat on the floor in groups, talking and slipping their amber chaplets through their fingers.

'Do the women ever come here?'

'Oh, yes,' Halal pointed to a heavy curtain stretched across a corner: 'They may sit behind there.'

Harriet was glad to have an escort. No one gave her curious looks or nudged against her or stared into her face with bold, provocative eyes. She was hidden, the concern only of her protector who was probably mistaken for her husband. Halal, for his part, held himself with an air of importance. As guide, he was almost too knowledgeable. Harriet became weary, standing about while he talked. He required her to 'give attention' to the lamps of which there had once been six hundred, each hanging from a golden chain. He started to count them but on reaching a hundred, gave up, saying apologetically, 'Many have been plundered, I fear. At times there has been much destruction, massacres and such things, and the mosque is very old. It was first a Greek temple – the temple of Rimmon spoken of in the Bible – then a Christian church, and now a mosque. They have beneath this floor a precious relic: the head of John the Baptist.'

'I'd like to see that.'

'I, too, but it is put away, I think because of the war. Still, there is another relic. Very interesting. Follow me.'

They came to an ancient doorway, the main doorway of the early Christian church. Halal stretched out his right arm: 'Behold what is written above! Can you read it?'

'No. I never learnt ancient Greek.'

'Then, I will translate for you.' Holding himself stiffly, his black case under his arm, he proclaimed with reverence: 'Thy kingdom, O Christ, is an everlasting Kingdom and thy dominion endureth through all generations.' He relaxed and smiled on her: 'That was true in the fourth century and still true, is it not?'

'Why do you think Christ let the Moslems take over?'

Halal thought it best to evade this question: 'We must not question the will of God. Now we will visit the old castle.'

Taken for a walk round the castle walls, Harriet was surprised by her own energy. She was recovering what she had lost in

Egypt: the will to exert herself. When Halal proposed 'a little drive into the Ghuta' next day, she said: 'That sounds pleasant.'

'It is pleasant,' Halal earnestly told her: 'The Ghuta is the Garden – the Garden of Damascus. You will come, then, Mrs Pringle? Good! I will call for you.'

That evening Dr Beltado leant towards her to say with a conniving smile: 'I see you have made a conquest.' Knowing he suspected a liaison had started, she was discomforted, chiefly because Halal had no attraction for her. She decided that the outing to the Ghuta must be their last.

The next day Harriet wished she had rejected it. The sky was overcast and the suburban greenery, heavy with the night's rain, seemed to her oppressive. She had become conditioned to desert, the nakedness of the earth, and the orchards and market gardens worried her. Anything might be hidden among their massed, lush leaves.

'We owe all this,' Halal complacently said, 'to our great rivers that in the Bible are called Abana and Pharphar.'

'The ones that couldn't cure Naaman?'

'Ah, I could take you to the house of Naaman. It is now a leper colony.'

'No thank you.'

Halal smiled but, discouraged by her manner, kept silent until they were beyond the town and driving into the grassy slopes of the Anti-Lebanon. The sun broke through, the mists cleared and the green about them became translucent. Harriet, now more appreciative of Halal's hospitality, said: 'It is beautiful here.'

'Yes, yes,' Halal became eagerly talkative again: 'And now we come to a very nice café from where we can see Damascus encircled by gardens as the moon by its halo.'

Harriet laughed: 'You're quite a poet, Halal.'

'Alas, it was not me but another that wrote that deathless tribute to our city.'

The café, a white clap-board bungalow, was hung on the hillside, its terrace built out over the slope below. Three young men, one with a guitar, were seated on the terrace and called to Halal as he passed them: 'You're out early Halal,' and they looked, not at Halal, but at Harriet.

Halal gave them a cold 'Good morning' and led Harriet to the rail so she might see rising above the 'halo' of foliage, the battlements of the castle and the gold-tipped domes and minarets of the Ummayad mosque.

'Mohammed was right, was he not? This is paradise. Some say it was indeed the Garden of Eden.'

When Harriet did not speak, he asked, 'Could you live your life in this place?'

'Yes, if I had to. I feel well here.'

'That is good. And now observe,' Halal pointed towards the minarets: 'See the very tall one? There Christ will alight on the Day of Judgement.'

'Christ? Not Mohammed?'

'No, not Mohammed. Mohammed will return to the rock in Jerusalem from which he leapt up to Heaven. It is in the Mosque of Omar and still bears the mark of his horse's hoof.'

Behind them, the young man with the guitar had started to strum a popular Arabic song. He sang quietly: 'Who is Romeo? Who is Julietta?' Harriet noticed two tortoises crawling near her feet and as she bent towards them, she caught the eye of the guitarist who gave her a sly, sidelong glance and smirked. So the song was directed at her.

Halal, seeing her attention diverted, frowned and spoke to regain it: 'The spring is already here! The anemones are coming out.'

Looking down at the grass, Harriet saw that a few buds were breaking and one, more sheltered than the rest, was opening, a gleam of scarlet.

'In summer, when the evenings are long, we walk by the river and many young men bring musical instruments. Such things are common here.'

Before Halal could instruct her further, a waiter called to him and he led her to a table set with cakes and coffee: 'I took the precaution of ordering by telephone so there would be no delay.'

The young men put their heads together in wonder at this precaution. Halal, becoming more confident, asked boldly: 'May I ask you, Mrs Pringle, why you came here alone to Damascus?'

Ready now for this question, Harriet said: 'Because I was ill in

Cairo. The climate did not agree with me. I developed amoebic dysentery and was advised to come here to regain my health.'

'Ah, I understand. And your husband could not come with you?'

'No, his work kept him in Egypt.'

'So you will stay till you are restored, is that it?'

'I will if I can but, to tell you the truth, I need to earn some money.'

'You need to earn money? E-e-e-e-e!' Halal made a noise that expressed his astonishment. 'But that is very difficult for an English lady. And yet it might be possible. I may have an idea.'

'Really?'

'We will say no more. I would not raise false hopes.'

Driving back into the city, Halal stopped the taxi and said to Harriet: 'Let us take a little stroll. There is something that may please you.'

The stroll, up a lane between the backs of houses, ended at the gate of a graveyard. The graves were so old, the stones had sunk almost out of sight but in the centre there was a prominent tomb, an oblong protected by iron railings. A rambler rose, just coming into leaf, sprawled over the rails and covered the tomb's upper surface. Halal crossed to it and put his hand affectionately on the stone.

'This is a Christian graveyard and this is the burial place of Al-Akhtal, a poet and a wild fellow. Because he was a Christian, he was free to drink wine and he loved to go with singing slave girls. These things inspired him and he wrote about them.' Halal tittered: 'It was very shocking, of course, but perhaps enjoyable. What do you think?'

'It sounds very innocent to me.'

'Indeed?' Halal looked pleasurably surprised: 'That, I agree, is how we should see it but most people here are not very advanced.' He smiled and lifted his eyes to the sky: 'There is the new moon. Do you know what the Moslems call it? The prophet's eyebrow.'

The moon was brilliant, a sliver of crystal in the green of the evening sky. Halal, lowering his gaze to her, said solemnly: 'You know, Mrs Pringle, you are like the new moon.'

'Meaning I'm thin and pale?'

'Meaning you are very delicate. When I saw you in the souk, I thought, "She is so delicate, these ruffians will sweep her away." Yet, though you are delicate, you shimmer like the moon. You are, if you will permit me to say it, the wife I wish I had.'

'Oh dear! Surely there are a great many ladies in Damascus who would do as well?'

'Yes, there are ladies here, very nice but very simple. For myself, I like them less nice and more intelligent. Tell me, will you come tomorrow and see the ravine through which the Abana flows?'

Harriet replied firmly: 'No. You have been very kind to me, Halal, but I cannot go out with you again. People will misunderstand.'

Halal's face lengthened with an expression of tragic melancholy and he slowly shook his head: 'It is true, they observe and do not understand. And I know, you are afraid of your husband. Gossip will reach him and he will be angry.'

Harriet laughed at the idea of Guy's anger. 'Nothing like that,' she assured Halal but he knew better.

'Believe me,' he said: 'I respect your prudence.'

Harriet laughed again but left it like that. Before they parted, she asked him: 'Please tell me, Halal, what do you keep in your black case?'

He gravely answered: 'My diplomas.'

As the days passed without Halal, Harriet wished she had not given him such a definite dismissal. Almost any company was better than none. In her solitude, it seemed to her that Dr Beltado was ignoring her, perhaps in disapproval of her separation from Halal. The women, once she had an escort of her own, had relented somewhat and had even given her a glance or two. Now all three seemed determined to stress her loneliness. But perhaps she imagined this for one evening Dr Beltado, his coffee cup in his hand, came over and sat in the chair beside her.

'Our friend Halal tells me you might like to help me out with my book?'

'Why, yes, I would.'

'Say, that's fine. You know we have the big room on the top floor? Every morning we work there together. Well, little lady, any time you feel like it, come up and join us.'

Overwhelmed by this proposal, Harriet wished Halal were there so she might show her gratitude.

The room that Beltado spoke of was very big; a long, low attic with two dormer windows. It was as sparsely furnished as Harriet's bedroom but the Beltados had brought in their own folding chairs and tables and the floor was heaped with their books.

Dr Jolly who had her work space at one end of the room, sat bent down in concentrated study and apparently deaf to her husband's voice. Dr Beltado and Miss Dora held the centre of the room where there was most light. Beltado dressed for breakfast and then apparently, undressed in order to do battle with his enormous task of correlating all cultures. The bed had been pulled forward to accommodate him and, resting on one elbow, he lay, wearing a Chinese robe that exposed more of him than it covered. He was dictating to Miss Dora when Harriet tapped on the door. He called to her to come in, obviously irritated by the interruption. He stared at her, bemused for some moments before he remembered why she was there.

Rather exasperated, he said: 'What are we going to do with you?' He ordered Miss Dora to show Harriet her shorthand notes: 'Think you can make a rough typescript of that?'

The shorthand was unlike any Harriet had seen before: 'I'm sorry, I can't.'

'You can't, eh? Sit down then and we'll find you something else.'

Harriet sat and listened and learnt about different cultures but she never learnt what she was employed to do. Or, indeed, if she were employed at all for, from first to last, there was no mention of a salary.

Forgetting Harriet, Dr Beltado dictated, waving his arms about and letting his robe slip so all might view his white legs, his belly and his large pudenda. Miss Dora, obviously used to this display, ignored it and meekly scribbled on. Advocating the co-ordination of all cultural disciplines, Dr Beltado said that the experts should work together like an orchestra gathered under the baton of one supreme conductor.

'And who,' Beltado asked, 'should that conductor be? I think I may, without undue conceit, suggest myself, a man widely travelled and experienced, and not one to flinch from responsibility. If invited to fill the role . . .' Gazing round, he caught Harriet's eye and came to a stop.

'What are you doing here?'

'I'm waiting for a job.'

Miss Dora was told to find Harriet a job. She produced a box of photographs that had to be sorted according to their countries of origin. There were some five hundred photographs and sorting them gave Harriet three days' work. That finished, she was set to making a fair copy of Miss Dora's rough typescript. At the end of the first week, she hoped Dr Beltado would mention money, but nothing was said. She spent the next week typing each day from nine in the morning until six in the evening and once, when Dr Beltado had gone to relieve himself, she spoke quietly to Miss Dora: 'Does Dr Beltado pay one weekly or monthly?'

'Pay?' Miss Dora seemed never to have heard of pay. Her homely face with its small eyes and thin, red nose quivered in embarrassment, but she asked: 'What did you arrange with him?'

'I didn't arrange anything but I need to earn some money.'

'If I get a chance, I'll mention it to Dr Jolly.' Miss Dora turned away as though the subject were distasteful and nothing more was said for the next three days. Then Harriet managed to trap her in the passage.

'Miss Dora, please! Have you asked Dr Jolly about my salary?'

'You're to send in your account.' Miss Dora dodged round Harriet and was gone. Harriet, used to a system of wages paid weekly for work done, had no idea what to charge or for how long. She bought some ruled paper and spent Friday evening in her room, concocting an account so modest no one could question it but when, on Saturday morning, she went up to the Beltado work-room, she found no one there.

Dr Beltado, Dr Jolly and Miss Dora, folding chairs and tables, books and papers – all had gone. The bed was back against the wall. The whole place had the abject nullity of a body from which life had departed. And Harriet, on the floor below, had not heard a sound.

She hurried down to ask Madame Vigo where Dr Beltado had

gone? He and his ladies had departed the pension soon after day-break, leaving no forwarding address.

'And when are they coming back?'

'One year, two year. I not know.'

'They did not pay me for my work.'

'They forgot?'

Perhaps they did forget; and Harriet felt the more disconsolate to think herself forgotten.

Eleven

The news reached Cairo that British and American forces had made contact in North Africa. At the same time Guy received official confirmation of Harriet's death. The letter stated that the name of Harriet Pringle was on a list of 530 persons granted passage on the evacuation ship, the *Queen of Sparta*, that sailed from Suez on 28 December 1942. The *Queen of Sparta* had been sunk by enemy action while in the Indian Ocean. Harriet Pringle, together with 528 other passengers, had been declared missing, believed drowned. One passenger and two members of the crew had survived. The passenger's name was given as Caroline Rutter.

Guy took the letter to Dobson who was still in his bedroom. 'It's been a long time coming.'

Dobson, quick to defend authority, said: 'There could be no absolute certainty about the ship's fate till it failed to turn up at Cape Town.'

'What about the survivors? Wouldn't they be conclusive proof?'

'No. We've had a longer report. The crewmen were lascars who scarcely knew what ship it was. The woman was too ill for weeks to tell anyone anything. Until there was proof, the rumours had to be treated as – well, rumours.'

'I see.' Guy put the letter into his pocket.

That morning, at breakfast, Edwina said she was thinking of marrying Tony Brody.

'Good heavens,' said Dobson; 'not Tony Brody!'

'Why not? He's a major and a nice man.'

'I should have thought you could do better than Brody.'

Edwina, sniffing behind her curtain of hair, said dismally: 'There's not much choice these days. The most exciting men have all gone to Tunisia and I don't think they're coming back.'

'Even so. Be sensible and wait. Someone will come along.'

'I have waited, perhaps too long. I'm not getting younger.'

Dobson observed her with a critical smile: 'True. The bees aren't buzzing around as they used to.'

'Oh, Dobbie, really! How beastly you are!' Edwina gave a sob and Dobson patted her hand.

'There, there, pet, your Uncle Dobbie was joking. You're still as beautiful as a dream and you don't want to marry Brody.'

'Oh, I might as well. If you can't marry the man you want, does it matter who you marry?'

'Why not stay peacefully unmarried, like me?'

'Because I don't want to spend the rest of my life working in a dreary office.'

While this conversation skirted his consciousness, Guy was thinking of Harriet missing, believed drowned. At an age when other girls were thinking of marriage, she was lying at the bottom of the Indian Ocean.

The letter, though it told him nothing he did not already know, hung over him during his morning classes. It was as though a final shutter had come down on his memories of his wife and he realized that all this time some irrational, tenuous hope had lingered in his mind.

He thought of another ill-fated ship, the ship on which Aidan Pratt had served as a steward when he was a conscientious objector. On its way to Canada, with evacuees, it was torpedoed and Aidan had shared a life-boat packed with children in their night clothes. They had died off one by one from cold and thirst and when thrown overboard, the little bodies had floated after the boat because they were too light to sink. Harriet had weighed scarcely more than a teenage girl and Guy could imagine her body floating and following the boat as though afraid of being left alone on that immense sea.

Still disconsolate when he reached the hospital, he found Simon in a mood very different from his own. That morning, Simon had managed to walk a few yards without a crutch. He had walked awkwardly but he had done it – he had walked on his own.

'You see what that means?'

86

Guy laughed, trying to lift his own spirits up to Simon's level: 'No wonder you're so cheerful.'

Simon, lying in a deck-chair on the veranda of his small ward, was cheerful to the point of light-headedness. Delighted with himself, he said: 'I was like this once before, when I first went into Plegics – but more so. In fact, I was pretty nearly bonkers and for no reason. But now I have a reason, haven't I? I *know* I'm going to walk like a normal man. I told you about those dreams I get, when I'm running for miles over green fields? Well, one day, after the war, I'm going to do that! I'll go into the country and run for miles, like a maniac.'

'Just to show you're as good as the rest of them? You could run in the desert just as well.'

'No, it has to be over fields. I want that green grass, that green English grass.'

'So it's England now, not India or Cyprus?'

Simon laughed wildly. He was in a state where everything amused him but he was particularly pleased by a joke he had heard the previous evening. There had been a lecture in the main hall of the hospital, intended for patients who were near recovery. They were told they would leave the hospital in perfect health and the army had expected them to stay in perfect health. They were to avoid brothels and street women and to keep themselves clean and fit.

'Just like a school pi-jaw,' Simon said, 'Except that the chap was funny. Oh, he was funny! What do you think he said at the end? He said: "Remember – flies spread disease. *Keep yours shut!*"'

Simon threw his head back in riotous enjoyment of this statement and Guy, smiling and frowning at the same time, thought: 'What a boy he is! Little more than a schoolboy in spite of all he's seen.' Guy himself was not yet twenty-five but, suffering the after-effects of bereavement, he felt a whole generation or more older than Simon. It occurred to him, too, that Simon returning to normal vitality, was a different person from the disabled youth whom he had adopted as a charge. Simon, helpless and dependent, had had the appeal of a child or a young animal but now, growing into independence, he had qualities that set him apart from his protector. Guy remembered his own boredom at the

87

Gezira pool while Simon felt only envy of an activity in which he could not join. Even now Simon, with his carefree ambition to run over green fields, was growing away from him and Guy, with the letter in his pocket, wondered what consolation he would find when Simon was gone altogether.

For some weeks now he had been avoiding public gatherings and the condolences of friends but that evening, feeling a need to talk to someone who had known Harriet, he went to the Anglo-Egyptian Union where he found Jake Jackman practising shots at the billiard table. They played a game of snooker then went into the club-room for drinks. Sitting with Jake at a table, Guy took out the letter and said casually: 'This came this morning.'

Jackman, as he read, grunted his sympathy until coming to the name of Caroline Rutter, he burst out: 'So that old crow Rutter's still alive!'

'Who is this Caroline Rutter?'

'Why, the impertinent old bloody bitch who had the cheek to ask me why I wasn't in uniform. To think of it! A nice-looking girl like Harriet dead and that old trout survives! She probably lived off her fat. The rich are like camels. They grow two stomachs and spend their time filling them so they've always got one to fall back on in case of emergencies.'

Jackman, drinking steadily, spent the evening dwelling on this fantasy and enlarging it until Castlebar's wife came to the table. He was now in a rage against the perversity of chance and he looked at Mona Castlebar with hatred. Not disconcerted, she sat down beside Guy. She had sung in his troop's entertainment and felt she had as good a right as anyone to his company. Having no quarrel with her, he bought her a drink.

She said: 'I suppose you've heard nothing from Bill?'

'I'm afraid, not a word.'

'Neither have I, and I haven't had a penny from him since he went. He neither knows nor cares how I'm managing.'

Jackman asked with gleeful malice: 'How *are* you managing?'

'That's my business.'

Both men knew that the university was allowing Mona to draw Castlebar's salary so Guy did not speak but Jackman, who had been eyeing her breasts and legs as though unable to credit their bulk, said: 'You're not starving, that's obvious.'

Mona, her glass empty, was tilting it about in her hand as though inviting a refill. Jackman said: 'I'll buy you a drink if you buy me one.'

'I'm not buying you anything. You've had more than enough as it is.'

'Oh!' Jackman straightened himself, his eyes glinting for a fight: 'No wonder Bill went off with the first woman who asked him. He always said you were a mean-natured lout.'

'He said you were a scrounging layabout.'

'That's good, coming from Lady Hooper's fancy man.'

Guy said: 'Shut up, both of you,' and Jackman, grumbling to himself, looked around as though seeking better company. Seeing Major Cookson at another table, he said: 'If that cow's staying, I'm going.'

Guy felt he, too, had had enough of Mona. As a taxi came in at the Union gates, he said he had to go home and correct students' essays.

Taking the chance, Mona rose with him: 'As you're going to Garden City, you can drop me off on the way.'

So it happened Guy missed an event that was long to be a subject of gossip in Cairo. Or, rather, he did not miss it, for had he remained it would never have occurred.

What Jake Jackman did after joining Major Cookson was recounted by Cookson whenever he found himself an audience.

Cookson had not been alone at his table. He had with him his two cronies: Tootsie and the ex-archaeologist Humphrey Taupin. Shouting so all could hear, Jackson told this group that he would not spend another minute with that 'grabby monstrosity' Mona Castlebar and continued to vilify her till she and Guy were gone. Then, curving forward in his chair, his right hand pulling at his nose, his left hanging between his knees, he subsided into morose silence. Cookson, who was spending Taupin's money, asked what Jake would drink.

'Whisky.'

Cookson called on Taupin to replenish funds but Taupin said he had nothing left. Jackman losing patience, called a safragi and ordered a double whisky: 'Put it down to Professor Pringle's account.'

'Not here Ploffesor Plingle.'

'He's coming back. And bring another for him. Put them both down to his account.'

Still pervaded by grievances, Jackman drank both whiskies rapidly and they brought him to the point of action. Leaning confidingly towards Cookson, he said: 'You know that Mrs Rutter who lives down the road?'

'I don't think I do.'

'She owns a swell place. Big house and garden, crowds of wogs to wait on her. Generous old girl, keeps open house. Told me to drop in for a drink any time. "Bring your friends," she said, "I'm always ready for a booze up."'

'Really!' Major Cookson's grey, peaked face lit with interest. 'She sounds a charming woman.'

'Charming? She's charming, all right. Like to come?'

'What, now? Oh, I don't think I can leave my friends.'

'All come, why not?' Jackman slapped the table to emphasize his magnanimity and jumped to his feet: 'It's no distance. We can walk there in half a minute.'

Cookson and Tootsie, unusually animated, got to their feet but Taupin was unable to move. He lay entranced, sliding out of his chair, eyes shut, a smile on his crumpled, curd-white face.

'Leave him,' Jackman said and walked off. After a moment's uncertainty, Tootsie and Cookson followed.

The house was, as Jake had said, no distance away. It was one of the privileged mansions of Gezira that shared the great central lawn with the Union, the Officers' Club and the Sporting Club. It stood dark amid the clouding darkness of tall trees and Cookson, seeing no light in any windows, said doubtfully: 'I don't think the lady's at home.'

'She's there all right. She's always home. Probably in the back parlour. Come on.' Jake led them through the cool, jasmine-scented garden to the front door where he gripped a large lion-headed knocker and hammered violently on its plate. If the noise roused no one else, it troubled Cookson who said: 'Oh dear, do you really think we should?'

They all peered through the coloured glass of the front door and saw the outline of a staircase curving up from a spacious hall. Jake hammered again and at last a light was switched on at the top of the stair. A white-clad figure began to make an uncertain descent.

'I'm afraid we've got her out of bed,' Cookson whispered.

'Nonsense. She's up till all hours.'

The figure, reaching the hall, paused half-way to the door and a nervous female voice called out: 'Who is it? What do you want?'

'We're friends. Open up.'

'If you want Mrs Rutter, she's not here. You can leave a message at the servants' quarters – they're at the bottom of the garden.'

Losing patience, Jackman bawled: 'I don't want the bloody servants. Open the door.'

'No. I'm just looking after things while she's away.' The girl began to back towards the stairs and Jackman became more persuasive:

'Look, it's important. I've something to deliver to Mrs Rutter. I'll leave it with you.'

The girl returned and opening the door a couple of inches, asked: 'What is it?'

The two inches allowed Jackman to force his foot in, then, using his shoulder, he flung the door open, sending the girl staggering back. Jackman was inside.

The destruction, Cookson said, began there and then. A six-foot-high Chinese ornament stood in the hall. Jackman overturned it with the decisive competence of a cinema stuntman and it crashed and splintered on the stone floor. He then marched into the drawing-room ('A treasure house' according to Cookson) and here he went to work as though carrying out a plan that had been burning in him for months.

Cookson and Tootsie had followed him, making weak protests, while the girl sobbed and asked: 'Why are you doing this? Why are you doing this?' Getting no reply, she tried to reach the telephone but Jake flung her away and then pulled the wire from the wall.

'Then,' said Cookson, 'he just went on smashing the place up.'

When everything breakable had been broken, he took a pair of cutting-out scissors the girl had been using and tried to cut up the velvet curtains. The scissors were not strong enough and, said

Cookson: 'Raging around, he found a diplomat's sword, a valuable piece, the hilt and sheath covered with brilliants, and pulling it out, he slashed the curtains, the upholstery and the furniture. Fine Venetian furniture, too. I kept saying: "For God's sake, stop it, Jake," but it was like trying to stop a tornado. For some reason the girl was more frightened by the sword than the general destruction. She started to scream for help and ran out of the house, but you know what Gezira's like at that time of night! There should have been a boab on duty but he'd cleared off somewhere. And even if she'd found a policeman, he'd simply have taken to his heels at the idea of tackling a lunatic.'

The girl reached the Anglo-Egyptian Union. The gates were shut but the safragis were still inside. She persuaded the head safragi to telephone the British Embassy and so, eventually, a posse of embassy servants arrived in a car and took charge of Jackman who by that time had fallen asleep, exhausted by his own activity.

Guy asked Dobson: 'Is it true Jackman's a prisoner at the Embassy?'

'Not any longer.'

'Then where is he?'

'At the moment in a military aircraft. If you must know, but keep it under your hat, he's been sent to Bizerta HQ for questioning.'

'To Bizerta HQ on a military aircraft! Why should the military concern themselves with Jackman? You don't mean he really was doing undercover work?'

'My dear fellow,' said Dobson, 'Who knows? Anybody could be doing anything in times like these.'

Twelve

During the three weeks that Harriet had spent working for Dr Beltado, Halal had come to the pension five times. These were social visits. He would arrive just as supper was ending and bowing to the doctor and the two women, would say: 'I hope I see you well!'

Dr Beltado always responded with a weary effort at good-fellowship, saying: 'Hi, there, Halal, how's tricks?' or, 'How's the world treating you?' and push forward a chair: 'Take the weight off your feet, Halal.'

Protesting that he had no wish to intrude, no wish to impose himself, Halal would sit down and Miss Dora would be sent to order coffee for him. While Beltado went on talking, Halal would give Harriet furtive glances, transmitting the fact that there he still was, patiently waiting, in case she had need of him.

Now, if she did not need Halal himself, she needed help of some sort. She was nearly penniless and, walking up and down the souk, she longed for circumstance to befriend her. She loitered at each stall, with the crowd pushing about her, and when she came to the Roman arcade, she turned and walked all the way back again. No one took much notice of her now. She had become a familiar figure, an English eccentric with endless time and no money to spend.

Three days after Beltado's departure, when she was nearing desperation, Halal came to the pension. She had finished breakfast and was wondering what to do with herself, when he edged round the dining-room door and without approaching further, began at once to explain and excuse his presence. Jamil had heard of Beltado's departure and had seen her walking in the souk, apparently with nothing to do.

'I asked myself "Could Mrs Pringle be bored? Would she care to look over the silk factory?"'

'That would be nice.' Harriet's manner was so subdued that Halal crossed to her, saying with concern: 'I hope, Mrs Pringle, you are not ill.'

'Sit down, Halal. No, I'm not ill, but I'm very worried. Have you any idea where Dr Beltado has gone?'

'I know nothing, but I see all is not well with you. Please, if I can help, what can I do?'

'I'd be glad of anyone's help but I don't know what you can do. Dr Beltado went without paying me for the work I did.'

'No?' Aghast, Halal declared in fierce tones: 'Such a thing is not heard of in our world.'

'You mean the Arab world? But Beltado isn't an Arab. Madame Vigo thinks he just forgot.'

'To forget one who has worked for three weeks! It is not possible.' Frowning, he considered the matter for some moments then said: 'This should be told to Jamil. He will be in his café at this time, discussing business. May I take you to see him?'

'Would it do any good?'

'Perhaps. He has known Dr Beltado longer than I have. He may know where to find him.'

Jamil's café was not, as Harriet supposed, one of the bazaar cafés where men sat all day over a cup of coffee. It was in the new city, a large modern establishment with marble table-tops and tubular chrome chairs. Jamil, as proprietor, sat among an admiring crowd of young men, one of them the guitarist who had sung 'Who is Romeo?' They all shouted Halal's name and Jamil, springing to his feet, placed a chair for Harriet, making it clear to the others that he was already acquainted with her. She realized that if they had not actually seen her with Halal, they had heard of her. Their welcoming laughter was not for Halal alone, it was for Halal accompanied by a lady. She might have a husband somewhere but if so, the fact merely enriched the drama of Halal's relationship with a foreign woman, and the courtesy bestowed on her was all the more courteous.

Halal's manner was serious but that did not affect the humour of his friends and several minutes passed before he could tell them of Beltado's perfidy. Even then, from habit, Jamil went on laughing, saying: 'That Beltado! It is like him, isn't it? You remember last time he was here he had long treatment for his stomach from Dr Amin, then one day he was gone and Amin was not paid?'

One of them prompted him: 'Tell us again what Amin said.'

'Yes, what he said!' This was so funny that Jamil could hardly speak for laughing: 'He said of Beltado: "Pale, bulky and offensive like a sprue patient's shit."'

'*Jamil*!' Halal raised his voice in anger: 'To tell such before a lady!'

Jamil collapsed in shame, red faced and abashed to the point of speechlessness. Harriet pretended that Dr Amin's remark had been beyond her comprehension and so Jamil gradually recovered and was able to discuss Beltado's departure. But the discussion did not help Harriet. Beltado with his large, powerful car might have gone anywhere. He might even have returned to Turkey and, as he had done in the past, disappeared into Axis territory. Soon the talk ceased to relate to Harriet's predicament and became an acclamation of Beltado's mysterious, almost supernatural, ability to cross frontiers closed to the subjects of the Allied powers.

'How is it done?' they asked each other. 'Is he British or American? If not, what is he?'

Harriet told them that Beltado had an Eire passport.

'But what is it, this Eire passport? How does it give him such powers?'

'It means he has Irish citizenship and as Ireland is not at war with the Axis, he can enter occupied countries, but he doesn't find it easy. The Axis officials can't believe that Ireland, being part of the British Isles, isn't an enemy country.'

This explanation merely puzzled them further and led them a long way from Harriet's problem. Halal, seeing that there was no help from Jamil, said: 'I am taking Mrs Pringle to see my father's silk factory.' They left amid regrets and good wishes.

Alone with her in the street, Halal said sadly: 'I fear now you will return to Cairo.'

'I don't know what I'll do. To tell you the truth, I can't return to Cairo. My husband thinks I'm on a ship going to England. I was supposed to go but instead of boarding the ship, I came here.'

Halal, baffled by this confession, stopped and stared at her:

'What you tell me is very strange, is it not? Do I mistake your meaning? Did you say you were to go in a ship to England but did not go? Ah, I understand! You could not bear to travel so far from Mr Pringle and yet, afraid to go back, you came here. Was that what happened?'

'That may have been the reason.'

The indecision of this reply puzzled him still further but sensing there was a rift between the Pringles, he walked on, staring down at his feet as though pondering what he had been told. He said at last: 'Do you wish to come to the silk factory?'

'Yes.'

The factory was in a series of sheds behind the souk. For a while she was distracted by the young workmen – very like Halal's friends except that the friends were idle while these men had to work – and the large spools of brilliantly coloured silks. She was shown rolls of the finished materials in ancient patterns, some enhanced with gold and silver. She forgot Beltado but Halal did not forget his concern for her. Walking with her back to the pension, he said earnestly:

'Mrs Pringle, my friends do not understand why I seek your company. They say: "Halal, you are foolish. We know such English ladies. They seem free but there will be nothing for you. All you do is waste your money." But I know better. I have in me ideals they do not know of. They talk much of romance but they are afraid. In the end they marry within the family. It is usual with them to marry a cousin.'

'And does it work out?'

'Oh yes, well enough. The girls do not expect much. There is something simple and good in these women. They have the childish outlook of nuns. And what criteria have they? What do they know of men? They know only a father or a brother. A cousin is the nearest thing; he is safe. And the female relatives are tactful. When the bridegroom is seen, they are full of admiration, or pretend to be, so the girl is content.'

'I suppose it is the criticism of the world that spoils things.'

'Well, for me, I don't fear criticism. I know what I want. I know what I am doing. I say to Jamil and the others: "If I spend money on this lady, I shall make a friend. One day I think she will reward me."'

He looked into Harriet's face, expecting her to applaud him and perhaps give him hope, but she had no hope to give. The rain started as they reached the pension garden and they stood for a few minutes under the mulberry tree. Halal put his hand out to her but she would not take it.

He said again: 'May I offer you my protection?'

She looked away, wondering how to escape him. When he tried to touch her arm, she said 'I'm sorry,' and hurried into the pension. Reaching her room she locked the door, not from fear that he would follow her but because she had to isolate herself. She had to face her own situation. She lay on the bed and closing her eyes, she projected her thoughts into space. With the resolution of despair, she cried to such powers as might be there: 'Tell me what to do now.' After a while she sank into a drowsy inertia, stupefied by her own failure.

In London, she had earned her own living and had told herself that any girl who could survive there, could survive anywhere in the world. Now she knew she had been wrong. Here her attempt at an independent life had reduced her to penury. She slept and woke with a name in her mind: Angela.

She knew only one Angela, her friend in Cairo who had gone off with the poet Castlebar. Remembering her with affection, she thought: 'Dear Angela, I know if you were here you would help me. But you're not here and I must help myself.' She jumped up and packed her suitcase. When she went to the dining-room, she told Madame Vigo she was leaving next day.

Unperturbed, Madame Vigo said: 'You want taxi?'

'No. I'll go to Beirut by train.'

'Not good train. Better taxi.'

Harriet could not afford a taxi to Beirut but she had to take one to the station. Driving through the main square, she saw Halal at the kerb, his case under his arm, his sallow, vulnerable face grave, waiting to cross the road. Safely past him, she said to herself: 'Goodbye, Halal. I'm afraid your friends were right.'

At the station, she spoke to the stationmaster who knew a little English. When was the next train to Beirut? He shrugged, putting out his hands: 'Mam'zell, who knows? Trains very bad. All stolen by army, better take taxi.'

'I can't. It would cost too much.'

'Then go Riyak and then go Baalbek. In Baalbek many tourists, some English. They take you Beirut.'

Here was a solution of a sort. She felt pleased, even excited, at the thought of seeing Baalbek. There was a local train to Riyak at one p.m. and she waited on the platform, fearful of missing it. There was no buffet, nowhere to sit, but she was getting away from Halal.

The train arrived at two o'clock and stood for an hour in the station before setting out again. As it climbed the foothills of the Anti-Lebanon, she could see through the dirty windows the foliage of the Ghuta and the golden crescents of the mosque, and she said again: 'Goodbye. Goodbye, Halal.' The oasis, a thick green carpet, was sliced off abruptly and then they were in the desert, grey under a grey sky. The train, like a mule unwilling to go farther, jerked and jolted and stopped every few miles.

Two old countrywomen shared Harriet's carriage, speaking a language that was strange to her. Halal had told her that in some outlying villages the people still spoke Aramaic and she listened intently, wondering if she were hearing the language of Christ.

When at last the train dragged itself into Riyak, the sky had cleared and a small tourists' shuttle marked 'Baalbek' stood at the next platform. The ease of this transfer brightened everything for her. As the shuttle ran between orchards burgeoning in the sunlight, she felt sure that succour awaited her in this brilliant and fruitful land.

Thirteen

Dobson said at breakfast: 'The navy's been bombarding Pantellaria. I think we can guess what that means.'

As Guy and Edwina had never heard of Pantellaria, he told them: 'It's an inoffensive little island shaped like a sperm whale. I suppose the Wops have it fortified.'

'So you think we're preparing to cross the Med?' Guy asked.

'My guess is as good as yours, but we're certainly preparing for something. The gen is that Axis troops have folded up in North Africa. Not a squeak out of them. So we're due for the next move which would be northwards. It could all be over quicker than anyone thinks. Home for Christmas, eh?'

'Not this Christmas, I shouldn't think.' Remembering the wet, empty streets of London at Christmas, Guy knew he had no home there. On his last Christmas in London, on his way to an evening party, he had passed men standing at street corners, waiting for the pubs to open. Lonely men, men without homes. But he would not be like that. He would always have friends. He had friends wherever he went, but the truth was: friends had lives of their own and were liable to disappear. Castlebar had gone off with the mad woman Angela Hooper and Jackman had been sent to Bizerta under arrest. And perhaps even Simon would not need him much longer. He was beginning to feel that the only permanent relationship was the relationship of marriage, if death or divorce did not end it. He sighed, thinking that his had been as good as any yet he had not known it at the time.

Fourteen

Baalbek was the end of the line. Though the little train still went hopefully to its destination, tourists were few and Harriet was the only passenger. When she descended at the empty station, it seemed that even the engine driver and the guard had disappeared. There were no porters. The platforms were empty. She was alone. She dragged her case out to the road then stopped, unable to take it farther. She hoped to find a taxi but there were no taxis.

At one side of the station entrance there was a primitive café with an outdoor table and bench. Pushing the case in front of her, she reached the bench and sat down in the late afternoon sunlight. Though the whole place looked unpopulated, she felt pleasure in being there.

A wide road ran from the station into the distance where rust-coloured hills rose from among green foliage. The road was light-coloured, dusty, and on either side stood trees, very tall and slender, drooping towards each other. There were a few old buildings here and there and neglected fields. Beyond the fields there were the remains of ancient ramparts. At one side of the road a clear and brilliant stream ran into a pool. The place, what there was of it, conveyed a sense of tranquillity and broken-down grandeur.

Tired, not knowing where to go, she let herself drift into the pleasing languor of the spirit that the Arabs called *khayf* and was startled when a man came out of the café and stood looking at her. He was short and though still young, stout. His dress, white shirt and black trousers, told her that he was a Christian. He asked in French what he could do for her. When she said she was looking for somewhere to stay, his plump, brown face became troubled.

'I bring you *mon frère* George.'

George, a large, red-haired, fair-skinned fellow, came from the café. From his appearance, he might have been an English yeoman and, as was fitting, he spoke some English. Harriet, deciding that the brothers were descended from a red-haired Crusader, was delighted with them for proving the Mendelian theory and tried to explain heredity, pointing out that while one brother was a brown-skinned Arab, the other was a copy of his English forebear. They did not know what she was talking about and she realized she was being absurd. Her situation was now so hopeless, she was almost light-headed.

She said to George: 'Where can I find an hotel?'

George stared at her for some moments before reaching the point of speech: 'Not any more hotel. Before war, two, but now all two are close-ed.'

'Is there a train to Beirut?'

'Tonight no train. Train tomorrow.'

A third brother, very like the first, appeared now and the three of them, speaking in Arabic, discussed her situation with expressions of concern. It did not occur to them to abandon her. Here was a young woman alone, in need of a bed for the night, and something must be done for her. They appeared to reach a conclusion and the red-haired brother, saying 'Come with me', beckoned her into the white-washed interior of the café. She was led upstairs to a landing that had the smell of an unaired sleeping place. He opened a door and showed her a small room with a bunk, a broken-backed chair and some hooks for clothing. There were no sheets but a grimy, padded cover thrown to one side showed that this was a bedroom. One of the brothers had given up his room to her.

The red-haired man offered this accommodation with a smile, apparently imagining it was as good as anything to be found in the world. She returned the smile, saying: 'Thank you, it is very nice.' What else could she do? Where else could she go? At least she had shelter for the night and next day there would be a train to Beirut.

The first brother carried up Harriet's suitcase and, left to herself, she went to look for a washroom. She found only a privy with a hole in the floor, high smelling and not over clean.

When she went downstairs, the brothers were waiting for her and George asked: 'You like to eat? We make kebabs.'

'Yes, but later. I must see the temples first.'

George came out to the road with her and waving at the long avenue of trees, said: 'Baalbek very old.'

She looked at the ruined remnant of fortifications and asked: 'Roman?'

He shook his head in forceful denial: 'No, no. Much more old. Cain lived here. He built a fort to hide in after he murdered Abel. Noah lived here. King Solomon sat beside this water. He built the temples for his ladies. You know he had many ladies, all many religions.'

Harriet laughed: 'Are you sure Solomon built the temples?'

'What other could do it? Solomon had them built by his genii. Not men.'

Harriet laughed again and started down the road. As she went, she could see columns rising in the distance, dark and ponderous, looking less like classical monuments than menhirs from a more primitive age. The sun was beginning to sink, the light was deepening and she hurried to see what she could before the night came down.

Inside the temple enclosure, she came to the steps on which the columns stood. Standing below them, she gazed up at them, overawed by their height and massive girth. Against the dense cerulean of the evening sky, their hot colour looked almost black.

Although there were walnut trees coming into leaf and pigeons taking flight and lizards rustling between the stones, there was a sinister atmosphere about the site. The platform had been a place of sacrifice: human sacrifice. Terror was imprinted on the atmosphere and Harriet felt afraid as she climbed up the steps and passed between the pillars on to the stretch of massive stones that now reflected the orange-gold of the sinking sun. She contemplated her own solitude and thought of the room in which she would have to spend the night. The men, however good their intentions, were strangers and she had seen no sign of a woman about the café.

Tomorrow she could go on to Beirut, but what would she do there? Without money and without future, she would be no better off than she had been in Damascus. Unnerved by her own situation, she cried out: 'Guy, why don't you come to look for me?'

But no one was coming to look for her. No one knew where she was to be found. For all anyone knew, she might be dead.

She walked to the temple at the other end of the platform. The interior was dark and, pausing at the entrance, she thought she heard a car come to a stop. She stood, listening intently, and after a few minutes heard someone coming up the steps to the platform. She felt the solace of not being alone, then she realized that she was alone and anything could happen to her.

She watched apprehensively as a fat man limped into view. He had on a faded khaki shirt and brown corduroy trousers and only his cap, worn at a jaunty angle, showed that he was an army officer. She recognized him and laughed at her own fears. Seeing her, he lifted his stick and waving it excitedly, shouted: 'What are you doing here?' Astonished by her presence, he came towards her, moving as quickly as he could, his round, pink face beaming at this unlikely encounter. She felt too much relief and thankfulness to say anything.

'You remember me, don't you? Old Lister who used to take you out to lunch at Groppi's?'

'Of course I remember you. It's just . . . I'm a bit stunned. It seems too good to be true.'

Delighted at seeing her, Lister scarcely heard this declaration but chattered on: 'It's amazing, how things happen. Only yesterday I saw a friend of Guy's, that poet fellow I met in Alex. I didn't speak to him because he's not alone. He's got a bint with him. Nice-looking, dark-haired girl, not too young.' Lister's round pink nose and fluff of fair moustache quivered as he spoke of the girl: 'Lucky chap, eh? Lucky chap!'

'Do you know where they're staying?'

'At my hotel. That's where I saw them.'

Lister, not understanding her wonder at this news, went on: 'And where's Guy? Not on your own, are you?'

'Yes, on my own. I was trying to get from Damascus to Beirut and arrived here. There's no train till tomorrow.'

'So you're stranded? Pretty god-forsaken place, if you ask me. Where are you staying?'

'There's no hotel but I've found a room, not very nice.'

'I bet it's not very nice. If you want to get to Beirut, how about coming back with me? Have a night at my hotel, see your friend

Castlebar and take the bus tomorrow. Have a convivial evening in the bar with old Lister. What do you say?'

A few hours ago this suggestion would have seemed to her her salvation, but now she thought of the brothers and their kindness and said: 'The people who've given me a room – I don't want to hurt their feelings.'

'Oh, don't worry. I'll explain to them.'

'And then, your hotel – I don't think I could afford it.'

'If you're short, I can lend you a few quid. Guy will always pay me back. Now, let's look round. Spooky place, isn't it? But those columns are pretty impressive. What's this temple?' Lister had a guide-book and led her from temple to temple, determined to see everything: 'Good lord, look at this – just like the inside of a city church. Wonder where the oracle had its abode!' Limping and groaning from the pain in his foot, Lister kept her among the temples till the air became chilly and the sun began to set. Then in twilight that was beautiful and pleasant now she was not alone, they went out to the waiting taxi and drove towards the station.

'Where's this pension of yours?'

'It's not exactly a pension. I'm in this café.'

The brothers showed only satisfaction that Harriet had found someone to look after her. Lister went upstairs to fetch her suitcase and came down looking blank. George, putting the suitcase into the taxi, said happily: 'You go Beirut. You like very much.'

Once out of hearing, Lister said in a shocked tone: 'My dear girl, you couldn't have stayed in a place like that. What do you think would have happened to you there?'

'What would be likely to happen?'

'God knows. You're too trusting.' Lister gasped and began to titter: 'A girl alone with three randy A-rabs! No wonder they said "Come into my parlour . . ."'

'Really, Lister! I'm sure they only wanted to help me.'

'Perhaps, perhaps,' Lister dropped the subject and said: 'I wish we could have found the oracle. It was much brighter than that affair at Delphi. Much more – well, what's the word? Snide. The Emperor Trajan tried to trick it by handing it a blank sheet of paper and in return, he got another blank sheet of paper. Then he asked about his expedition to conquer Parthia and the oracle handed him a bundle of sticks wrapped in a piece of cloth.'

'What did that mean?'

'What indeed! Probably nothing, but he died on the way and his bones were sent to Rome wrapped in a piece of cloth.'

'Did oracles ever give anyone good news?'

'I doubt it. They were always hinting at something nasty.'

The road carried them in deepening twilight over the bare rocky pass between the Anti-Lebanon and the Lebanon. The journey was not long and there was still a glint on the western horizon as they dropped down among gardens and orchards, and Lister pointed: 'There! That's the hotel, The Cedars.'

Seeing the hotel, its windows radiant, set on a hill spur above Beirut, Harriet said: 'It's much too grand for me.'

'Nonsense. Guy's not badly off. We can't have you staying in places like that café.' As the taxi stopped, Lister struggled out, saying: 'I'll see you're properly fixed up. Room and bath, eh?'

He was gone before Harriet could reply and she stood in the garden, among a scent of orange blossom, and wondered how she would manage to pay.

She entered the vestibule as Angela Hooper was coming down the stairs. Angela glanced at Harriet, glanced away then jerked her head back and gave a scream: 'Harriet Pringle! But you went on that evacuation ship.'

'No, I didn't go. I came to Syria instead.'

'Good heavens, what a shock you gave me! And you're staying here?'

'Only for one night . . .'

'No, you must stay longer than that. I want to hear what's been happening in Cairo and a lot of other things.'

'I'll have to find a cheaper place. The truth is, I'm almost out of cash.'

'Oh, cash. You're always worrying about cash . . .'

Angela stopped abruptly as Lister, coming from the desk, joined them. Stiffening slightly, she looked suspiciously at him then said to Harriet: 'I thought you were alone.'

Angela did not move but Harriet felt that in her mind she took a step away and a distance of disapproval had come between them. Harriet said: 'I was alone but I met Major Lister in Baalbek and he was kind enough to give me a lift in his taxi. And now I'm here.'

'So you are!' Angela smiled but there was still uncertainty in her manner: 'And where's Guy?'

'In Cairo.'

'Too busy to come with you, I suppose.' Angela gave Lister another look and realizing that her suspicions were absurd, laughed: 'Well, it's lovely to have you here. Let's all have a drink after supper. See you in the Winter Garden.'

When she had left them, Lister said: 'I don't think your friend liked me.'

'It was just that she thought at first I'd gone off with you.'

Lister shook with wheezy laughter: 'Would it were true! Dear me, dear me! Would it were true!'

Harriet laughed too: 'She went off with Castlebar. It's funny how often people disapprove of others doing what they have done themselves.'

Angela and Castlebar were seated at a small table in an alcove of the dining-room that Angela, with her habit of lavish tipping, had probably kept reserved for them. Glancing across at their enclosed intimacy, Harriet could not suppose that Angela would want her to be with them for very long. She had found friends but that did not solve anything. She might borrow from Angela, she might even borrow from Lister, but borrowing merely put off the day when she must face up to her situation. She glanced again towards the lovers and caught Castlebar's eye. As though he understood her dilemma, he smiled and raised his hand reassuringly. She had never understood his attraction for Angela but now, warmed by his greeting, she felt him to be an old friend in a strange, unhelpful world.

'What are we going to drink?' Lister offered her the wine list.

'Not for me.'

'Oh, come on,' Lister rallied her: 'must have a glass,' and added as though admitting to a curious virtue, 'I always have wine with my meals.' He ordered a bottle of Cyprus red and watching the cork being drawn, he flushed with impatience and pushed his glass forward.

Harriet remembered his eagerness for food and drink. Based in Jerusalem, he would come to Cairo whenever he could to treat himself to what he called 'the fleshpots'. He sometimes took Harriet out for a meal, feeling that a companion gave him licence to indulge himself.

His glass filled, he lifted it quickly and drank, holding the wine in his mouth and sluicing it round and round his teeth, then as he swallowed it, giving a long drawn 'Ah-h-h.' Before the meal was over, Lister had drunk the whole bottle.

As Angela and Castlebar left the room, Angela called across: 'See you in the Winter Garden.'

'You think they want me?' Lister asked with tremulous lips and bulging wet blue eyes.

'Of course. You saw she meant both of us.'

The Winter Garden, that stretched out from the main building, was a large, glass gazebo that gave a view of the lights of Beirut and the dark glimmer of the distant sea. Lister followed Harriet with timorous expectancy as though fearing Angela would order him away.

Angela and Castlebar were seated in a corner behind a screen of blue plumbago flowers. Again Harriet felt they had made this seclusion their own, but Castlebar rose eagerly to welcome her and went to find extra chairs. During his absence from Cairo, it seemed he had taken on the function of host while Angela, who paid the bills, kept in the background. Their nightly bottle of whisky was on the table. Angela pushed it towards Lister who, after conventional demur, filled his glass and lifting it towards her, said: 'Here's seeing you, mem.'

Angela watched him with critical attention as he put down the whisky and refilled his glass. She did not look at Harriet but Castlebar, devoting himself to an old friend, insisted that evening she must have something more festive than her usual glass of white wine: 'How about a Pimm's? They do it very nicely here.'

When the Pimm's arrived, expertly dressed with fruit and borage, he handed it to her with a conniving smile and she felt he would not be at all displeased if she remained to share Angela's liberality. She was sure they had discussed the oddity of her presence here when she was supposed to be on the *Queen of Sparta*. And why was she short of money when she could send to her husband for help? She realized that if she stayed there, she would have a lot of explaining to do.

Angela, leaning her delicate, pretty head back among the flowers, gave Harriet a quizzical smile then, perhaps remembering their past friendship, suddenly leant forward and squeezed Harriet's hand: 'Dear Harriet, I thought I would never see you again.'

Angela had not changed in appearance since she left Cairo but Castlebar was not quite the Castlebar of the Anglo-Egyptian Union. He not only had more confidence and more to say for himself but he had lost the seedy look of the alcoholic for whom any money not spent on drink was money wasted. He was wearing an expensively tailored suit and silk shirt. Rich living had enhanced his looks but he still chain-smoked, placing the pack open in front of him with a cigarette pulled out ready to succeed the one he held in his hand. He still hung over the table, his thick, pale eyelids covering his eyes, his full, mauvish under-lip hanging slightly with one yellow eye-tooth tending to slip into view. Not really very different from the Castlebar of the Anglo-Egyptian Union.

Harriet asked where they had been since leaving Cairo.

'W-w-we went to Cyprus,' Castlebar said. 'S-s-stayed in Kyrenia.'

'At the Dome?' asked Lister: 'Great hotel the Dome. Got more public rooms, and *bigger* public rooms, than anywhere else in the Eastern Med. And the teas,' Lister's eyes watered at the thought of them, 'real old English teas – scones, jam, cream, plum-cake! Oh, my goodness!'

'Yes, we stayed at the Dome. But Cyprus is a small place and we got b-b-bored. We took the boat back to Haifa and Angie bought a second-hand car and drove us up here.'

Angela said: 'We thought we'd stay here a bit.' She smiled at Harriet: 'It's quite a nice hotel, isn't it?' and Harriet wondered what she would have thought of the Baalbek café.

Offered the bottle again, Lister said: 'Can't drink all your booze,' but, pressed, took a larger glass than before and, sipping, sighed: 'Back to the grindstone tomorrow. Only had four days' leave but managed to see a few things. Ever been to the Dog River?'

Angela, beginning to relent towards him, asked: 'What is the Dog River?'

'Oh, quite fantastic. There's this great headland where all the conquerors since Nebuchadnezzar have carved inscriptions. I wanted to see the earliest, the Babylonian one, but it's all over-grown with bramble. Silly people these Lebanese, no sense of history. I'd've climbed up and cleared it but couldn't get across the river. I've been told that at the river mouth there's a dog – not a real dog, of course – that used to howl so loudly at the sight of an enemy, it could be heard in Cyprus.'

Castlebar lifted his eyelids with interest: 'W-w-what was it? Some sort of siren?'

'Don't know. Drove down and looked for it but couldn't see hide or hair.' In an absent-minded way, Lister refilled his glass again and fell silent. He was beginning to droop and had to cling to his stick to keep himself from falling. He sighed and lifted the bottle but finding it empty, he put it down and his infantile nose and fat cheeks fell together with disappointment: 'Walked a long way . . . foot very bad . . . no dog anywhere. Never been able to find anything, really. Always deprived, always ill-treated. My nurse – what d'you think she used to do? She used to pull down m'knickers and beat m'bum with a hairbrush. Bristle side. Used to pull down little knickers and beat little bum. Poor little bum! What a thing to do to a child!' He drew in a long breath and let it out painfully: 'Never got over it. Never. Never shall.'

He sniffed and as he gave a sob, Angela sat up briskly and looking from Castlebar to Harriet, said: 'Time for bed.'

Making their excuses and goodnights, the three left Lister to brood on his wrongs and went out to the hall, where Angela asked: 'How did you come to pick that one up? Or, rather, how did Guy pick him up? I take it, it was Guy.'

'Of course. And how does Guy come to pick anyone up?'

'Well, Major Lister's going tomorrow, thank goodness, but Harriet you must stay on. I can't let you go so soon. We haven't had a chance to talk yet.'

'Angela dear, I've less than five pounds in the world.'

Angela went upstairs. Putting a hand out to stop the argument, she said: 'I'll settle your bill and you pay me back in Cairo,' then passed from view.

Harriet turned to Castlebar: 'You know, Bill, I can't afford to stay here.'

Castlebar grinned: 'Leave it to Angie. You're silly to worry, she loves to do the honours.' He followed Angela upstairs.

He did not worry himself. His attitude towards Angela's money had been determined early on when his friend Jake Jackman told him: 'If Angela takes us to places we can't afford, there's nothing for it. We'll have to let her pay.'

For Harriet, too, there was nothing for it. She had to borrow or starve. She could only hope that one day she would be able to repay what she owed.

When she went down to breakfast next morning, she found that Lister had already gone. There was no sign of Angela and Castlebar so, having eaten alone, she walked round the hotel garden that was lush with semi-tropical plants and early orange trees. The end, unfenced, fell for several hundred feet sheer to the road into Beirut. She saw Beirut itself stretched beneath her, a sharply-drawn maze of streets set with pink and cream buildings, delicately coloured in the early sunlight. The streets, flashing with traffic, converged towards the water-front where ships were gathered on the glittering Mediterranean. On the southern side of the town, beside the road, there was a wood of dark trees, each a stiff arrangement of branches with wings of closely packed foliage, standing like crows in affected attitudes. These, she realized, were the Cedars for which the hotel was named. And the hotel, of course, was one of the most famous in the Middle East – and here she was, living in idleness with no means of keeping herself. How long could it go on? Angela had said 'pay me back in Cairo' and now that their relationship had established itself, she and Castlebar would, sooner or later, return to Egypt. Then what would become of Harriet? The future was too ominous to contemplate and, turning her back on it, she went out to the road and walked between the orchards.

Angela and Castlebar were down for luncheon. Angela had asked for a larger table and, leaving their alcove, they seemed content to have Harriet with them. If they had suffered headaches or hangover, they had had time to recover and Angela began to consider the afternoon.

'Supposing we go and find this Dog River! What do you think, Harriet?'

Harriet said she was ready for anything. After luncheon, Angela said:

'Let's have our coffee in the Winter Garden. You, Bill darling, you want to work on a poem, don't you?'

Castlebar said, 'Yes', and went upstairs, as no doubt prearranged, and Angela took Harriet to the secluded spot behind the plumbago plants.

'Now, Harriet, when you say you're near penury, you're playing a little game with yourself, aren't you? I'm sure if you write to your husband, he'll send you what you need?'

'I can't write to him, that's the trouble. I can't ask him for anything.'

'Well, you can rely on me. I'll do all I can to help – but I must know the truth. What are you doing here? You're obviously not on holiday. Have you left Guy?'

'I think you could ask, rather, has he left me. Things happened that made me feel I'd be better elsewhere. I decided to go to England but, instead, I came here.'

'What happened? What sort of things?'

'Small things that seemed important at the time. You remember that brooch you gave me: the rose-diamond heart? Guy took it from me and gave it to Edwina.'

'To Edwina?' Angela gave a shocked laugh but added: 'If he did, surely it didn't mean anything?'

'It meant something to me.'

'I'm sorry. Oh, Harriet, I'm truly sorry. I wish I'd never bought the wretched thing.'

'I loved it. But if it hadn't been that, it would have been something else. I was ill and depressed. Guy's devotion to the outside world was more than I could stand. I felt I was tied up to him yet I was always alone. I sometimes think I would have done better to go on the evacuation ship. In England I could have earned a living. I would have had a life of my own.'

'But how did you get here from Suez? Not by train, I'm sure.'

'I was given a lift in a lorry. I came on an impulse, without stopping to ask myself how I was going to live when I got here. I had fifty pounds with me but it didn't last long. I'm in a silly predicament which I've brought on myself and I don't know what to do next.'

'Well, I won't abandon you, now that I've found you. As for money, you needn't worry about that. We're moving around and if you'd like to come with us, then come with us.'

'I'd like nothing better but I'd feel like an intruder. You and Bill are soon going to get tired of having me trailing after you.'

'No, you wouldn't be an intruder. We see quite enough of each other, and when we surface, we're glad to have someone else to talk to.'

'Yes, but for how long?'

Angela laughed and said: 'You know, Bill likes you, and he's not averse to having two females in tow. Men are like that. Women, too, probably. I wouldn't mind having an extra man around if he were amusing. But, for goodness' sake, no more Major Listers. He was impossible. Bill and I may not be very exciting company but at least we don't cry about our little bums.'

'Angela darling, it is lovely to be back with you. My only fear is I'll never be able to repay you.'

'Oh yes, you will. I'll chalk it up, every penny. But, please, no more about money. You've no idea how boring it is. It's a bore to be without it, and a bore to have it and have to look after it. There should be a more satisfactory system of exchange.'

Angela stood up and now, with explanations over, Harriet supposed they were going to the Dog River, but no. Angela said, 'I'd better see how Bill's getting on', and going upstairs did not come down again.

Harriet, giving up hope of her, returned to the garden to look at Beirut far below. Wondering how much it would cost to take a taxi down to the sea-front, she went and asked the hotel clerk who said: 'There and back, a wait for you between? I fear, very much.'

'More than five pounds.'

'More, yes, I fear. The taxis are not here. They come up from Beirut and they must return. It is a bad mountain road so they charge more. And then this very nice hotel and drivers think, "All rich people," and charge more. So it is.'

Harriet, contemplating the penalties of affluence, said: 'I see. Thank you,' and gave up the idea of going to Beirut on her own.

The days passed in monotonous inactivity. Angela might say: 'Let's go to Baalbek,' or the Beirut bazaars, or the Dog River, but in the end, she and Castlebar would retire to their room and not reappear until suppertime. Harriet's only diversion was to walk along the country road to a small village where there was nothing to do or see.

Still, here, on the seaward side of the mountain, the spring was advancing. The fruit trees were beginning to flower and small cyclamen were opening in the grass verges. The middays were so warm that Angela and Harriet could take their coffee in the garden. Castlebar, who did not take coffee, always went upstairs 'to work' and Angela would follow him there.

It had not occurred to Harriet that Castlebar was entertaining but now, escorted by what he called his 'two birds', he would tell stories and repeat conversations he had overheard and, at Angela's request, repeat his limericks, all of them well known to Harriet. The first hour after dinner was the time for these performances. Later his stammer grew worse, his speech slurred and he began to yawn. When he was at his best, Angela kept him going, reminding him of this story and that.

'Darling one, tell Harriet about the two officers at the Mohammed Ali Club.'

Castlebar snuffled and tittered, apparently reluctant until coaxed further: 'Do tell it, darling, it's my favourite story.'

'W-w-well, it was like this. These two young officers were discussing the arrival of a Sikh regiment in Cairo: "Nuisance their being here. Means, if the city's overrun, we'll have to shoot our women."

'"Shoot our women, old chap, why'd we do that?"

'"Done thing, old chap. Obligatory, y'know."'

Delighted, Angela threw her arms round Castlebar: 'You'd enjoy shooting me, wouldn't you, you great, big, glorious brute?'

Every night, she insisted on at least one of Castlebar's own limericks and she was as indignant as he was that the Cairo poetry magazine *Personal Landscape* had rejected them as too obscene for publication.

Harriet had discovered that beneath the mists of alcohol, Castlebar's creativity had its own separate life. During their days at The Cedars, he was, he said, working on a poem.

'When do you do it? In the afternoon?'

'W-w-well, no. Angie and I tend to get drowsy in the afternoon.' He took out of his pocket a page from a small, ruled note-book: 'I have it here. Before lunch, when I'm shaving, I put it up on the shaving-mirror and look at it, and I alter a word here and there, and gradually it builds up. In a couple of weeks, it will be a poem.'

'When it's finished, what will you do with it?'

'Just keep it, and one day I'll have enough for a slim vol.'

As Harriet gazed at him in a wakening admiration, Castlebar patted her knee: 'Don't worry about money. You'll be all right with us. Angie's a great giver. She loves to feel she's got us captive.'

'And you don't mind being a captive?'

'I don't mind anything so long as I can work at my poetry.'

He smiled and put the paper back in his pocket. She could see he had his own integrity and though he might be under Angela's heel, a part of him remained aloof and intact.

She envied him his talent and decided that an occupation so intensive it made all else unimportant was very much what she needed herself. She wondered if she could write. During the empty afternoons, she read through the books in the writing-room bookcase. They had been left behind by visitors and were mostly forgotten French novels, stilted and dull, but there was a Tauchnitz edition of *Romolo*. Though she thought it laboured in style and lifeless in content, she read it for lack of anything else to do.

A week after her arrival, Harriet heard a familiar voice as she entered the dining-room. Dr Beltado, seated with Dr Jolly and Miss Dora, was declaiming on the possible fusion of all cultures. Glancing up at Harriet as she passed, he looked puzzled as though wondering if he had seen her before. Dr Jolly did not notice her but she saw that Miss Dora had seen her and had no wish to see her.

As the doctor's voice filled the room throughout dinner, Harriet questioned herself whether she dare intercept him before he got away again. Angela, seeing her abstracted, asked what was the matter and heard the whole story.

Swinging round, giving the trio a fierce stare, she asked at the top of her voice: 'You mean that lot over there? You must make them pay up. If you don't, I will.'

The other diners, alerted to an interesting situation, stared at Angela then at Beltado, and again at Angela and back to Beltado, until Beltado, his voice failing him, began to realize he was a centre of unwelcome attention.

'I'll just have a word with him,' Angela said and, crossing to his table, she made her accusations in a voice that could be heard by all. He had bolted without paying the sum owed to an employee.

Beltado gave Harriet another look and recalled what this was all about. He began to bluster: 'How was I to know what I owed her? She was told to put in her account . . .' Bluster had no effect on Angela. Extravagant though she was, she would not tolerate misdealing, and she demanded that the money be paid there and then. She came back to Harriet with more than was due to her.

'But I didn't earn all that.'

'Never mind.' Angela closed Harriet's fingers over the bundle of notes and, alight with victory, kissed her on the cheek: 'You take it. It's your money plus interest. Next time he'll decide it's cheaper to pay when the money is due.'

Fifteen

Simon was reaching the point of complete recovery. Guy, on his next visit to the hospital, found he had given up his crutch and was moving firmly on a stick. His walk was normal except, as he explained to Guy, his left foot tended to drag a little and his right toe had a trick of doubling under itself.

The trick came at unexpected moments but he had it under control. Whenever the toe seemed about to pitch him forward on to his face, he squared his shoulders and jerked them back and the toe was frustrated.

Simon laughed as though he had outwitted an enemy: 'Neat that. Greening says the toe's the last hurdle. He said: "Get your muscles into trim and your feet will serve you OK." He told me to just go on working at it, so I'm working at it. I say to myself: "See that rope over there? You've to shin right to the top."'

'And can you do it?'

'I have done it. It's a bit of a sweat but I make myself do it. I think Greening's pretty pleased with me.'

'You like him better these days?'

'Oh, Greening's all right.'

Simon was not only physically better, he had thrown off the shock to his system and had a new belief in himself.

'I'll be out of here as soon as the toe clears up. I don't intend to hang around in the convalescent centre. Lots of chaps stay there for weeks, afraid of going back to the desert, but I'm not like that. I want to go back.'

Guy still hired the car and took Simon to the Gezira gardens or the sports fields, but the heat was becoming too oppressive for these afternoon outings and Simon no longer wanted to be treated as an invalid. As for Guy himself, he had other things he should be doing.

When he next arrived with the car, Simon said: 'I want to go to the pyramids.'

Not much drawn to the pyramids, Guy said: 'We could go to Mena and have a drink in the bar.'

Driving through the suburbs where flame trees held out plates of flowers the colour of tomato soup, Simon was reminded of his first day in Cairo and his first trip into the desert. That had been a month or so later than this, but already the wind blowing into the car had the sparking heat of mid-year and the chromium was too hot to touch. The climate had seemed to him intolerable yet during his year in Egypt, he had learnt to tolerate it.

The car stopped outside Mena House. When they stepped into the brazen sunlight, Guy's one thought was to reach the air-conditioned bar but Simon, without pause or explanation, hurried away in the opposite direction. Guy followed him, calling, but he did not look round. Striding across the stone floor on which the pyramids were built, he stopped at a corner of the Great Pyramid where the stone showed white from the scraping of many feet. This was the usual place of ascent. Shielding his eyes with his hands, he looked up to the apex above which the sun was poised, blazing and scintillating in a sky white with heat.

When Guy caught him up, he said: 'I'm going to climb it.'

'Not now, surely?'

'Yes, now.' He turned to look at Guy with an exultant determination and Guy could only try and reason with him.

'Simon, you know, this is foolhardy. If you slipped, you could undo all the work they've done on you.'

'I won't slip.' He held out his stick: 'If you'd just look after that . . .'

Guy took the stick and put it on the ground: 'You don't imagine I'd let you go alone?'

Simon laughed: 'Good show. Let's see who gets there first.'

The blocks that formed the pyramid were about three feet in height. Guy, with his face towards the stonework, put his hands on the first block and pulled himself up till he could kneel on top of it. He got to his feet and tackled the second block.

Simon shouted to him: 'Look, this is how Harriet did it.' Turning his back on the pyramid, he jumped his backside up on to the block, swung his legs after him, stood up and sat himself on the second block.

To Guy, watching, it seemed to be done with one movement and he remembered Harriet going up in the same way, wearing her black velvet evening-dress that had never been the same again.

'It's easy,' Simon said and Guy agreed. It looked extraordinarily easy but he preferred to keep his eyes on Simon and laboured up in his own way, keeping immediately below his companion with some idea of acting as a safety net.

Simon, in high spirits, laughed with pleasure at the speed of his ascent and the noise brought out the 'guides' who bawled: 'Not allowed. Must have guide,' and shook their fists when they were ignored. But it was too hot for indignation and they soon retreated to whatever shelter they had found.

Half-way up, Simon's pace slackened. Both men were soaked with sweat and Simon, pausing to get his breath, took off his shirt and spread it on the stone. Guy did the same thing and while they stood for a few minutes, he hoped Simon would now give up. Instead, he went on at a less furious pace. Guy, below him, could see the scar of his wound rising above the waistband of his slacks. It was red and the skin looked thin. Guy, fearing it might break open, wondered where he could go for help if help were needed. But Simon did not need help. He was well ahead of Guy and reaching the top where the apex stones had been removed, he passed out of sight. Guy, moving more quickly, followed and found him lying spreadeagled on his back, his arms over his eyes.

Throwing himself down beside him, Guy asked: 'How do you feel?'

'Fine.' He was too breathless to say much and lay for so long without moving that Guy became uneasy again. How was Simon to be transported down if he could not transport himself? Before this unease could become anxiety, Simon lifted his arms and seeing Guy's worried expression, burst out laughing.

'I did it.'

'Yes. It was pretty impressive.'

'I feel a bit dizzy, though.'

Guy felt dizzy, too. Looking around him at the dazzle of the desert, he wondered why anyone should want to come up here. There was little to see. In the distance, wavering and floating in the liquid heat, were the odd shapes of the Saccara Pyramids. Not much else. The two men might have been on a raft in a yellow sea; or rather, on a grill beneath an intense and dangerous flame.

He shook Simon by the shoulder: 'Come on. If we don't move out of this, we'll both get sun-stroke.'

Without speaking, Simon rolled over and over till he reached the edge of the floor then he let himself down to the step below. Here an edge of shade was stretching out but not enough.

'If you can manage it,' Guy said, 'we'd better get down to the hotel and have that drink.'

'Oh, I can manage it.' Standing up, Simon staggered slightly and made a face at Guy: 'Muscles stiff. Not yet in tip-top form, but they soon will be.' He sat on the edge of the block and dropped down to the one below: 'Piece of cake, this. I wish Greening could see me.' His shirt was dry again and at the bottom, he picked up his stick: 'I don't think I'll need this much longer.'

'What about the toe?'

'The toe? Good Lord, I'd forgotten about it. That's what Greening said. I'd only to forget I couldn't do it.'

He talked on a note of triumphant assurance but for all that, he was glad enough to sink into a chair in the bar and take the glass Guy put into his hand: 'Cheers. Just the job.'

There were half a dozen or so officers in the bar and Guy noticed that as Simon entered, leaning lightly on his stick, they had reacted very differently from the men at the swimming-pool. There, pallid and strained, he had been a dismal reminder of the reality of war. Here, his young face still flushed from the climb, he was the shining hero.

He and Guy sat for a while, silent and glad of rest, drinking their chilled beer, then Simon put his hand into his shirt pocket and took out a thin piece of card: 'This came two days ago.'

It was one of the new air-mail letters, photographed and reduced, and Guy had to tilt his glasses in order to read the miniature handwriting:

Dear Simon, Sorry I can't say 'darling' any more. I know you'll be upset but it's a long time since you went away and you didn't write much, did you? I don't suppose it was much fun in the desert but it isn't much fun here, either. I've been lonely and what did you expect? Well, the long and the short of it is I've met someone else. Not getting letters from you, my thoughts turned to Another. I like him very much and he makes me happy and I want a divorce.

It wasn't much of a marriage, was it?

Ever yours,
ANNE

P.S. Your mum tells me you were wounded. I'm sorry but you didn't even let me know that.

Guy read it through twice before he said: 'You didn't tell me you were married.'

'Yes. We rushed into it before I went to join the draft. We only had a week at the Russell Hotel before I left. She's right, it wasn't much of a marriage. She came to see me off at the station. All I remember is her standing there crying and waiting for the train to take me away. I thought: "poor little thing" – that's all: a girl crying and me looking at her out of the carriage window. I wouldn't know her now if I passed her in the street.'

'Have you a photograph?'

'No. I had a snap but it fell out of my wallet somewhere in the desert. I don't even know when it went. I just found one day it wasn't there. Well, I don't need to feel sorry for her any more. I'm glad she's found someone who makes her happy. I only hope he's a decent bloke.'

'I wouldn't take it too seriously. People get carried away in wartime. Probably, when you get back, you'll find she's waiting for you.'

'Oh, no. It's better as it is. She can have a divorce and welcome. It's the best thing for both of us.' Simon, with Edwina's face glowing in his thoughts, smiled and pushed the letter back into his pocket.

'Have you decided yet what you'll do when the war's over?'

'I don't know. What is there left to do?'

'Everything. You've got a whole lifetime ahead of you. Even if you were accepted for the regular army, it would only be a short-term commission. You still have to face the future. I suppose, whatever happens, you'll return to England?'

'I suppose so, but I'm not going to stay any longer than I can help. It's my Mum and Dad. Every letter I get from them, they say they're just waiting for me to come back and tell them about Hugo. They say that's all that's keeping them alive. They say, "We know you'll tell us everything," as though there was something secret about his death. I've told them everything. Everything I know, that is. What else is there to tell? It's all in the past now. I don't want to talk about it. I don't want to be reminded of it. I feel I can't go through it all again.'

'But if it means so much to them . . .'

'They should try to forget it. Instead, they keep on as though I'd be bringing him back with me.'

'In a way you will be bringing him back, because you looked so much alike.'

'Still, I'm not Hugo. When they see me, it will make things worse for them. They'll realize they used to have two boys and now there's only one. They make me feel responsible. Can't you imagine what it will be like, going over it all again and again. I feel sorry for them but somehow, I don't know, they've become strangers.'

'It will be different once you get home. You'll feel you've never been away.'

'I don't know that I want to feel like that. I can't pretend nothing has changed. I've changed. I don't feel I belong there any more.' Simon's mouth, that during the days of his dependence, had seemed tenderly young and defenceless, now closed itself firmly. He had been a sick, despondent boy; now he was a young man conscious of his strength and his individuality in the world. Guy did not feel altogether pleased by this developing self-reliance which hinted of selfishness and he said sternly: 'Still, they are your parents. You will have to let them talk about Hugo; you owe it to them. It will be a comfort to them. And, remember, you're all they've got now.'

Simon finished his beer and put down his glass: 'Yes, I suppose you're right. Of course I'll go home and do what I can for them. I didn't mean I wouldn't, but I'm not staying in England. I feel now as though the whole world's waiting for me.'

Driving back to the hospital, he said gleefully: 'You know, I told myself if I did it, if I got to the top, I'd apply for a return to active service. They may stick me in an office at first but anything's better than hanging round being treated like an invalid.'

'I suppose you'll be sent to Tunisia.'

'Hope so. I wouldn't want to be kicking my heels like those chaps we saw in the bar.'

Guy felt a drop in spirits, thinking that Simon, too, would be lost to him. But that had to happen sooner or later. Simon had reached the last stage of recovery and must return to normal life; or rather, to the killing, destruction and turbulent hatred that these days passed for normal life. As he considered the emotions of violence that must blot out all other emotions, Guy said: 'War is an abomination yet I could almost envy you.'

Sixteen

The day after they were routed, the Beltados left the hotel and Angela and Harriet, returned to the ease of their old amity, began to talk of going elsewhere, but it was only talk. Angela was content at The Cedars and the days went on as before with the after-dinner whisky bottle and the drowsy retreat to bed. Then one day she said: 'We'll leave tomorrow. Where shall we go?' She turned to Castlebar: 'Where do you want to go, you great, domineering brute?'

Castlebar beamed on her: 'Wherever you take me, my pet.'

'We'll go back to Palestine. We'll make an early start and drive to Jerusalem. Bill, tell them to wake us at eight a.m.'

Castlebar nodded: 'Right. Troops will parade at eight a.m.' But when Harriet, having been wakened, went down to breakfast, there was no sign of Angela and Castlebar. They appeared, as usual, for luncheon and the party set out at three in the afternoon.

Angela's car was an old Alvis and as she drove, she complained continually: 'Wretched car. Steering all wrong. On the way here it nearly had us over a precipice.' Yet it brought them safely up on the downlands of the frontier and Angela stopped for a rest beside a curious pair of rocks that rose like horns from the grass.

Castlebar said: 'This was where the great battle was fought in 1187 when Saladin defeated the Crusaders and captured the true cross.'

Whether this was true or not, they stood and admired the innocent rocks because men had fought around them.

They were in Galilee. The new grass that Harriet had seen on her way through Palestine had now grown tall and the whole countryside had become a rich meadow choked with flowers. She exclaimed in wonder at a field of blue lupins and Angela, stopping the car, said they would walk for a while and see what was to be seen.

Hidden among the lupins were irises of a maroon shade so deep they looked black. Farther on there were other irises, purple and pink, and a buff colour veined with brown. The field ended in a downslope of grass starred like the Damascus Ghuta with red, white and purple anemones, and in the distance there was a lake of pure lapis blue.

'Do you realize what that is?' Angela said: 'It's the Sea of Galilee.'

Castlebar, who had been trailing after the women, stopped at the edge of the lupin field and said he needed a drink.

'Yes, my poor lamb needs a drink and I feel I've driven far enough. That little town down there looks entrancing. It might do us for the night.'

The town, when they drove down to it, was less entrancing than it had seemed from the heights. Like everywhere else in the Levant, it had been blighted by war. The hotels were boarded up. A notice said 'Thermal baths' but another notice said 'Closed'. The whole place, with its white villas and waterside buildings, had the air of a resort but it was a rundown resort and most of the inhabitants had gone away. Castlebar was sent to enquire about accommodation in a shop and came back to say there was a pension somewhere in the long, lakeside main road. The pension was owned by a very old Jewish woman who talked with Angela in Arabic, explaining that people usually came there in summertime but nowadays hardly anyone came. Still, she agreed to put up the English visitors and she opened rooms where the blinds were drawn, the bedding folded away and the air smelled of dust. She smiled at them, friendly and encouraging, and said if they cared to walk round the town, all would be ready for them on their return.

Angela appealed to Castlebar: 'What do you think, loved one?'

Castlebar did not think at all but shook his head and said: 'Won't it do, darling? We don't want to drive all night.'

The old woman asked for their passports and required Castlebar to sign a register. His fountain-pen was dry and she said, 'Wait, wait,' and brought a small ink bottle. When the bottle was opened, there was nothing inside but a little black sediment.

Resignedly spreading her hands, she said, 'Never mind,' and shut the register up.

The English visitors started down the main street but did not get very far. Coming to a stone quay where an Arab café owner had put his tables and chairs by the lake edge, Castlebar sat down and took out his cigarette pack.

The sun was low, the water placid. There was no noise except the click of the tric-trac counters from inside the café. A slight breeze blew cool across the lake and Castlebar, drinking arak and smoking his cigarettes, smiled contentedly and put his hand out to Angela. She slipped her hand into his, then he smiled at Harriet and she smiled back. She knew he did not want her to be excluded and she had begun not only to appreciate him but to feel affection for him. She could understand Angela's love for him. He might not dazzle the outside world but he was Angela's own man. He devoted himself to her and to her comfort. He was kind, and not only to Angela. He carried his kindness over to Harriet so she, an admirer of wit, intelligence and looks in a man, was beginning to realize that kindness, if you had the luck to find it, was an even more desirable quality.

They sat for some time with nothing to say then Castlebar, no doubt prompted by their being in the Holy Land, told the women a story he had not told before: 'Y-y-you know that in the Far East every Jew is called Sassoon? Well, it's the Jewish name there. Someone told me that one of the embassy chaps was coming back from safari on a Good Friday and saw the embassy flag at half-mast. He said to his bearer: "What d'you think's the matter, Chang?" And Chang told him: "Two thousand years ago, Sassoon man kill white man's joss. White man still velly solly."'

Angela gave a shriek of appreciation: 'Oh, Bill, you are wonderful!' and leaning towards him, she kissed his ear.

How pleasant it would be, Harriet thought, if Guy were here with them, not talking his head off or looking around for additional company, but happy to be with her in the way Angela and Castlebar were happy.

As the sun sank lower, a remarkable thing happened. First, Mount Hermon appeared, its silver crest hanging in mid-air, a disembodied ghost of a mountain, then the hills round the lake were emblazoned with colour, turning from an orange-pink to crimson then a crimson-purple so vivid it scarcely seemed a part of nature.

They had all seen the splendours of the Egyptian sunsets and Harriet had seen the famed violet light on the Athenian hills, but none of them had seen before this luscious, syrupy richness of light that suffused the hills, the town and the waters of the lake. Their faces were brilliant with it and Angela cried: 'If this is Galilee, we will stay here for ever!'

They sat, amazed, until the colour faded and the wind blew cold, then they went to a restaurant where a card in the window said: 'Steak sandwiches.' Steak sandwiches, Castlebar said, were just what his inside had in mind. His inside was also thinking of a privy and while he was away, Harriet said: 'I can understand why you are so fond of Bill. He's kind. Perhaps the kindest man I've ever known.'

'Wasn't your Guy supposed to be the epitome of kindness?'

'Supposed to be, yes.'

Angela laughed, saying quietly: '"If he be not kind to me, what care I how kind he be?" To tell you the truth, I thought he was the most selfish man I've ever known. I often wondered why you didn't box his ears.'

Harriet smiled. She knew if Guy were to hear Angela's opinion of him, it would merely confirm his belief that she was mad.

'It's not exactly selfishness. It's . . . well, he doesn't stop to think.'

'You should pull him up short: *make* him think. The trouble is that with his charm, he has had things too easy.'

'That's true; but at the same time he feels deprived. He feels he should have fought in Spain. He venerates the men who did go there, especially the ones who died. I don't know why it should have been more heroic to fight in Spain than, say, the western desert, but apparently it was.'

'Is that why some of them bolted to the States when the war started?'

'Probably. They didn't want to be involved in anything so trivial as a Second World War.'

Angela, laughing, put her hands on Harriet's shoulder: 'Dear Harriet, I'm so glad you're with us. You really do add to the gaiety of nations.'

The restaurant was a long room with a row of tables against each wall. There was a bar at one end with a surprising variety of bottles. Small though the place was, it appeared to be the centre of life in Tiberias. Local boys were gathered there, drinking beer and mead. Angela was able to buy her bottle of whisky and Harriet was served with white Cyprus wine. The steak sandwiches were very good and Castlebar was able to buy a new pack of Camels. He and the two women imagined themselves comfortably settled in for the evening when there was a commotion in the street. Dozens of Australian soldiers were making an unsteady way down the centre of the road. The restaurant door crashed open and a bunched crowd of men elbowed each other into the narrow path between the tables. After staring about, befuddled and belligerent, they settled down at the few unoccupied tables and the arguments began.

The men wanted whisky. The young waitress, a refugee Jewess with little English, tried to tell them there was no whisky but they pointed to Angela's bottle and the other bottles behind the bar.

The girl appealed to Castlebar: 'What to do? Officers say no whisky for troops. Troops have beer but troops say: "Give whisky." What to do?'

Castlebar, feeling himself in a weak position, grinned uneasily at the angry men but had no suggestion to make. More Australians were crowding in but there was nowhere for them to sit. They lurched about, vaguely threatening, before wandering out again. One, as he left, scooped up a heap of small change from a table by the door. The rightful owner, finding it gone, began to shout that no change had been given to him. The waitress argued and wept while more arrivals pushed her this way and that.

Getting no help from her, the Australians took over the bar and began to serve themselves. They filled tumblers with spirits and started to sing. The girl brought out an older woman who demanded: 'You pay, you hear? You drink our drink and now you pay,' while the men, ignoring her, quarrelled, shouted and sang in hard, throaty voices.

In the midst of this uproar, Angela said: 'Let's go.' Castlebar hid the half-empty whisky bottle under his coat and they tried to push out between the tables but the way was blocked by a solitary Australian who had taken the empty fourth chair, which was beside Harriet. As she rose, he pushed her back into her seat and said: 'You're not going.'

Finding themselves trapped, Angela and Castlebar sat down again. The Australian, having looked Harriet over, said: 'Like to dance?'

'There's not much room for dancing.'

'Y'could be right.' He brought out a wallet and offered Harriet pictures of his parents. When she had admired them, she asked, 'What are you all doing here?'

'Three-day tour,' he said but could not tell her where they had been or where they were going. The men, it seemed, had arrived drunk the night before and having spent the day asleep, were intent on getting drunk again.

'So you haven't seen much?'

The Australian shook his head and again brought out his wallet: 'Wan' to see m'old mum and dad?'

'I've seen them. How long will you be here?'

'Don't know. Three-day tour.'

At that moment, a local boy at the next table, over-stimulated by events, gave a scream and fell to the floor. Shuddering, snorting, chattering, foaming at the mouth, he lay near Harriet's feet, a piteous and horrible sight. When she tried to move out of his way, the Australian pushed her down again.

'Take no notice of him; he's showing off. Wants to get ya to notice him. 'Ave another look at me old mum and dad.'

'For God's sake,' Angela shouted to Castlebar, 'make them let us out.'

Rising, holding the table before her like a battering ram, Angela thrust it into the aisle, pushing Harriet and the Australian in front of her. The Australian tried to force her back, but with the strength of anger, she gave him a violent blow across the mouth and he burst into tears. Castlebar, taking Harriet by the hand, pulled her after him while the Australian wailed: 'Nobody loves poor Aussies. Nobody loves poor Aussies.'

Somehow or other, the three English reached the street.

Harriet said: 'They'll be gone tomorrow.'

'So will we,' Angela spoke with furious decision and Harriet began to feel resentful of Angela's directives. The lakeside town

128

attracted her and she wanted to stay there a few days. At the pension, finding her room cleaned and the bed made, she thought of saying to Angela: 'You go. I will stay. I'm used to making my own decisions and I'm tired of being told where I shall go and when.' But supposing she did stay, how would she live? If she could not find work in Damascus, she certainly would not find it here.

During the night a storm broke and, wakened by the thunder, she went to the window and looked out on a small garden that ran down to the lake. She could see the water in tumult and a palm tree, lashed by the wind, bending from side to side, pliable as rubber, its fronds touching the ground this way and that. Serpents of lightning zig-zagged across the sky and flashed in sheets, illuming the scene with unnatural brilliance. The grass had been flattened by rain and, as she imagined the lupin field laid low by the torrent, she ceased to think of staying on in Galilee.

Next morning, the air glittered and the palm tree stood upright in the sun. No sound came from the room occupied by Angela and Castlebar. The next door was marked 'Bad' but when Harriet tried to open it, the old woman ran from her kitchen, holding up ten fingers to indicate the cost of a bath. Inside there was no bath but an old, rusted shower that creaked and gasped and gave out irregular bursts of cold, brown water.

The restaurant was shut till mid-day. Walking in the opposite direction, Harriet found beside the lake an open area planted with pepper trees. Beneath the trees were some iron tables and chairs, wet from the storm and as they dried, a mist rose into the delicate, lacy foliage of the trees. The lake water was flat and clear as glass and the surrounding trees motionless in the early morning air. A few people were sitting at the tables drinking coffee and as Harriet waited, a waitress came with a towel and mopped the rain from a chair and offered it to her.

Sitting happily alone beneath the shifting sun and shade of the trees, Harriet was diverted by a flying-boat that circled the lake and settled on the surface some fifty yards away from her. A rowing-boat went out to pick up the passengers. They were brought to the café, a collection of civilians with one army officer. The civilians, government officials or journalists, passed quickly between the tables and were gone while the officer, trudging up over the sandy floor, was left behind. He stopped in front of Harriet.

'Well, I never, I know the Middle East is a small world but surely the hand of fate is bringing us together.'

Wheezing and coughing through his big, fluffy moustache, Lister dropped on to a chair and tried to seize Harriet's hand. She slid it away from him, asking: 'What are you doing, arriving by sea-plane? Who were the other men?'

'Box-wallahs,' Lister panted, exhausted by the walk through the heavy sand: 'Secret mission. Trying to solve the food situation. Very hush-hush. Everyone knows about it, of course. Everyone knows everything here.' He coughed and spluttered before finding his voice again: 'The other day I got into a taxi and said to the driver: "Take me to the broadcasting station." "What you want, sah?" he asked. "You want PBS or you want Secret Broadcasting Station?" I said: "How d'you know there's a secret broadcasting station?" and the fellow roared with laughter: "Oh, sah, everyone know secret broadcasting station."' Lister, too, roared with laughter, his big, soft body straining against his washed-out khaki shirt and faded corduroy trousers. His eyes streamed and as he began coughing again, he took out a hip flask and drank from it: 'That's better. Have to go. There's a bus picking us up at 10.00 hours. See you in the Holy City, I expect. Oh, by the way, that actor fellow Pratt is there. Did I tell you?'

'No. If we come, where can I find him?'

'He's at the same bunkhouse as I am, the YMCA. I see a lot of him but he doesn't approve of poor old Lister. Thinks I'm fast or something. Look me up, won't you? We'll have a blow-out. Must go. Must go.' Shifting about and squirming, he managed to rise from his chair then, with a wave of his stick, he plodded on, his desert boots sinking into the sand, his trousers splitting over his big buttocks.

Jerusalem, Harriet decided, was the place for her. With the help of Aidan and Lister, she would be able to find work in a government office. Imagining all her problems were solved, she hurried back to the pension and found Angela, too, preparing to set out for Jerusalem. Castlebar had been sent to buy steak sandwiches and, soon after midday, they had left behind them the flowers and meadows of Galilee. Angela drove up on to the cen-

130

tral ridge of hills to reach Nazareth where Castlebar thought they might stop for a drink. Angela said: 'Not here. Dim little place. We'll go on to Nablous.'

Nablous did not look much better but there was a pool, a large tank, where boys were splashing about and making a lot of noise.

'Now this is fun,' Angela said, 'we'll stop here.' When they had eaten their steak sandwiches, she wandered down and spoke to the boys in Arabic. She asked how they had come by the pool and the boys told her that a rich man had presented it to the town.

She asked when did the girls have their turn in the water?

The girls? The boys looked confounded until one, older than the others, as though talking to someone simple-minded, told her the girls did not come to the pool. The girls had to stay at home and help their mothers.

Angela came back to the car in a rage and said: 'This is a one-sex town. Let's push on to civilization.'

As they reached the end of the ridge, they glimpsed distant towers and spires but it was not till they overlooked the valley of Latrun that they saw the Holy City complete and radiant on its hills. It seemed to float on a basin of mist and within its crenellated walls, the golden dome of the Mosque of Omar radiated the evening sunlight.

There was a downdrop of hairpin bends. 'The Seven Sisters,' Castlebar told the women. 'Notorious place for accidents, designed by the silly Turks. This is where the horses would smell the stables and make a dash and take the whole caboose over the edge. I hope our old moke doesn't smell a garage.'

Angela smiled indulgently on him. 'You awful idiot,' she said and bending to kiss him, nearly took the Alvis over the edge.

They drove down into olive groves then, rising again, reached the outskirts of the city and came on to the Jaffa Road.

'Here we are,' Angela said and stopped the car outside the King David Hotel.

Seventeen

The Jerusalem weather was still unsettled. Heavy showers came and went, leaving on the air the scent of rosemary, but the rains were nearly over. The sun, when it appeared, had the pleasant heat of an English summer.

Settling down to their old routine, Harriet, Angela and Castlebar would sit before dinner in the hotel garden and watch the mist clear over the Jordan valley and the mountains of Moab appear, purple-brown and wrinkled like prunes.

On the first evening, Angela was so pleased by her surroundings that she said: 'We might spend the summer here,' and Harriet, hoping soon to find work and pay her way, said she could think of no more agreeable place.

'What about you, loved one?' Angela turned to Castlebar and Castlebar, as usual, agreed with Angela.

But at dinner, her enthusiasm waned at the sight of the strange, dark meat on her plate. She called their waiter, an Armenian, and said: 'What on earth is it?'

The waiter was not sure. He said it could be mutton or it could be camel.

'Mutton? Camel?' Angela cried out indignantly, attracting the attention of the other diners: 'No one eats mutton these days. As for camel!'

'Here, madam, we must be glad for what we can get.' The waiter explained that the different communities conserved their food for their own people. The Arabs fed the Arabs, the Jews the Jews, but the British, having no one to provide for them, were always half-starved and the hotels had to take what they could get. He, an Armenian, was not much better off than the British so he was lucky to work where food was provided. His manner, modest and considerate, disarmed Angela who smiled into his old, sad, wrinkled face and said with humorous resignation: 'There's always a something, isn't there? And I suppose you're going to tell me there's no Scotch whisky.'

'Oh, madam, there is whisky. Many kinds. You like whisky, madam?' He asked as one asking a child if it liked chocolate. Angela threw back her head and laughed, then said to all the interested diners: 'Isn't he sweet!' She told him he was her favourite waiter, her favourite of all the waiters she had ever known and he smiled at her with gentle, adoring eyes.

The Holy City was protected by a town planner. The city was built of grey, local stone, and new buildings had to conform, but opposite the hotel there was a red, stark structure that had some-how evaded regulations. It was fronted by the small, neat rose-mary hedges that scented the air in wet weather. Harriet thought it was a block of municipal offices but found it was the YMCA.

When Angela and Castlebar were settled in the bar, she crossed the road to enquire for Aidan Pratt.

The porter told her: 'Captain Pratt gone away.'

'And not coming back?'

'Yes, indeed, coming back. We keep his room. He come when he come. When? Any time now, I think.'

Harriet, eager to start work, left with a sense of hope deferred. Outside on the steps, she met Lister who gave her a riotous welcome: 'Here she is, my lovely girl. Come to find her old Lister.'

'Well, not exactly. To tell you the truth, I was looking for Aidan Pratt but he's away.'

'That one is always away. He thinks the War Office sent him out on a joy-ride. Do you want him for anything special?'

'Only to see him. It's just that he's a friend of Guy.'

'Aren't we all? Everyone's a friend of Guy.'

'When do you think Aidan will be back?'

'I don't know but I could find out. Why worry about him when you've got your old Lister to show you round. How long will you be in Jerusalem?'

'I'm not sure.' There was, Harriet realized, a flaw in her plan to live and work here. Guy had friends in the city and sooner or later, one of them would tell him where she was. She had been prepared to take Aidan into her confidence but Lister was another matter. She could not trust him to keep her presence secret.

He said: 'Come over to the bar and have a drink.'

Having no reason to refuse, Harriet went with him to the hotel, discomforted by the thought that Angela did not want to see him again. But Angela seemed to be amused by the sight of him and when he pressed his damp moustache ardently against the back of her hand, she asked: 'And how's the little bum tonight?'

'Ho, ho, ho,' Lister shook all over and on the strength of their previous acquaintance, sat down and helped himself from the whisky bottle. His hand was shaky. It was obvious he had already reached the talkative stage of inebriation but he said: 'First today.' Then: 'Just met this girl looking for that actor fellow Pratt. She said he was a friend of Guy. "Aren't we all?" I said: "Aren't we all?" Eh, eh? Not surprising, eh?' He eulogized Guy's good fellowship, his gift of making people feel wanted, his readiness to help anyone who needed help and so on. While he talked, his eyes slid loosely in their sockets and several times looked to Harriet for confirmation of what he said, expecting her to be gratified.

And, in a way, she was. Guy deserved this praise, she could even feel proud of his deserving but the fact remained, she had not been included in this widely bestowed generosity.

Angela listened but said nothing. Castlebar smiled and gave Harriet a sly glance. Lister, catching the glance, shouted: 'Eh, you poetaster? What do you think? Do you agree or disagree?'

'I agree, of course.'

'Ever hear that story about the two men on the desert island? Neither knew the other but they both knew Guy Pringle?'

'Oh, y-y-yes, frequently.'

'There you are, then! The man's a legend. Isn't he a legend, eh?'

'Y-y-yes. Very lively legend, though.'

Mollified, Lister subsided: 'Glad you've turned up. Nice to have someone who talks one's own language. You'll be here most nights, I expect. Nowhere else to go, is there?'

Lister helped himself again from the bottle and in return for hospitality, set out on a survey of Palestine as it looked to him.

'Ideal climate this, never too hot, but awful place, everyone hating everyone else. The Polish Jews hate the German Jews, and the Russians hate the Polish and the German. They're all in small communities, each one trying to corner everything for themselves: jobs, food, flats, houses. Then there's the Orthodox Jews – they got here first and want to control the show. The sophisticated western Jews hate the Old City types with their fur hats and kaftans and bugger-grips. See them going round on the Sabbath trying the shop doors to make sure no one's opened up on the quiet. All they do is pray and bump their heads against the Wailing Wall. Their wives have to keep them. Then all the Jews combine in hating the Arabs and the Arabs and Jews combine in hating the British police, and the police hate the government officials who look down on them and won't let them join the Club. What a place! God knows who'll get it in the end but whoever it is, I don't envy them.'

Castlebar said: 'I s-s-suppose things'll settle down when the Jews feel more secure?'

'Don't know,' Lister had said his piece and had now started to droop. 'Hatred,' he muttered. 'Terrible thing: hatred! My nurse used to hate me, never knew why. She used the brush on me. Bristle side. Used to pull down m'little knickers...'

'Not that little bum again,' Angela interrupted sharply and Lister gave her a hurt look, then sank forward on his stick. A tear trickled down his cheek.

'No sympathy. No understanding...'

'Come on,' Angela ordered Castlebar who protested: 'But the bottle's still a quarter full.'

'Let him have it. You drink too much, anyway. How about you, Harriet?'

'I'm coming.' Looking back, Harriet saw Lister abstractedly refilling his glass. She expected a reprimand from Angela but Angela said only: 'I suppose we'll have him every night,' and sighed as she went into the lift.

Lister was, as she had feared, a nightly visitor to the bar but he also escorted Harriet on sight-seeing trips while Angela and Castlebar spent the afternoons in their room. Angela lent Lister the car and he drove Harriet to Bethlehem to see the Church of the Nativity and a cave made gaudy with velvets, brocades, ikons, holy pictures and bejewelled gewgaws that claimed to be the manger where Christ was born. They went westward down through the orange groves to Jaffa and eastward through the desert to Jericho and the Dead Sea. All these trips were described in the evening to Angela who was content to listen and see nothing, but there was one event that roused her interest. The Armenian waiter had told her about the great ceremony of the Greek church, the Ceremony of the Holy Fire.

Lister eagerly agreed: 'Mustn't miss it, even if you have to camp in the church all night.' He said nothing more but a few days later he arrived with an air of smiling complacency that had in it a slight hauteur. Even his limp had acquired majesty. Bowing first to Angela, then to Harriet and to Castlebar, he said: 'I have done the impossible. I have obtained tickets for the Holy Fire; and ask you to honour me by coming as my guests.'

Gratified by their grateful acceptance, he went to the bar and bought drinks for everyone. 'This year,' he explained in a somewhat lofty fashion, 'the police are going to control the show. There will be no fighting to get in, no violence or people getting killed. Admission will be by invitation only.'

'But won't that spoil things?' Angela said.

'Not a bit. The hoi-polloi will simply have to wait till the ticket holders are seated then they'll be admitted in an orderly manner. There'll be a special entrance for distinguished visitors, among whom will be . . .' he lifted Angela's hand, then Harriet's, and having kissed them both, simpered at them: '. . . will be these two lovely ladies.'

Harriet asked: 'How did you get the tickets?'

'Never mind. There are ways and means, *if* one has influence.' Lister maintained his dignity for the rest of the evening, leaving the bar while still reasonably sober and making no further mention of his little bum. He refused to disclose how he had obtained the tickets but Angela learnt from her friend, the Armenian waiter, that batches of invitations had been sent out to the different orders of Jerusalem society: the government officials, the military and the religious sects – the Greeks, the Roman Catholics, the Copts, the Armenians and even the lowly Abyssinians who were so poor, they had been pushed out of the interior of the church but had managed to keep a foothold on the roof.

'The roof of what?' Angela asked.

'Why, madam, the roof of the church. The Holy Sepulchre.'

Lister, when tackled by Angela, admitted he had applied for four of the military allotment and had been granted them. 'Quite an achievement, eh? Getting all four?' He produced the tickets and allowed his guests to examine them then, with the air of a munificent host, put them back in his wallet. He impressed on them the need to make an early start. Though the onlookers would be organized, nothing could organize the Greek patriarch.

'The show begins when the old boy chooses to turn up, and that could be any time. Want to get in at the start, don't we? It'll be a great occasion, a great occasion.'

Lister, in his state of expansive authority, remained as near sober as he ever was. The only thing troubling him was his gout.

Eighteen

Edwina had announced her engagement to Tony Brody but she still had doubts about the marriage. Creeping her hand towards Guy and gently touching his arm, she sighed and said: 'Guy darling, what do you think? *Should* I marry Tony?'

'Don't you want to marry him?'

'I wish I knew. I'm fond of him, of course, but he's so stingy about money. I told him I wanted a big wedding in the cathedral and an arch of swords but he won't hear of it. He says a simple ceremony at the Consulate will do for him. Isn't that mean? I've always wanted an arch of swords but he refuses to speak to his colonel. Just think of it! A simple ceremony at the Consulate! We might as well not be married at all. What was your wedding like, Guy?'

'Very simple. We went to a registry office.'

'Oh yes, people did that in England with the war coming. But next time you'd want something better than that.'

'There won't be a next time.'

'Oh Guy, really!' The evening in the fish restaurant had faded into the past and Edwina again considered Guy as a likely match: 'You're too young to be on your own. I keep thinking how silly it would be if I married Tony and then you changed your mind and started looking . . . well, you know what I mean!'

Guy smiled: 'I won't change my mind. I'm not the marrying kind.'

'You married Harriet.'

'Harriet was different.'

'How horrid you are!' Edwina, growing pink, shook her hair down to hide her face and said in a small voice: 'Well, Harriet's gone, now. Poor Harriet! You weren't all that nice to her when she was alive. She must have spent a good many nights alone here just as I do when Tony's on duty. I know how beastly it is.'

Guy rose without speaking and went to his room to sort his books. Dobson said to Edwina: 'That was cruel and uncalled for, Edwina.'

'I don't think it was uncalled for. Why is Guy so rude and horrid these days? He used to be sweet but now you never know what he'll say.'

'Then don't provoke him. If you've settled for Tony Brody, you must put Guy out of your mind.'

'You don't care what happens to me, do you? It's miserable being engaged. Nobody takes me out now except Tony.'

'You mean there's loyalty among men even in these lean times?'

'No, it's not that. All the best men have gone to Tunisia.'

'If you're marrying Tony simply because there's no one else, you'd be wise to wait. There are always better fish in the sea.'

'Oh, but we can't wait because we're going to Assuan. I've always wanted to stay at the Cataract and it'll soon be too hot.'

Marrying in haste, Edwina went around in taxis, shopping for her trousseau, buying evening dresses at Cicurel and having fittings for her bridal gown. She occasionally looked in at her office because she had decided to keep her job. It was, in its way, war work and, in a less enthusiastic mood, she admitted Tony had said the money would be useful. As she was still arguing and pleading for a cathedral wedding and a reception at the Semiramus, Tony had to tell her that he was a divorced man. Though there might be no ban by the cathedral authorities, he felt that a quiet civil ceremony would be more fitting for a second marriage. Edwina, stunned by this disclosure, was left with nothing but the honeymoon at the Cataract; and Upper Egypt was already uncomfortably hot.

'Poor girl,' Dobson said to Guy: 'I'll have to do something for her. We could have a little reception here. It won't be very grand but it will be better than nothing.'

Offered a party of thirty guests with Cyprus champagne and a cake from Groppi's, Edwina was moved to tears: 'Oh, Dobbie, what a darling you are! What a darling you've always been to me! Guy, too.' She dabbed at her eyes and both men felt the pathos of lost hopes. All her lavish plans had gone down in disappointment. She had hoped to marry Peter Lisdoonvarna and have a title, even if only an Irish one, and she had ended with a major past his first youth who already had one wife to keep.

Meanwhile Dobson had decided to write his memoirs. 'With the war out of the way, one has to do something,' he said and at the breakfast table, while Edwina was trying to discuss the details of her reception, he would call on Guy to approve some theory about empire or advise on some anecdote or other. He kept a collection of used envelopes on which he made notes.

Guy, giving an ear to each of them, inclined towards Dobson, having some interest in the uses of diplomacy and none in Tony Brody.

It was Dobson's belief that the British empire began to decay when the speed-up of communications gave the Colonial Office dominion over the colonial governors.

'That will be my theme,' he said.

Guy considered it: 'You mean, individuality became answerable to the machine?'

'Excellently put,' Dobson scribbled on an envelope: 'We no longer have great men like Bentinck, the Wellesleys, Henry Laurence, James Kirk: men who developed their initiative by exercising it. Now the service is dependent on a pack of nonentities. You agree?'

'I'm not sure that I do. One can develop bad judgement as well as good.'

'True, but now we have no judgement at all. We administer by statistics.'

'That's not necessarily harmful. Think of the mayhem that's been caused by putting a Hitler in control.'

'Well, yes. Strong measures don't always work. Would you say that HE did any good when he drove a tank through the gates of Abdin Palace?'

'You know more about that than I do.'

Dobson consulted another envelope: 'I've said the results weren't up to much. HE thought he'd taught Farouk a lesson but Farouk has his own ideas. He's no fool. The other day he said to HE: "When are you going to take the last of your damn troops out of my country." HE gave him a lecture on Egypt being the front line of defence of the Gulf oil-fields. Farouk listened in sulky silence and at the end said: "Oh, stay if you must, but when the war's over, for God's sake put down the white man's burden and go."'

When Guy laughed, Dobson added quickly: 'But keep that under your hat. It's my story. Those bloody journalists are a pack of thieves. If you're fool enough to tell them anything, they'll print it as their own next day. Your friend Jackman is the biggest crook.'

'Jackman's no longer here.'

'Umm, I forgot. Now listen to this: King Farouk said to me: "Egypt, you know, is part of Europe." "Indeed," I replied: "Which part?" I wasn't going to put it in but I think it's too good to leave out.'

Edwina, weary of this talk, broke in on it: 'Oh, Dobbie, you're becoming a bore. No wonder Harriet described you as a master of impersonal conversation.'

'Did she?' Dobson spoke in a high note of satisfaction and scribbled down: 'Master of impersonal conversation.'

'I don't think you've any real feeling for anyone. You know how worried I am. Here am I on the very eve of marrying Tony and I'm not sure I'll go ahead with it.'

'Then I'd better cancel the order for champagne.'

'Oh, I don't think you should do that,' Edwina said.

When Edwina had accused him of leaving Harriet too much on her own, Guy had been offended, yet the accusation was justified. Harriet must have spent many nights on her own and he had never asked her what she did with herself. Loneliness was something outside his experience. He had his work and his friends, and he had sacrificed Harriet to both. The truth was, the war had given his work too much importance. Work had condoned his civilian status. Its demands had left him no time for his wife and he had instigated her return on the doomed ship. But had the demands of his work been so intensive? Didn't he inflate them to save his civilian face?

Now, no longer challenged by the nearness of war, he could see the futility of his reserved occupation. Lecturing on English literature, teaching the English language, he had been peddling the idea of empire to a country that only wanted one thing; to be rid of the British for good and all. And, to add to the absurdity of the situation, he himself had no belief in empire.

But if he did not have his work, what would be left to him? He thought it no wonder that people were giving themselves to such absurdities as Dobson's memoirs and Edwina's perfunctory marriage. The war had abandoned them, leaving them in a vacuum that had been filled by everyday worries. But everyday worries were not enough. They had to invent excitements to make life bearable. Now it seemed to him the only excitement left in life was work.

He still had friends, of course. Almost everyone who knew him, claimed him as a friend. Simon was still on hand, glad of an outing now and then. And Aidan Pratt, though given little encouragement, came to Cairo with the sole purpose of seeing him.

Aidan, taking two weeks' leave, had spent the whole time at Shepherd's, telephoning Guy every day and begging his company when Guy had time to spare.

On his last day, he invited Guy to dinner at the Hermitage. 'Just to say "goodbye",' he said with unconvincing cheerfulness and Guy, feeling bound to him by his affection for Harriet, accepted the invitation but said he would probably arrive late.

'However late you are, I'll wait for you,' Aidan replied and Guy, tired of his company, felt the relationship was being augmented by a sort of blackmail.

Crossing the Midan to the restaurant door, Guy could see through the glass into the brightly-lit interior where Aidan was sitting on a sofa. He was, as he promised, waiting for his guest, looking for him but looking in the wrong direction, his dark, sombre eyes betraying a longing that brought Guy to a stop.

Guy, reaching the pavement, paused in the darkness of the street, reluctant to enter, knowing he was the longed-for object. He had tolerated Aidan, feeling indebted to him for grief shared, but now he had had enough. As he stood, half inclined to make his escape, Aidan turned, saw him and at once played another role. He had been sitting in the sofa corner like a caged, unhappy bird. Now, rising with an actor's grace, he lifted a hand as Guy joined him and said: 'So there you are!'

'Sorry I'm late.'

'I'm quite used to your being late,' Aidan spoke lightly, with a self-denigratory smile as though resigned to his unimportance in Guy's scheme of things. The smile still lingered on his face as they went to the table he had booked and sat down.

During dinner, he did not try to establish any sort of intimacy. He talked, as most people did, about the war. He had heard, he said, that plans were in hand for a combined British and American attack across the Mediterranean.

Guy said: 'I knew it was on the cards but if it's imminent, surely it would be top secret?'

'It is top secret. Naturally. But things get round. That fellow Lister who works at Sharq al Adna, you've only to give him a few drinks and he'll tell you anything. He got a signal about the preparations for an attack across the Med, but there's more to it than that. There's a rumour that the Vichy government has started to evacuate children from the Channel ports. That could mean a concerted attack, north and south. If there were two sudden blows, the whole centre could disintegrate quite suddenly. It might mean a complete German collapse.'

'You think so?' Guy could not believe it. He did not even want to believe it. He was in no fit state to face peace at that time: 'If by the centre, you mean the occupied countries, an area of that size doesn't collapse in a hurry. Except for Switzerland and Sweden, it's the whole of Europe.'

'What about Spain?'

'Spain's part of the Axis.'

'I wouldn't say that. The Germans haven't found Franco as docile as they'd hoped, and we should be grateful for it. If the government had won, Spain would have been occupied when war broke out. It would have been an important stronghold for the enemy. We would certainly have lost Gibraltar.'

Guy, frowning, said: 'That's merely supposition.'

Aware that he had annoyed Guy, Aidan left the question of Spain and said mildly: 'I have a feeling the war could be over this year.'

'That's ridiculous. The Germans will fight from town to town, from house to house, doorway to doorway. It could drag on for years. By the time we get back – if we ever do get back – there may be nothing left of Europe but rat-ridden, plague-stricken ruins, and, don't forget, there are other war zones. I can't imagine the Japanese ever giving in. It could be like the Hundred Years War. There may never be peace in our time.'

Aidan gave a bleak laugh: 'You're very gloomy tonight. Why shouldn't we pull out? – make a separate peace?'

'Pull out? We're allied to Russia and the United States. Do you imagine we could pull out and leave them to fight without us? Would you want such a thing?'

'I don't know. Perhaps.'

Guy could see that Aidan did want it, though he had little hope of it. The smile that had lingered on his face faded as he contemplated a lifetime of war and he said: 'I believe a good many people want it but, of course, they won't admit it. Look what the war has done to us all! You've lost Harriet. I've lost my future as an actor, everything that mattered to me. Do you remember that night in Alex when Harriet said she had seen me as Konstantin in *The Seagull*? How moved she had been! She said she was spellbound. On the first night, I said to myself, "Now it's all beginning," and less than three months later, it had ended. I declared myself a conscientious objector and I was directed on to that ship taking the children to Canada . . .' Aidan's voice failed and Guy, not unfeeling, said: 'It'll end sometime. We'll begin again.'

'But too late for me. I'll just be another out-of-work actor.'

'You think you'll be forgotten so soon?'

'I'd scarcely done enough to be remembered as more than promising. And I'll be edging into middle-age. Too late to be promising. In the theatre, if you don't start young, you might as well not start at all.'

Guy shook his head slowly, having no consolation to offer. As they walked to the station, Aidan broke their silence to ask: 'Did you mean that about the Hundred Years War?'

'Not really, no. But however long it lasts, what is lost, is lost. Things won't be returned to us. I forgot to tell you: Harriet left something for you – one of those Egyptian votive figures. A cat. She said you'd asked her to keep it for you.'

'Yes, I bought it for my mother.'

'Well, it's at the flat. I'll send it to you.'

They became silent again for some minutes then Guy said:

'I've been reading Pater's *Imaginary Portraits*. He says that the Greeks had a special word for the Fate that leads one to a violent end. It's Κήρ – the extraordinary destiny. It comes out to the cradle and follows the doomed man all the way: "over the waves, through powder and shot, through the rose gardens..."'

'The rose gardens!' Aidan jerked out a laugh: 'Aren't we all being followed through the rose gardens? One way or another, we're all due for a violent end. But do you think Harriet suffered an extraordinary destiny?'

'Who knows what happened on that ship?'

'Do you mean cannibalism? I assure you that in our boat, no one even thought of it.'

'No, I didn't mean cannibalism. She probably didn't even get into the life-boat. Just think of them all fighting for their lives. She was thin and weak. She'd been ill. She wouldn't've stood a chance.'

Aidan did not answer. They had reached the station and when he had found his berth in the sleeping-car, he stood in the corridor to say goodbye. Guy, looking at him from the platform, said: 'If you give me your address in Jerusalem, I'll post the cat to you.'

'Why don't you bring it yourself? You must have some leave due to you. Come and spend a week in Palestine. Jerusalem is a lovely place, just like a Cotswold town. A holiday will do you good. Take your mind off things.'

'No.' Guy spoke firmly. He had seen enough of Aidan for the time being and the remarks about Spain still irked him. He had decided to see less of him in future. There would be no scope for personal fantasies about a relationship that could never exist. Stepping back from the carriage, he said: 'I won't wait any longer. I'll be off.'

Aidan could not let him go so easily. Putting his arm out through the open window, he leant forward to touch Guy, pleading with him: 'Do come to Jerusalem...' Before Aidan's hand could touch him, Guy took another step back.

Looking at Aidan's eager, unhappy face, he shook his head: 'It's out of the question. I'm much too busy. What is your address?'

'I'm at the YMCA. Are you sure you won't come?'

'Quite sure.'

'Perhaps later. In the summer. It's an ideal summer climate.'

'No, I haven't time for holidays.'

'Or for me?'

Guy laughed, treating the question as a joke, and Aidan, his dark eyes pained, stared at him and gave a long sigh. Saying, 'Then goodbye, Guy,' he turned and shut himself in his berth.

Guy sensed the finality in that 'goodbye' and approved it. He would prefer not to see Aidan again. He had no wish to hurt him but what was more hurtful than the pursuit of hopeless illusions? Outside the station, he realized he had not answered Aidan and he said to himself: 'Goodbye, goodbye'.

A clean break, a tidy break, he thought as he set out on the long walk through the town to Garden City.

Nineteen

The invitation to the Holy Fire completely changed Angela's attitude towards Lister. Castlebar sometimes grumbled about him, saying: 'Do we want that fat fool drinking our whisky every night?' Angela now put a stop to these complaints. 'I won't hear a word against him. He's my favourite man.'

Lister, flattered by her, seemed to melt into self-satisfaction and was constantly lifting her hand to his wet moustache. Everything he did seemed to amuse her. She made him repeat his limericks that were less witty and more scatalogical than Castlebar's. Harriet thought them abject but to Angela they were wildly funny and she demanded more and more. Lister's pride rose to such a point, he decided to give a party.

'Small party. Nothing grand. Hope to see you in my room at 18.00 hours. Eh?'

Lister's room could not have held a larger party. He had invited a Wren officer on leave from Alexandria and the guests were somehow packed in with the bed, wardrobe, small table and single chair. The Wren, as newcomer, was given the chair and Castlebar stood, hanging over her. A strip of carpet ran from chair to table and on the table there was a bottle of gin.

Harriet and Angela were to sit beside Lister on the bed. Before sitting down, Angela examined the ornamental label on the gin bottle and read:

IN MEMORIAM GIN

Bottled by H M King George VI at Balmoral, England and Shipped by Messrs Ramatoola, New Delhi, India.

She asked: 'Where on earth did you get that?'

In a lofty tone, Lister said: 'I have my contacts.'

Angela told Castlebar: 'Gin doesn't agree with you,' but Castlebar was not listening. Standing very close to the pretty Wren, he said that as she was a sailor, she ought to know some sea shanties. Cheerful and obliging, the girl sang 'Roll out the Barrel' while Castlebar kept time with his forefinger. Though he seemed absorbed by the singing, he slipped away every few minutes and tip-toed along the carpet to top up his glass. Returning with the same tip-tippity step, he kept his finger waving to cover his excursions to the bottle.

Angela watched anxiously as the line of his steps was impressed on the carpet and whispered to Harriet: 'That stuff will kill him.'

It was also having an effect upon Lister who was beginning to hark back to ancient wrongs. He told the room that there had been a 'super tart' staying at the King David the previous Christmas. He had decided to give himself a Christmas present of a session with the lady but – here his voice started to break: 'She wanted so much money, I couldn't afford it. I said: "Season of good-will. Come on, do a chap a good turn," but she wouldn't drop her...' Lister ended on a sob.

'Wouldn't drop her what?' Angela asked crossly.

'Price,' Lister gulped.

Angela shouted to Castlebar: 'Time to go, Bill.'

He was led out of the YMCA in a dazed state and half-way across the road he sank down on to his knees. Pulling him to his feet, Angela demanded: 'What was that stuff you were drinking? Some sort of bootleg poison, from the look of it.'

'Very strong,' Castlebar mumbled: 'Only needed a sip to knock a fellow out.'

Angela ordered him to bed. When he was not well enough to appear for supper, she confided to Harriet: 'I don't know what I'd do if anything happened to Bill.'

The next day was the day of the ceremony. Before Harriet had finished her breakfast, Lister arrived, eager to be off. In his impatience, he left the hotel and walked up and down in the early sunlight while Harriet telephoned through to Angela, urging her to come down.

Lister was wearing his cap at a jaunty angle, the peak over one eye, but beneath it, his face was strained and he paused every now and then to look down at the desert boot which held his gouty toe.

It was nearly nine before the party set out. When they reached the Jaffa Gate, crowds were passing through it on their way to the Holy Sepulchre – or so Lister said. He had forgotten that the ceremony had been organized by the police and kept saying there would be no room for them in the church.

Just inside the gate, where meat stalls imbued the air with a smell like a rotting corpse, Angela stopped to laugh at a single piece of black meat which hung in a mist of flies. The owner, supposing her to be a customer, hurried out with his flit gun and sprayed the meat. Angela started to chaff him in Arabic and Lister, beside himself with anxiety, gripped her upper arm and urged her on, saying: 'It'll be your fault if we miss the show.'

Elbowed by all the races of Palestine, they pushed a way through the main alley that ran deeply between buildings that almost touched in the upper air. Lister, hurrying his party on, realized he did not know the way to the basilica. He began to force them wildly this way and that, first through the fruit market, then the spice market, then into the bazaar of the metal workers where the air rasped with the smell of white hot steel.

Lister, his voice thin, cried: 'This isn't right. Where are we? Where are we?'

Angela stopped at a curio shop and began to pick over antique fire-arms, their butts decorated with silver and brass and semi-precious stones. When she said: 'One of these might frighten Bill's wife,' Lister limped on in disgust.

'We're lost,' he said. 'We've taken the wrong turning,' and he looked for someone who might give them directions. A camel passed, shaking its tasselled head; donkeys were pushed through spaces too small for their loads. Female beggars, their faces covered with black and white veils, plucked at his arm and he shied away, thinking they were lepers. At last a man in a European suit came round a corner and Lister stopped in front of him. The man was a Greek. Finding that Lister understood modern Greek, the man began to rage at him then, suddenly becoming all courtesy and smiles, directed him to the basilica.

'What was that about?' Angela asked.

'Oh, he was complaining about police interference. He said no person of decent feeling would go near the basilica this year. It's his opinion that if people want to be trampled underfoot, no one has a right to stop them. Anyway, he thinks we should go through the Via Dolorosa.'

In the Via Dolorosa a procession was advancing slowly over the spacious, creamy flagstones, led by a bespectacled cardinal in magenta canonicals. Lister saluted and the cardinal bowed towards him.

'Who was that?' Harriet whispered.

Lister replied with modest satisfaction: 'Spellman. Friend of mine.'

They came into the Greek quarter which was strangely clean, empty and silent. Immense black coffin lids stood upright by the doors of undertakers and small shops were filled with silk vestments and olive wood camels. There was a scent of incense in the air and Lister said: 'At last.'

Somewhere, hidden by the buildings that crowded about it, was the basilica. They found it at the bottom of a narrow turning. Seeing the great, carved door amidst the crumbling splendour of the façade, Lister gave a shout of triumph: 'Here we are, and not a soul going in. We'll have the whole place to ourselves.'

But the door was shut. A barrier had been erected across it and two policemen sat in front of it. They observed Lister with a contemptuous blankness as he took out his tickets and advanced upon them. The door was not an entrance; it was an exit. Lister and his party must return to the Via Dolorosa and start again.

Lister stood for a moment, stunned, then tried to pull rank. He claimed friendship with the Greek Metropolitan and with Cardinal Spellman. He said he knew the Chief of Police. He said the ladies were tired and one of them had been very ill. The police could not be moved. Ticket-holders, like everyone else, must enter by the main door.

Lister, who had advanced so confidently, now limped back with a pained and foolish air. Reaching his guests, he said in a low voice: 'Damned self-important nobodys. Just as I told you. Everyone despises them so they try to get their own back. Bunch of conchies, most of them. Shipped out here because they're no good for anything else. One of them was a ballet dancer. Think of it, a policeman ballet dancer!' Lister tried to laugh and Harriet was sadly aware that he had suffered such defeats all his life.

The din around the main door was heard long before they

found the way to it. Almost at once they came up against a closely packed crowd and could go no farther. Lister, trying to push through, demanded passage for ticket-holders. No one moved.

A Greek in the back row turned to tell him that people were wedged together for half a mile or more. Some had been waiting since dawn. Some had been there all night.

'But why are they waiting?' Lister asked: 'Why don't they go into the church?'

'Because the door's locked and there's a barrier across it. A police barrier,' said the Greek, spitting his contempt.

'How long are they going to keep us here?'

He was told they would have to remain till the Armenian patriarch arrived. The door belonged to the Armenians, the patriarch kept the key, and only he had the right to unlock it.

While this talk went on, more people had arrived so Lister's party had ceased to be at the back of the crowd and now was in the midst of it. As those at the rear tried to push forward, the English visitors were wedged into a solid mass of bodies and Harriet, more frail than the others, could not free her arms. Her face was pressed against sweaty clothing and she had to rise on tiptoe to get air to breathe.

More and more people arrived and as the pressure grew, some of the older women began to moan, fearful of what would happen when there was a move. A batch of Greek soldiers, finding the way blocked, tried to prise themselves into the crowd with their elbows. Eyes were struck, arms came down like hammer blows on heads and shoulders, and there were screams of pain and wrath. A woman began to pray and others took up her prayer. The screaming, the prayers of the women, the moans of those held prisoner and gasping for breath, caused waves of panic to pass backward and forward through the congested bodies.

Angela clung to Castlebar. Harriet, crushed and nearly senseless, remained upright simply because there was no room to fall. Lister, pressing his arm in between her body and the one behind, gripped her round the waist and catching her elbow on the other side, whispered: 'When the rush starts, hold on to me.'

There was a cannonade of hisses and enraged insults and word came back that the Armenian patriarch was about to unlock the door. Lister, a head taller than those about him, laughed and

151

said: 'The old fool's skipped inside pretty quick. Scared out of his black socks. *Now*! Keep hold of me!' But the door was shut again and the enraged Greeks shouted: 'Break down the barrier!' As a drive like a battering ram struck the rear of the crowd, one old woman began to call on God and her cry was taken up by men as well as women. People pleaded: 'Let us out. Let us out,' and Harriet, clinging to Lister, felt the same primitive urge to call on God, the last resort of them all.

The barrier crashed down. The crowd toppled forward and as the police shouted warnings and the Greek soldiers howled as though rushing into battle, Lister gathered Harriet into his arms and shouted to her: 'Stay upright. Whatever you do, don't let them knock you down.'

People pelted past them, striking against them like rocks rushing downhill. One furious blow knocked Harriet out of Lister's arms but he caught her wrist as she fell and held on to her until she was afraid the bone would break. Then another blow sent them spinning together into a curio shop. Crashing through the candles that hung over the doorway, scattering rosaries, crucifixes, olive wood boxes, baskets of Jericho roses, they fell into a corner with a table on top of them.

Shaken but unhurt, they were helped up by the shopkeeper who said: 'The police will pay for this. They caused this trouble, so we'll make them pay.'

'And serve them bloody well right,' said Lister.

Laughing and forgetting to limp, he kept his arm round Harriet as they made their way to the churchyard where the soldiers were breaking up a paling intended to keep the visitors in an orderly queue. The police had taken themselves off, leaving the Greeks free to smash whatever could be smashed. The front of the basilica, riven by age and earthquakes, was held up by wooden struts and these, too, were attacked until a priest came out and demanded a stop.

There was no sign of Angela and Castlebar. 'How will they get in?' asked Lister anxiously as he brought out his tickets, but no one was taking tickets. Inside the porch, a black-clad Armenian monk stood guard over the Armenian door, fiercely observing everyone who passed through it. Inside the church there was chill and quiet. To add to the drama of the occasion, all the candles had been extinguished and the place was in darkness. As Harriet and Lister made their way blindly forward, they were met by a major-domo with a silver-headed stick. Finding they had tickets, he conducted them in a formal manner to the chairs reserved for distinguished visitors. So far the only distinguished visitor present was Angela. She had lost Castlebar and Lister was sent off in search of him.

Angela had seated herself in the centre of the front row and Harriet, discomposed by the fall, sank down beside her. There were about fifty chairs, placed in a square and roped in with a heavy cord. Outside the cord, a mass of people stood together, awaiting events. For the first half an hour, they waited patiently, then the soldiers and young men, growing restless, began to climb the scaffolding that shored up the interior walls. Boredom produced noise and the noise grew as time passed. Occasionally someone, seeing himself more privileged than the rest, attempted to breach the cordon and sit on the empty chairs. Some were sternly ordered back to the crowd, others, for no obvious reason, were allowed to remain. An Egyptian family, the father in a fez, was left undisturbed while an old, fat Greek, gasping, sweating and pleading, was helped to a chair by one major-domo and thrown out by another.

After a long interval, Lister returned with Castlebar, both men smelling strongly of arak. They sat on either side of the two women and at first were circumspect, quietly gazing at the monument of gold and coloured marbles that was said to mark the burial place of Christ. Lister told them that the rotunda over it, shored up by girders and struts, had been placed there by the Crusaders. They returned to silence. Fifteen or twenty minutes passed then Castlebar, beguiled by the twilight, put his arm round Angela and Lister fumbled for Harriet's hand. Harriet, grateful for the protection he had afforded her, let him hold it for a while. Lister was kind but, thinking of his fat, pink face, his ridiculous moustache, his wet eyes and baby nose, she told herself that kindness was not enough.

The church was now so full that people were taking places in the topmost galleries and some had managed to join the poor Abyssinians on the roof. Faces were pressed against the small windows in the dome. The young men on the girders climbed higher to allow others to take their places. The most adventurous went up and up until one slipped and fell screaming to the crowd below. The girders, hung with a weight of humanity, creaked and shuddered and some of the women shouted warnings and the young men shouted back. Gradually losing all restraint, the congregation talked and laughed and began to sing Greek songs.

Lister's hand was plump and small with small, fat fingers, an enlarged baby's hand, that seemed to Harriet much too soft. He was not more than thirty but was deteriorating early. Defeat, though he resented it, had got its hold on him and Harriet felt sorry for him. She, too, could be kind and when he squeezed her hand, she squeezed back. Lister whispered: 'You may get a better-looking one but a more loving one, you'll never find.' Harriet laughed and slid her hand away.

The hubbub came to an abrupt stop. A minor procession was entering the church. Representatives of leading Greek and Christian Arab families, all male of course, were making a circuit of the sepulchre, the more prosperous in dark suits and pointed, patent leather shoes, the very poor in dirty galabiahs.

'A ruffianly lot,' Lister whispered as rich and poor went round with no sense of status, linking fingers and smiling at each other.

Seeing three people led to the doorway of the sepulchre, Lister became grave: 'My goodness, look who we've got here! Prince Peter and Prince Paul. The woman is Peter's Russian wife. He's a nice chap; looks like an English gent.'

Harriet, turning her head away from Lister's arak smell, saw a group of English officials being led to the chairs, among them a woman she had seen somewhere before. But where? The woman chose to sit by herself in the front row. Harriet watched her as she took her seat. She had a large crocodile handbag which she placed on her knee, putting her hands on it as though to shield it from all comers. This gesture confirmed Harriet's certainty that the woman was known to her. Some occasion when there had been a similar shielding of an object stirred vividly at the back of her mind but would not present itself. The occasion, she knew, was associated with unhappiness. She felt the unhappiness again, but that was all. The occasion itself eluded her.

She remained puzzled until distracted by the excitement around her. The major-domos were clearing a passage for the

Greek patriarch. Using their silver-headed sticks, they pushed and prodded people out of the way. The congregation moved, if it moved at all, unwillingly, craning necks for a sight of the great figure of the day.

As he appeared in the doorway, a shout of welcome filled the church and he stopped, making the most of his entry, then moved slowly forward. In robes of white brocade, wearing a large, golden, onion dome on his head, the patriarch held himself with dignity, his white beard parted from chin to waist so all might see the display of gold and gems that covered his chest. The priests behind him were in cloth of gold, some of it ragged with age, some new and gleaming. After the priests, came the choir boys. They were singing, mouths opening and shutting, but the sound was lost in the general din. After the choir boys, it was just anyone who happened to own a religious banner. These rearguard upstarts were treated with little respect. The crowd closed in on them, swamping them, throwing down their banners which they used as weapons to keep the mob at bay.

The patriarch, with an eye open for press photographers, pulled back his beard and arranged his jewels whenever he saw a camera. The procession was to go three times round the church but in the third round, all was confusion. The patriarch himself was untouched but his retinue had degenerated into a rabble of shouts, scuffles and blows. Arriving intact at the door to the sepulchre, he shook hands with the royal visitors then, mounting the steps to the door itself, he stood benign and smiling, while acolytes removed his onion dome and outer robes, leaving him in a black cassock, a humble priest like any other priest. Then came the search for matches or any means of making fire. He lifted his arms and the acolytes patted him lightly on either side. No matches were found.

The search completed, the door to the tomb was unsealed. The patriarch, with two priests to act as witnesses, entered the sepulchre. The door was shut. There was silence as everyone awaited the miracle.

'How long will it take?' Harriet whispered.

Lister nodded portentously: 'A decent interval.'

It was scarcely that. There were two smoke-blackened holes through which the fire would appear. As it shot out, a wild paean

155

of joy bellowed from the crowd. A man had waited at each hole to seize the cylinders that held the fire and at once, as the church vibrated with the yells of the faithful, the fire was passed from hand to hand. The cordon was broken and the congregation, stumbling over chairs and falling against the distinguished visitors, rushed forward, holding out candles and tapers to receive the fire. All inhibitions were lost in the intoxication of the miracle. The patriarch had brought them the divine gift of fire.

Faintly above the uproar, the church bells could be heard pounding away, telling the world the miracle was accomplished and bringing down the plaster from the ceiling. Bunches of lighted candles were given to the men on the scaffolding and passed up and up to the topmost balconies and out to the Abyssinians on the roof so, in no time, the whole interior of the church was festooned with light.

Two enormous, painted candles, guardians of the tomb, lit only on this special occasion, spouted enormous flames. Dark outlying chapels became bright with the fire and the crypt, where Helena had discovered the true cross, threw a refulgence from the depths.

Harriet, caught up in all the excitement, jumped on to the seat of her chair and stood among a dazzling swirl of lights.

The door of the sepulchre opened and the patriarch, his hands full of lighted candles, burst forth just ahead of the witness priests who, holding him on either side, ran him from the church and out of sight.

But that was not the end of the ceremony. A sort of burlesque or harlequinade followed the miracle. Priests in tattered, grimy robes now walked round shaking poles from which hung silver plates surrounded by bells. After the priests came men with boys perched on their shoulders. The boys had whips and lashing out, struck anyone who could not dodge away from them. The men on the scaffolding leant forward to lunge at the boys and two of them lost their footing and went down among the crowd.

A new, less pleasing animation had come over the scene. The royal visitors prepared to leave and the English thought it best to follow them. As Harriet stepped down from the chair, the woman at the end of the row glanced towards her and she knew it was Mrs Rutter.

Mrs Rutter did not recognize Harriet. Their only meeting had been brief. With her jewel case on her knee, she had sat near Harriet in the train going to Suez. She had been in the queue moving on to the *Queen of Sparta* when Harriet saw Mortimer and Phillips. By now she should have been half-way to England.

She hurried towards her friends and Harriet went after her, catching her up in the church porch.

'Excuse me.'

Mrs Rutter, turning and seeing what she took to be a stranger, frowned to discourage her: 'Yes?'

'Surely you are Mrs Rutter?'

'I am Mrs Rutter, yes.'

'We went to Suez in the same carriage. I was with Marion Dixon and her little boy.'

Mrs Rutter let out her breath and, lifting a hand to ward Harriet away, she went at a half-run out to the churchyard where her friends awaited her. Disturbed and puzzled, Harriet pursued her and caught her by the shoulder.

'Mrs Rutter, please, you must tell me why you are here. You boarded the ship for England, didn't you? Then how did you get back? Is Marion here, too?'

'Don't speak of it.' Mrs Rutter had lost what colour she had and her voice was hoarse: 'I can't speak of it. I don't want to speak of it. Go away,' then seeing Harriet's perplexed face, she relented a little: 'Anyway, I can't speak of it here.' She moved over to the churchyard wall and leant against it as though about to faint.

The casualties of the ceremony – two men on stretchers, one shrouded in death – lay nearby but she seemed unaware of them. Her friends, standing apart, stared at Harriet, realizing there was something very odd about the encounter.

Breathless and still hoarse, Mrs Rutter said: 'You didn't know what happened? You don't know that we were torpedoed? Some of us got into a life-boat. Marion and me and poor little Richard . . .' She choked and gasped before asking: 'You didn't know any of this?'

'No.'

'But it was in the *Egyptian Mail*.'

'I didn't return to Egypt. I heard nothing.'

'The boat drifted. There was something wrong with the steering. We had two lascars on board but they didn't know what to do. We had no water, nothing to eat . . . It went on for days. We caught some rainwater in a tarpaulin and drank it, but it wasn't enough. People started dying . . . Poor little Richard was one of the first.'

'And Marion?'

Mrs Rutter shook her head, unable to speak, then whispered: 'All dead except me and the lascars. The children first, then the women . . . I don't want to talk about it. I came here to forget it.'

'I'm sorry if I've upset you but I had to know.'

Mrs Rutter, like an invalid in need of help, looked towards her friends and one of the men, giving Harriet a look of reproach, crossed to her and led her away.

Harriet remained by the wall, shock-bound by Mrs Rutter's story. Angela, seeing she was alone, came to ask: 'What's the matter?'

'Guy thinks I'm dead.'

'Is that what that woman told you?'

'No. She told me the evacuation ship was torpedoed and she was the only woman who survived. Marion and Richard were lost. Guy thinks I was on the ship.'

'But he may not have heard . . .'

'Yes, it was in the *Egyptian Mail*.' As Harriet absorbed this fact, tears came into her eyes and she broke down, sobbing: 'Poor Guy. Oh, poor Guy, he thinks I'm dead.'

Angela led her over to Castlebar and Lister. Walking back to the Jaffa Gate, all three tried to comfort her by giving different unfounded reasons for supposing Guy would know nothing of the sinking. Harriet was too tense to listen. She wanted only one thing: to contact Guy and assure him she was alive and well.

They stood together in the foyer of the King David discussing how best to deal with the situation. Lister had been invited to luncheon at the hotel but Harriet would not join the party. She said: 'I'd better ring the Institute first.'

Castlebar said: 'It's Saturday. Isn't that Guy's day off?'

Angela said to Lister: 'Is it easy to ring Egypt?'

'Not very. The lines are always engaged. The military used to have an emergency line but that closed down when the army moved west. Better put the hotel porter on to it. Tell him to ring every two minutes till he gets a line.'

Angela said to Harriet: 'It may be ages before he gets through. You might as well come and eat.'

'I can't eat.'

Harriet sat through the afternoon in the foyer, awaiting a summons to the telephone. It was six in the evening before the porter was connected to the Garden City flat. Smiling at his achievement, he called Harriet and handed her the receiver. Her impatience, that had lapsed during the hours of waiting, now filled her with such perturbation, she felt sick. A strange safragi answered the telephone. In a remote, small voice, she asked for Professor Pringle.

'Not here, Blofessor Blingle.'

'Where is he?'

'How do I know, lady?'

How, indeed! How did anyone ever know where Guy was?

'Who is there?'

'Not no one. All out, lady.'

Desperately, she asked for the safragi she had known: 'Where's Hassan? Tell him to come to the 'phone.'

'No, no Hassan. Hassan gone away. Me Awad, me do all now.'

'I see. Thank you, Awad.'

Downcast with disappointment, she went to the bar to join Angela and Castlebar. She said: 'He's not at the flat. I can't find anyone.'

Angela looked at Castlebar: 'If we took the train tonight, we'd be in Cairo tomorrow morning.'

Scarcely understanding, Harriet stared at her: 'Do you mean you'd come with me?'

'Of course. We can't let you go alone.'

'Angela, you're the best friend I've ever had.'

'Thanks: but the truth is we want to go to Cairo. Bill can't stand the food here. If it hadn't meant leaving you to fend for yourself, we would have gone before this.'

After supper, when Lister came to the hotel, he found Harriet, Angela and Castlebar packed and ready to set out for the station. They would take the train to Jaffa and there change to the Kantara train which would reach the canal before day-break. They would not be in Cairo as soon as Angela supposed, but they would be there soon enough.

'And you're taking all this baggage? You travel like a Russian princess.' Lister smiled at Angela but his manner was unusually subdued. He offered to arrange sleepers for them. Most of the wagon-lits were permanently reserved for army officers and usually left empty. He went to the telephone and came back saying: 'I've fixed it,' then he helped carry the bags to Angela's car. At the station, Angela put the car keys into his hand.

'I'll leave it with you.'

'A loan?'

'In a way. I don't suppose I'll ever ask for it back.'

'A car's always useful.' Lister looked down at the keys for some moments before he said: 'I'm afraid I've bad news for you, Harriet. Your friend Aidan Pratt has been shot.'

'But not dead?'

'Well, yes. It was on the train coming back from Cairo. In the corridor.'

'Who would shoot him? He had no enemies.'

'No, no enemies. He shot himself.' Lister raised his wet, blue eyes and looked at Harriet: 'I'm sorry. Bad time to tell you, but thought you ought to know.'

The whistle blew and Harriet, too confused by her own problem to give Aidan the attention due to his memory, embarked with Angela and Castlebar on her return to Egypt.

Twenty

The news of Aidan Pratt's suicide reached Guy with unusual speed. The commanding officer at Kantara had telephoned the Embassy where Dobson was on night duty and Dobson, coming in to breakfast next morning, said: 'You know that actor chap, Aidan Sheridan! He seems to have gone berserk on the train to Palestine. Killed himself in the corridor of the sleeping-car. Put his gun to his head and blew his brains out. I imagine we'll hear from the Minister of Transport about the mess. Why couldn't he have waited till he got to his own quarters.' Then, observing Guy's face, he apologized: 'Didn't mean to upset you. He wasn't a particular friend, was he?'

'I saw him fairly often. He used to ring up when he came here. In fact, I had supper with him last night. He was attached to Harriet and upset by her death, but not to that extent. I'm afraid he was rather a one for dramatic gestures.'

'Unstable sort of chap, was he?'

Bemused by this second tragedy, Guy said: 'I don't know. I don't think I'd say unstable. The war had trapped him in an intolerable situation and he probably took this way out.'

'The war's trapped a good many of us but death's a pretty desperate escape route.'

Guy could feel little more than exasperation at Aidan's death. Too much was being imposed on him. He tried to put it out of his mind but for the rest of the day Aidan's dark, appealing gaze followed him as he went about his work. Aidan had wanted response, reassurance and affection, perhaps even love, and Guy had made it clear that he would give none of those things. He remembered that Harriet had accused him of taking up with inadequate people so for the first time they felt understood and appreciated. Then, their dependence becoming tedious, he would leave her to cope with them. She had, apparently, coped with Aidan. Guy, having talked him out of his defences, had become bored with him and wished him away. He had gone, and gone for good.

Edwina, told of his death, dismissed Aidan without a tear: 'You mean that actor who came to the fish restaurant? I'm not surprised he shot himself. He was an absolute misery.'

It was the eve of her wedding and she passed at once to the much more important subject of the reception.

'You're coming, aren't you, Guy darling?'

Guy, in no mood for parties, tried to excuse himself: 'I'm afraid I can't. I promised to go and see Simon.'

'Oh, but Guy, you can see Simon any time. This is a special occasion; I don't get married every day.'

'Well, the arrangements have been rather sudden, and I'm committed to Simon. He's leaving the hospital. It may be some time before I see him again.'

'Bring him with you. I'd love him to come. Now, Guy, you've no excuse. You're to come to my reception. I'll never forgive you if you don't. You're such a close friend, if you weren't there, people would think we'd had a row or something.'

Realizing it would be wise to put in an appearance, Guy telephoned Simon at the hospital and asked if he would like to come to a party in Garden City.

'Will Edwina be there?'

Simon's voice was eager and Guy said: 'Of course,' forgetting to tell him that the party was to be Edwina's wedding reception.

Simon was hoping to leave the hospital soon. He refused all offers of rest in convalescent homes and intended to take himself to Kasr el Nil barracks before being posted to an office job. What the job would be, he did not know but it was to be temporary. The party in Garden City had come at the right time. It would be for him a celebration of his complete recovery.

He had brought from England, as part of his kit, a dress uniform of fawn twill which, packed in an insect-proof tin trunk, had followed him about in the regimental baggage train. Now, for the first time, he had a use for it. The tin trunk had been sent after him to the hospital. He dragged it out from under his bed and Greening found him trying to smooth out the creases in the twill.

'Dressing ourselves up, are we, sir? Come on, I'll get that pressed for you.'

Guy, when he reached the hospital, found Simon dressed and ready, a handsome and elegant young officer, in high spirits and aglow with health. Guy had brought a taxi which took them to Garden City earlier than they were expected.

Simon, breathless at the thought of seeing Edwina again, bounded up the long flight of steps to the upper flat with Guy some way behind. Shown into the living-room, Simon was deflated at finding they were alone.

'But where is Edwina?'

'Don't worry. She'll be along soon.'

They waited with the appurtenances of the party all round them. There was a table with cold meats and a cake from Groppi's, five rented champagne buckets and three cases of champagne. There were also vases of tuberoses, white asters, lilies and ferns.

'I say, it's quite a party, isn't it?' Simon said.

It was some time before the other guests came, and they came all together. Simon, unaware of the nature of the occasion, was surprised that there should be so much laughter in the street; then came an inrush of young people, mostly from the British Embassy, all wearing white carnations. There was still no sign of Edwina but her name was repeatedly mentioned and when most of the guests hurried out to the balcony, Simon realized they were watching for her. He guessed that this was a wedding party yet it did not occur to him that it could be Edwina's wedding.

There was the sound of a car door banging below. The guests on the balcony shouted a noisy welcome. Two girls entered, dressed in pink chiffon and carrying bouquets of Parma violets. Then, at last, Edwina herself appeared. She stood posed in the doorway of the room so all might admire her in her dress of white slipper satin, a veil thrown back, a wreath of gardenias crowning her resplendent hair. She remained there for nearly a minute, the day's bright star, then the dazzled audience thought to applaud. She burst out laughing and the young men crowded about her, clamouring for a kiss.

Simon, stunned, realized there was a man looking over her

shoulder: the dim, grinning face of Major Brody, the man in possession. As Edwina was drawn into the room, the safragis started bringing round the champagne in ice buckets. Simon, given a glass, whispered to Guy: 'You didn't tell me.'

Edwina was now making her way round the room. The effusive hostess, she greeted each guest in turn, kissing the girls who were her office friends. The guests embraced her and she gave squeals of excitement, declaring her love for all of them. Coming to Simon, she was stopped, astonished by the change in him. She gasped before she said: 'But you look wonderful!'

As she bent to kiss him, a confusion of emotion strained her face and she said under her breath: 'You're so like Hugo . . . so like Hugo!' then turned quickly away and gave her attention to Guy. '*Dear* Guy, so glad you're here,' speaking his name as though there existed between them a particular intimacy. He kissed her lightly and she passed on.

The cake was a large cream sponge but Edwina, using Tony Brody's dress sword, cut it as though it were a real bridal cake. As this performance went on, Simon said pleadingly to Guy: 'Please, let's go.'

Guy was about to make their excuses to the wedded couple when he became aware that the room had grown silent. People were staring towards the door and a figure, apparently uninvited and unexpected, was sidling into the room, self-consciously smirking, as surprised at finding himself at a party as the party was at seeing him. The new arrival was Castlebar.

Guy pushed forward, saying: 'But this is wonderful! Jake's been taken from us and you've come to console us.'

'Y-y-yes,' Castlebar was fumbling for his cigarette pack: 'Y-y-you're right. I have come to console you.'

Edwina, asserting her importance, said: 'Good gracious, where have you come from? Where have you been all this time?'

'Oh, swanning around,' Castlebar managed to get a cigarette into his mouth and his speech became clearer, 'I came to see Guy. Didn't know there was something on. Angie's downstairs in a taxi and she sent me up to break it to you. She thought I should come up first and t-t-tell you, she's not alone.' Whatever Castlebar intended to say to Guy, he had obviously been warned to say it without undue haste. He lit his cigarette before adding: 'It . . . it's about Harriet.'

There was an uncomfortable movement throughout the room. This was no time for recalling the dead and Guy, going close to him, said urgently: 'You don't know, of course, but Harriet was lost . . .'

'But that's just it. That's what I came to tell you. She wasn't. She kept trying to telephone you yesterday but couldn't get hold of you, so we thought we'd better come straight here and . . .'

Dobson asked sternly: 'What are you talking about, Castlebar?'

'I'm not doing very well, am I? I wanted Angela to come up first but she decided to stay with Harriet.'

'What do you mean?' Guy, agitated, took Castlebar by the shoulders and shook him: 'Are you trying to say Harriet is alive?'

'Yes. I've been telling you – she's downstairs with Angela.'

Dobson pulled Castlebar away from Guy and gave him another shake: 'If you're lying, I think I'll murder you.'

'I'm not lying. Don't be an ass. Who would lie about such a thing? She *is* alive. She didn't get on to the ship for some reason, I don't know why. She went to Syria and we found her there and brought her back. That's the truth. If you go downstairs, you'll find her with Angie in the taxi.'

Guy did not seem able to move and Edwina, elevated by all that had happened that day and was still happening, darted forward: 'I'll go. I'll bring her up. I was her best friend.'

Guy, his face creased in an expression of longing and disbelief, stared at the door until Edwina returned holding Harriet tightly, Angela following behind. Edwina cried out to the room: 'Isn't this marvellous! To think it should happen at my wedding! The whole of Cairo will be talking about it.'

Harriet took a step towards Guy then stopped in uncertainty: 'I wasn't sure you'd want me back.'

Guy put out his arms. She ran to him and he clutched her against his breast and broke into a convulsive sob. Dropping his head down to her head, he wept loudly and wildly while people watched him, amazed. He was known as a good-humoured fellow, a generous and helpful fellow but no one expected him to show any depths of emotion.

Harriet kept saying: 'I'm sorry. I didn't know the ship went down. If I'd known, I wouldn't have stayed away.' She tried to explain her action but Guy did not want an explanation. His paroxysm subsided and, finding his voice, he said: 'What does it matter? You're safe. You're alive. You're here,' and, his face still wet with tears, he started into laughter.

Simon, caught up in the drama of Harriet's return, no longer wanted to leave the party. Had Guy offered to go with him, he would have said: 'It doesn't matter,' and it did not matter. A part of his mind had been returned to him. His vision of Edwina had dropped out of it, just as Anne's photograph had dropped from his wallet, and he knew he was free of her. His sudden freedom produced in him an emptiness like an empty gift box that in time would be filled with gifts.

Looking at her now, he saw the glow had faded. Her hair was still lustrous, her skin smooth, yet it was as though a film of dust had settled on the golden image.

She had been a fantasy of his adolescence but now he had not only reached his majority, he was verging on maturity. He had been the younger son, Hugo's admirer and imitator, and Edwina's attraction had lain not only in her beauty but the fact he had believed her to be Hugo's girl. He had wanted to be Hugo and he had wanted Hugo's girl, but now he was on his own. And Edwina had been no more Hugo's girl than she could be his.

He realized he was becoming less like Hugo. He was losing the qualities that had made him Hugo's counterpart. He was becoming less simple, less gentle, less considerate of others. He had, he feared, been tainted by experience, but he did not greatly care. Hugo did not have to face the future; he could remain innocent for ever. But there was no knowing what he, Simon, might still have to endure.

Harriet came over to speak to him. Not knowing he had been wounded, she asked: 'How are you, Simon?'

'Very well, thank you.' And that was the truth. He had passed through the ordeal of slow recovery and he was very well.

There was a flurry as Edwina, having gone to change, reappeared in a suit of white corded silk; a pretty girl, a very pretty girl, but the magic was no longer there. Her departure left Simon unmoved. For him, she had already gone.

The party dwindled; the guests went off to their different offices. Dobson, before returning to the embassy, came close to Harriet and, surprisingly, squeezed her round the waist.

There remained only Guy and Harriet, Simon, Angela and Castlebar, together with the debris of the feast. They sat down with little to say, exhausted by events.

Guy began to think of the day's work. He said he would take Simon back to the hospital and then go on to his class at the Institute.

'Oh no!' Angela sat up in protest: 'You can ditch the Institute for one night. We'll all take Simon back and then we must do something special. Mark the occasion. Make a night of it.'

Guy, looking blank, said nothing. For him the excitement was over. Harriet was safely back and there was no reason why life should not resume its everyday order. But Angela, imagining he would agree with her, had other plans for the evening. She and Castlebar intended to book in at the Semiramis, so she said: 'We'll have dinner at the hotel and then go on somewhere, perhaps to the Extase.'

Guy frowned but still said nothing. Harriet, with the Semiramis in mind, said she must go and change. Awad had put her suitcase in the room she had shared with Guy. Now it was her room again.

She thought: 'Our room. Our very own room!' She had gone away in despair but could not think why she had ever despaired. The room was as it had always been; very hot, the woodwork like parched bone, the air filled with the scent of the dry herbage in the next-door garden. It was the day for the snake-charmer and the thin, wavering note of his pipe rose above the hiss of the garden hose.

She opened her case and threw the clothes out. They were the summer things she had intended to wear while voyaging down the coast of Africa. They were very creased but one dress, a light mercerised cotton, was still fit to wear. She shook it out and spread it on the bed, then opened the top drawer of the chest. It had been her underwear drawer and Guy had left it unused. There was only one object in it – the diamond heart brooch that Angela had given her. She ran with it to the living-room.

'Look what I've found.'

She held it out to Guy who gave it an uninterested glance. She asked: 'Did Edwina return it to you?'

'I don't know. I think I asked for it.'

'Why did you ask her for it?'

'I can't remember.' Guy turned to Simon, saying: 'We must go', then to Angela: 'I'm afraid dinner isn't on tonight. I've too much to do. After the Institute, I have to meet some young Egyptians and give them a talk about self-determination. I was invited by Harriet's doctor, Shafik, and I can't let him down. You can see that. We'll have dinner another night.'

This did not satisfy Angela who said: 'This is absurd. Surely on a night like this, you can ditch all this nonsense you get up to. So far as you're concerned, Harriet has returned from the dead and you want to leave her and go and talk to a lot of Egyptians.'

'They're expecting me.'

'You can put them off.'

'It wouldn't be fair to them.'

Defeated by his belief in his own reasonableness, Angela gave up the argument. Guy, bending to kiss Harriet, became aware of her despondency and relented enough to say: 'Very well. I won't stay long at the meeting. You go and have dinner at the Semiramis and I'll come and join you afterwards. We'll all have a celebratory drink. How's that?'

'Try not to be late.'

'No. I'll come as soon as I can.'

When Guy had gone cheerfully away, taking Simon with him, Harriet said: 'Nothing has changed.'

'No. I told you you ought to box his ears. It would serve him right if you went away again.'

'Where would I go? I'm not much good at being alone. My home is where Guy is and the truth is, he's more than he seems to you. You saw how he cried when he saw me. And he made Edwina return the brooch.'

'I'd like to know how that happened,' Angela said, then she turned to look at Castlebar who had fallen asleep with his mouth open: 'Poor Bill, champers doesn't agree with him.' She kissed the top of his head and he, lifting his pale, heavy eyelids, smiled at her. 'Wake up, you gorgeous brute,' she said. 'We're going to the Semiramis. And you, Harriet, if you're going to change,

hurry up. We must feed Bill. He badly needs a proper meal after
all those awful weeks in the Holy Land.'

At the Semiramis, Angela booked into a famous suite on the
top floor that was called the Royal Suite. There, protected by the
hotel servants, she hoped they would be safe from the assaults of
Castlebar's wife. The main room overlooked the Nile and Angela
decided that before they went down to the dining-room, they
would have drinks by the window and wait for the pyramids to
appear.

Castlebar, lying on a long chair, smiled in lazy content and
said: 'Suppose we just stay here! Have supper sent up!'

'What a good idea!' Angela went to the house phone and asked
for the menu.

The little black triangles of the pyramids came out of the mist
as they had done every evening for some four thousand years.
They came like the evening star, magically, just as the red-gold of
the sunset was changing to green. Twilight fell and the star was
there, a single brilliance that for a few minutes hung in the west
then was lost among the myriad stars that crowded the firma-
ment. While all this was happening, Castlebar kept his eyes on
his plate, eating smoked salmon, veal cutlets and a mound of
fresh, glistening dates. Harriet, who had not yet regained her
appetite, ate frugally and watched the spectacle outside.

Angela's whisky bottle had come up with the meal and, when
they had eaten, the two of them sat over it as Harriet had seen
them sit so many evenings before. The lights of Gezira came on
and darkness fell. It was time for Guy to arrive. Castlebar,
replete, yawned once or twice and Harriet became anxious, feeling she should leave but having to stay. At last, when the bottle
was nearly empty and Angela and Castlebar were nodding with
sleep, Guy was shown into the room.

'Sorry I'm late.'

Angela roused herself and laughed towards Harriet: 'You're
right: nothing has changed.'

Guy, surprised by the laughter, asked: 'What should change?'
He was himself again, relieved not only of grief but remorse and
a nagging sense of guilt, free to pursue his activities without
being tripped at every turn by the memory of his loss. He said:

'Life is perfect. Harriet and I are together again. No one would want things different, would they?' He took Harriet's hand and bent to kiss her.

'And how were your Gyppos?' Angela asked.

'Fine!' Guy had had a brilliant evening and being given a vote of thanks, the leader of the group had said: '"Blofessor Blingle has blought his influence to bear on many knotty bloblems."'

Guy reproduced the Egyptian accent with such exactitude that Angela had to laugh as she said: 'Knotty problems, indeed! Do they hope to solve anything? The Gyppos play around with hazy ideals instead of learning to govern themselves.' She had given Guy the last of the whisky and when he had drunk it, she said: 'We must go to bed.'

'I've only just arrived. I want to talk with my friend Bill.'

'Not now. Bill's exhausted. It's nearly midnight. I'm afraid you'll have to talk another night.'

Guy, feeling he had been uncivilly ejected, said when they were in the street: 'You see what I mean about Angela? She asks me to dinner then turns me out as soon as I arrive.'

'You were very late.'

'Not unreasonably. She really is the most irrational of women. Crazy. Pixillated. Mad as a hatter. I don't know what you see in her.'

Twenty-one

In July, while Cairo wearied under its blanket of heat, the British and American forces left North Africa and crossed the sea to Sicily. So far as the Egyptians were concerned, the war was over. But the British, bored and restless, with no hope of going home till hostilities ceased, knew it was not over.

Guy, who now took a much more favourable view of the future, told Harriet it might be over in year or eighteen months, then what were they going to do?

That was something to be thought out. Harriet said to Angela: 'What will you and Bill do when the war ends?'

Angela smiled and said: 'Humph!' as though the end of the war were a remote and fantastic concept. Still, she was willing to consider it.

'Bill ought to start work again. They've kept his job open here but I doubt if he'll go back. He'd be willing to live like this for ever but is it good for him? I'd like him to apply for a lectureship in England. Of course he'd only get one in a minor university but what fun to settle down in a provincial town and act the professor's wife: make friends with the vicar and the local nobs, have a nice, old house and cultivate one's garden! Would you come and see us?'

'Of course. We might even come and live near you.' Harriet, too, could see herself settling down in a provincial town. 'Make it a cathedral town,' she said. 'What about Salisbury?'

'You goose, Salisbury has no university. I'm afraid we'll all end up in somewhere grimmer than that.'

Harriet was the only visitor admitted to the Royal Suite. News that the runaways had returned, bringing Harriet with them, had been spread by the wedding guests. When it was known that Angela and Castlebar were living in opulent seclusion at the top of the Semiramis, Angela's old friends called at the hotel but were turned away.

Angela said: 'One of them might prove to be Bill's wife in disguise. She'd do anything to get in here. Even dress up as a man.'

'With her figure,' said Harriet, 'she'd look extremely odd.'

'Still, I'm not risking it. I've got Bill in safe-keeping and that's where he's going to stay.'

'For how long?'

'As long as need be. If she gets in here, it'll be over my dead body.'

The suite was air-conditioned and during the fiery days of summer, while the British and American forces occupied Sicily, Angela and Castlebar scarcely moved from their retreat. The windows were fitted with jalousies in the far-eastern manner. During the day, while the city shimmered in a glare of sunlight, the rooms were shaded and the occupants as cool as sea-creatures in a rock pool.

The hotel servants, heavily tipped, would allow no intruder to reach the suite. Harriet they saw as belonging to it and she came and went as she pleased. She need no longer spend her evenings alone in Garden City. When the sun began to sink, she could take the riverside walk to the hotel and join her friends on the top floor for a drink, for supper, for as long as she cared to stay. As the heat slackened, a safragi came to pull back the jalousies and they could watch for the pyramids on the western horizon. When it became dark, the safragi returned to open the windows and admit the evening air.

It was a pleasant routine but on the night that Italy surrendered, there was a disturbing break. When Harriet arrived, Castlebar was not in the long chair with his drink and cigarettes, but sprawled on the bed with Angela pouring iced water for him and persuading him to take two aspirin.

'What is wrong with Bill?'

'He has a headache. I think we've been shut in here too long. He needs a change of scene. Why don't we all go out for a drive?' Angela, looking anxiously at him, put her hand to his brow: 'Better?'

He gave her a languid smile: 'A little better.' He had taken the aspirin and after a while said: 'The pain's lifting. We'll go out if you like.'

A gharry was sent for and they drove by the river beneath the glowing sky. As they turned on to Bulacq Bridge, boys jumped on to the gharry steps and offered them necklaces made of jasmin flowers. Begging and laughing, they swung the heavily scented necklaces into Castlebar's face and Castlebar, usually amused by this sort of play, shuddered back: 'Tell them to go away.'

Angela paid off the boys then asked: 'Where shall we go?' When Castlebar said he did not care, she turned to Harriet who remembered an excavated village she had seen during her first days in Cairo. She said: 'If we drive to the pyramids, I'll show you something you've never seen before.'

They passed through the delicate evening scent of the bean fields out to Mena where the pyramids stood and beyond them to the desert that stretched away to the horizon. Angela said: 'Surely there's nothing to see here?'

'Wait.' Harriet stopped the gharry and Angela descended with her, but Castlebar shook his head. Smiling slightly, he put his face against the grimy padding at the back of the seat and closed his eyes.

The two women crossed the flat, stony mardam and reached a depression that was invisible from the road. Below they could see a whole village of narrow streets and empty, roofless houses that had been excavated from the sand.

Angela jumped down at once and said: 'Let's explore.' Watching her, Harriet felt an odd apprehension. She and the others had been shown this village on the day Angela's child had died. Putting this from her, she followed Angela. They wandered about the lanes and looked into small rooms, amazed that lives had once been lived here in these confined quarters. They asked each other why this isolated village should exist at all, without water or any reason for being there.

'But, of course,' Angela said, 'before the dam was built, the Nile would have come very near. There could have been cultivated land here. Or, more likely, the people who lived here built the pyramids. You know they were not slaves as scholars once thought. They were peasants, ordinary workmen, doing a job for a daily wage. And they were fed on onions and radishes – not much of a diet, if you had to lug blocks of stone about.'

The twilight had begun to fall between the houses and as the women returned to the road, a wind sprang up and sand hit their faces. They started to run as the storm roared upon them, the sand grains striking into their flesh and blinding them. Clinging together, lost in the dark enveloping sand, they heard the gharry driver shouting to them above the noise of the wind.

They found Castlebar still lying back, eyes closed, unaware of sand and wind, while the driver gestured wildly, warning them that they must get back before the road was covered. Castlebar did not move and Angela, sitting close to him, lifting his limp hand, said: 'The aspirin have made him sleepy.' At Mena, she said they must go into the cloakroom and tidy themselves before facing the guests in the Semiramis foyer. In the cloakroom, the women looked at each other, seeing their faces coated with a grey mask of sand. Angela threw back her head with a howl of laughter and it was to be a very long time before Harriet heard her laugh again.

At the Semiramis, Castlebar said he did not want supper. He would go straight to bed.

'But you'll have a whisky, won't you?'

'No, I don't fancy it. I might take a drop of vodka.'

'Oh well, so long as you have something!' Angela was relieved.

Food for Harriet and Angela was sent up to the living-room. As they ate, Angela said: 'It's probably just a touch of gyppy. What should he take, do you think?'

Harriet recalled all the remedies that were part of the mythology of the Middle East. She recommended that great comforter Dr Collis Browne's Chlorodyne, but it was not easy to find. One cure was to eat only apples and bananas and drink a mixture of port and brandy. Then there was kaolin, intended to block the gut, but a more rapid cure, in Harriet's opinion, was a spoonful of Dettol taken neat.

'Neat?'

'Yes. It's not difficult to swallow, and it's nice and warming.'

'I'd never get Bill to swallow it.' Angela sent down for apples, bananas, port and brandy and when they arrived, said: 'Let's go and look at him and see what he'll take.'

Castlebar, in bed, his throat visible above his pyjama jacket, looked gaunt and tired but not seriously ill. Harriet left early and Angela, walking with her to the lift, said: 'Do you think it might be jaundice? A lot of officers have had it. He might have picked it up in one of these low bars.'

'Good heavens, does he go to bars?'

'I know he sneaks out when I'm in the bath. Poor old thing, he wants a drink with the boys. I don't say anything.'

Harriet agreed with Angela that Castlebar would be all right in a day or two, but two days passed and his condition was unchanged. He was indifferent to food, and nauseated by the things that had once pleased him most. And there were other symptoms.

Castlebar did not want company so Angela now came down to sit with Harriet in the foyer or the dining-room. She said: 'His temperature goes up and down; up in the evening and down in the morning. He says his tum is sore. He doesn't like me to touch it. I want him to see a doctor but he says "No".'

'Gyppy is painful, you know.'

'His stomach is not so much painful as tender, and it's swollen – or, rather, it's puffy.'

'It could be food poisoning.'

'I thought of that. He sometimes slips into a place that sells shell-fish. I've told him not to touch it but he doesn't always do what he's told.'

At the end of a week Castlebar had developed a rash that covered his chest and belly and Angela, now agitated, rang Harriet and said he must see a doctor whether he liked it or not.

She shouted into the telephone: 'It could be smallpox.'

'No. Believe me, he'd be much more ill. He'd have high fever and be delirious; and he'd be vomiting. I know because I read it up when I was in quarantine.'

'He has been vomiting. Oh God, Harriet, what am I to do?'

'Is he well enough to walk? Could we get him into a taxi?'

'Yes, he goes to the bathroom. He even took a few bites of chicken at lunch time.' Angela's voice shook with the attempt to reassure herself: 'He says he's not ill, only not well.'

'Then let's take him to Shafik at the American Hospital. Shafik is a good doctor; he'll set your mind at rest.'

'You'll come with me?'

'Of course I'll come with you. Get him dressed and I'll be round by the time you're ready to go.'

Harriet was uneasy, less for Castlebar who might not be very ill, than for Angela who had known despair and could not face it again. Harriet had seen her in a state of anxiety that was near frenzy and knew that at such moments she was, as Guy maintained, crazy. It was important to get Castlebar's illness diagnosed before Angela again lost control of her reason.

She took a taxi to the hotel and waited in the hall. As Castlebar came from the lift, she was shocked by the sight of him. He could walk, but with the shuffle of an old man, leaning on Angela who was maintaining a precarious calm. He looked weary beyond endurance. The sweat of exhaustion beaded his face and when Harriet spoke to him, he could scarcely lift the lids from his sunken eyes. He smiled at her but it was a weak and frightened smile.

The porter took his arm and helped him to the taxi. Angela, following behind, whispered to Harriet: 'His temperature's up again. It's 102°.'

Harriet said: 'That's not bad,' but she knew it was bad enough.

The white hospital building and the avenue of gum trees glimmering in the afternoon sun gave them the sense that all would now be well. There would be no more doubts and confusion of hope and dread. Help was at hand. Castlebar's ailment, whatever it was, would be treated and cured.

The hospital porter, opening the taxi door, insisted that the patient must stay where he was till a wheel-chair was brought for him. Then, with the sympathy that the Egyptian poor show to the sick, three male nurses came out to lift him into the chair. Castlebar tried to grin, suggesting that all this attention was a joke, and inside the hospital, took out his cigarettes but did not try to light one.

Harriet sent her name up to Dr Shafik. Shafik came down at once, his handsome face beaming with astonished delight: 'How is it you are here, Mrs Pringle? Have you been so quickly to England and back again? Or did you decide you could not leave your Dr Shafik after all?' He was eager to renew their past flirtatious relationship but Harriet was too worried to respond to him. She said: 'Dr Shafik, I've brought my friends to you because they need your help.'

Shafik turned to observe Harriet's friends and his manner changed at once. He crossed to Castlebar, stared at him and asked: 'How long has he been like this?'

Angela said: 'About ten days.'

'He should have been brought here sooner.'

'What is it?' Angela's voice was shrill with alarm: 'What is the matter? What can you do for him?'

'That, madam, I do not know.' Shafik had reverted to the iron-ical formality that was his professional manner. 'We must make tests. May I ask: are you his wife? No? I understand. Well, it is necessary that he remain here and when his malady is known, we will do what we can.'

'May I stay with him?'

'No, no. Impossible. He must be alone. He needs rest and quiet.'

Castlebar, languishing in his chair, showed no awareness of what was being said. He did not open his eyes or move as Angela clung to him for some moments before he was wheeled away. The chair was put into a lift. Angela stood so long, staring as the lift rose up out of sight, that Harriet put an arm round her shoul-der: 'Angela dear, I think we should go.'

'Go? Go where?'

'We could have tea at Groppi's and then come back and ask if there's any news!'

'No, I can't leave here. I must stay until I know what is wrong with him.' She looked round for Shafik but Shafik had left them. 'Stay with me,' she said to Harriet.

At the farther end of the hall there was a waiting area where french windows opened on to the hospital grounds. The grounds joined up with the Gezira polo fields and they sat and stared out at the great vista of grassland that floated and wavered in the haze of heat. Angela, by nature a restless woman, was so still that no creak came from the basket chair in which she sat.

Harriet, remembering how long she had had to wait for the result of her own tests, said: 'You probably won't hear anything until tomorrow or even the day after.'

Angela turned her head slowly and looked at Harriet, her eyes glazed and uncomprehending. So they sat on. Sister Metrebian, who had nursed Harriet through amœbic dysentery, came down to speak with her: 'But you are looking very well!'

Harriet, rising and leading the nurse away from Angela, whispered: 'The new patient – is he as ill as he looks?'

'Yes, he is ill, but it is for Dr Shafik to say. He must first make the diagnosis.'

'What do you think yourself?'

Sister Metrebian shook her head and was soon gone, unwilling to talk. Angela and Harriet sat in silence until six o'clock when the porter told Angela she might go to Castlebar's room. While she was away, Shafik came and spoke to Harriet in a subdued voice: 'Mrs Pringle, you must look after your friend. She is, I think, of an hysterical temperament and will need support. I have allowed her to see the patient but I cannot let you go up. You have been ill too recently. You must not risk an infection.'

'What infection? What is wrong with him?'

'I cannot say yet. He has what is called the "typhoid" state. That is: he has a fever, rapid pulse, low blood pressure and other symptoms we will not speak of.'

Harriet could guess that the other symptoms were, in Shafik's opinion, either too distasteful or too profound for the female mind. Cutting through his constraint, she said: 'So he has typhoid?'

'I did not say so. He has been ill only ten days. It is the second week which is critical.'

'Poor Angela, what can I do for her? She will be beside herself.'

'I will prescribe sedatives. I have told her nothing but if she suspects, you can say that typhoid is endemic here and we know how to treat it. Tell me, do you know, has Mr Castlebar been injected against typhoid?'

'He probably was when he first came out. We're supposed to have a booster each year but I'm afraid most of us forget.'

'So I feared. Mrs Pringle, you and your friend must go today to the Out Patients' Department and be given an anti-typhoid injection. You, please, go now and I will send your friend to join you.'

*

Angela, sedated, remained as though benumbed until the end of the second week when she telephoned Harriet and begged her in a frantic whisper: 'Come, Harriet, come at once.'

It was nine in the morning and Harriet asked: 'Come where?'

'To the hospital.'

'What has happened?'

'You will see when you come.'

Harriet, her taxi delayed again and again by the early morning traffic, was taut with apprehension. Shafik had said the second week was critical but typhoid, notorious for its long fever, was not necessarily fatal. In spite of Angela's entreating tone, she could not believe that Castlebar was dead. As she entered the main hospital door, Angela rushed at her and said hoarsely: 'That woman! That terrible woman!' She pointed to the waiting area where a woman was sitting, upright and purposeful, her massive, tubular legs planted so she could rise in an instant.

Harriet recognized the red hair that accentuated the clammy pallor of the face: 'Mona Castlebar! How long has she been here?'

'She was here when I came this morning. As soon as she saw me, she bawled: "Clear out, you bitch, you're nothing better than a whore." She tried to push me out through the door but I fought back and the porter went to fetch Shafik. Shafik ordered us both out. She said she'd fetch the consul to prove that she's Bill's legal wife and Shafik said he didn't care what she was, she must go. But she wouldn't go and I wouldn't go, either. Bill needs me. He's mine. I can't be kept from him. Harriet, Shafik's your friend. He'll listen to you. Please, Harriet, *please* go and explain that Bill left that woman months ago. She has no right to claim him. He never wants to see her again.'

'But is he well enough to see anyone?'

'The sister says he's a bit better today. I know if that woman forces her way in on him, he'll have a relapse. Oh, Harriet, please go.'

Harriet found Shafik still indignant at the uproar caused by the two women. Before she could speak, he shouted at her: 'So Mr Castlebar has two wives! That is nothing to me. He can have three. If he is rich enough, he can have all the prophet allows, but he is a sick man. I will not allow these ladies to come and disturb him.'

'Is he very sick?'

'Yes, he is very sick. He is now entering the third week and any day there will come the crisis. There could be perforation, peritonitis, pneumonia, cardiac failure – all such things are brought on by shock. These ladies must be kept from him.'

'But his wife! Can she be kept out – legally, I mean? She has threatened to call the British Consul to establish her rights.'

Dr Shafik, angry that the consul or anyone else might try to broach his authority, brought his hand down on his desk: 'In a case of life or death, the doctor's decision is final.'

'Dr Shafik, I'd be grateful if you'd let Lady Hooper just look in on him. She will be quiet, I promise you. They love one another. The sight of her will help him.'

Shafik, placated as Arabs usually were by a suggestion of romance, reflected for a moment then said: 'Very well. If you take her to the back entrance, I will send the porter to show her to his room. She will have five minutes, no more.'

Returning to the hall, Harriet said: 'Come, Angela, there is no point in staying here.' Angela, realizing that this summons meant more than was said, followed Harriet out to the porch and gazed hopefully at her.

'Back entrance. He's letting you see Bill for five minutes.'

Angela held on to Harriet's hand as they went up the staff staircase and were led to the door of Castlebar's room. As the door opened, Harriet had a glimpse of the patient propped up with pillows, ice bags on his head and brow, his eyes shut, his skin yellow, his face drawn. A low muttering was coming from his lips that hung open, swollen, cracked and dark with fever.

The door was shut behind Angela and Sister Metrebian stood guard before it.

Harriet said: 'Lady Hooper told me he is a little better today.'

'Not much better. His temperature will not come down. That is bad.'

'Is he in pain?'

Sister Metrebian put her thin little hand on to her abdomen: 'He is . . . pouf!' She moved her hand out to show how Castlebar's middle was distended: 'Here is discomfort.'

'Poor Bill!' Harriet said, thinking of his gentle compliance with

Angela's demands, his kindness and his sympathy: 'Will he recover?'

'I cannot say.'

Angela came out, too perturbed to weep, and Harriet led her down to the taxi. Put to bed in the Royal Suite, she lay so long silent that Harriet thought she was asleep and began to leave. Alert at once, she said: 'Don't go, Harriet, don't go.' She rang down for smoked salmon and a bottle of white wine. When it was brought up, she refused to eat.

'No, Harriet, it is for you.'

She lay as before until late in the afternoon when the telephone rang. The hospital porter had promised to keep in touch with her. After a few words, she replaced the receiver with a sigh.

'How is he, Angela?'

'No change.' After another period of silence, she raised herself on her elbow and said in a firm, clear voice: 'He will get better. I have faith. They say if you have faith, you can move mountains. I have profound faith.'

Angela was not allowed in to see Castlebar again. The porter, who rang two or three times a day, told her that Mrs Castlebar was always at the hospital but excluded from the sick room. Three days after Angela's profession of faith, it seemed that faith had prevailed. The porter told Angela that the patient's temperature had fallen at last. It was under 100°.

Angela, in a state of euphoria, telephoned Harriet, who was at breakfast, and told her to come at once to the hotel. She was to bring a taxi and together they would enter the hospital by the back door and, unknown to Shafik and unseen by Mona, make their way to Castlebar's room.

As soon as she saw Harriet, Angela began to talk at manic speed, and went on talking all the way to the hospital, planning Castlebar's convalescence. They would go back to Cyprus and stay at Kyrenia in the Dome, or perhaps he would prefer to remain in Famagusta where the sands were perfect and white lilies grew on the dunes. Or they might go to Paphos where Venus rose from the sea.

When they reached the corridor that led to Castlebar's room,

Angela came to a stop. Mona Castlebar was stationed outside the door. Angela, pulling Harriet round a corner, out of sight, said: 'Get her away somehow. Tell her Shafik wants her in his office.'

'Wouldn't she wonder what I was doing here?'

'You can tell her you were a patient here once. You've come in for a check-up. Go on, *do*!'

'She wouldn't believe me.'

'She would. Oh, Harriet, get rid of her. Flatter her, charm her, fool her for my sake.'

'For your sake, then . . .'

Harriet approached Mona with a smiling attempt at friendliness: 'I hear Bill is improving. I'm so glad.'

'I don't know who told you that.' There was cold aggression in Mona's tone but before anything more could be said, Sister Metrebian came from the room.

Harriet asked her: 'How is Mr Castlebar?'

Sister Metrebian answered gravely: 'He is in the operating theatre. The bowel perforated. He was in much pain. I heard him cry out and went at once to Dr Shafik. Now they perform the laparotomy.'

'So he has a chance?'

'A chance, yes. There was no delay.'

Mona, asserting her position as Castlebar's wife, said: 'I was allowed in for a minute but he did not recognize me.'

Which was as well, Harriet thought. Aloud she said for the sake of saying something: 'Do you think he'll get better?'

'Your guess is as good as mine.' Mona's manner was suitably serious but she could not suppress a hint of triumph, a twitch of satisfaction that Angela should lose out in this way.

Harriet returned to Angela who was avid for news of her lover: 'He's not in his room.'

'Why? Where is he? He's not dead, is he?'

'No. We can't talk here. Mona is full of suspicion. I'll tell you outside.'

Standing under the gum trees that shivered and glistened in the early sunlight, Harriet said: 'They're having to operate. There was no delay – Sister Metrebian says he stands a chance . . .' As Angela's lips trembled, Harriet added: 'A *good* chance.'

'What shall I do? What *can* I do?'

'Angela dear, you can't do anything. Only wait.'

'Stay with me, Harriet.'

'Of course I will stay,' Harriet said.

Castlebar died just after three a.m. the following morning.

The porter, when he telephoned Angela the previous evening, said: 'Mis' Castlebar not so well,' and Angela, going at once to the hospital, was told that Mona had been admitted to the sick room. Angela herself was refused entry. Prepared for any contingency, Mona had obtained from the consul written confirmation that she was Castlebar's legal wife. She must be permitted to visit him and in the event of his death, she alone had the right to dispose of his remains. Angela, having no rights at all, walked back to her hotel.

Dobson, as usual the first to hear whatever news there was, received from the consul an entertaining account of 'the whole damn fool imbroglio – two women squabbling over a dying man. And one of them no less a person than Lady Hooper. Now that he's gone, he's eluded both of them but Mrs C will be awarded the cadaver.'

Harriet felt it unlikely that the porter, with the Arab dislike of conveying bad news, had told Angela that Castlebar was dead. Harriet went at once to the Royal Suite and found Angela lying, fully dressed and awake, on the bed.

'What have you come to tell me, Harriet?'

'I'm afraid you've guessed right.'

'He's dead?'

Harriet nodded. Angela stared at her with an expression of distraught vacancy bereft, it seemed, of anything that made life possible. Knowing there could be no comfort in anything she might say, Harriet sat on the edge of the bed and held out her arms. Angela collapsed against her.

Harriet remained with her till late in the evening. For most of the time Angela lay as though in a stupor but twice she started to talk, rapidly, almost vivaciously, going over the details of Castlebar's illness and its possible cause.

'The shellfish! If I had been with him, he would be alive now. But, who knows, it may not have been the shellfish. Yet I'm sure it was the shellfish . . .'

When she lapsed into silence the second time, Harriet persuaded her to undress and take her sedative tablets. Leaving her sleeping, Harriet walked to Garden City by the river and was astonished to find Mona Castlebar with Dobson in the living-room. She had a drink in her hand and from her manner, seemed to see it as a gala occasion. Having no one else on whom to impose herself, she had come to the flat, ostensibly seeking advice about the funeral.

Had Castlebar died anywhere but in the American Hospital, he would have been already buried. The hospital, with all its modern equipment, had a refrigerated mortuary cabinet and there the dead man could stay till Mona claimed him.

This, she said, was very satisfactory. She would have time to arrange a funeral befitting a well-known poet and university lecturer.

'The service will be in the cathedral, of course. Fully choral. I'm having invitations printed but these will only go out to a select few. If other people want to attend, they can sit at the back. Now, as to timing, I suggest we have the coffin carried in about mid-day then allow an interval of, say, fifteen minutes, after which I'll walk slowly up the aisle. There should be someone for me to lean on,' Mona glanced at Harriet, 'Guy would do.'

Harriet did not speak. Dobson, who had maintained a decorous face until then, could scarcely keep from laughing: 'My dear lady, this is a funeral, not a wedding. If you must make an entrance, you should come in immediately after the coffin.'

Mona's face fell. She tried to argue but had in the end to agree that Dobson, an authority on protocol, probably knew best.

Angela, to Harriet's surprise, wanted to attend the funeral service. 'I must go. Of course I must. What would Bill think if he didn't see me there? You'll come and call for me, won't you? We'll go together.'

Harriet, calling for Angela, found her in a short dress that looked too fashionably chic for a funeral.

She said: 'It's my only black. I know it's not suitable, but what does it matter? I suppose I'll have to wear a hat!' She pulled a milliner's box from the wardrobe and brought out a wide-brimmed hat of black lace trimmed with pink roses: 'This will do, won't it?' She sat it on her head without looking in her glass. 'Is it all right?' she turned to Harriet, her face red, swollen and dejected beneath the pretty hat.

'It will do,' Harriet said.

In the cathedral, the three front rows of pews were filled by Mona's selected guests: a few members of the embassy staff and some senior lecturers from the university.

Guy, though he had received an invitation, had chosen to sit at the back and Harriet and Angela sat beside him. Almost at once the congregation rose. There was a shuffle of feet in the porch, then the coffin began its journey down the aisle. Mona's invitations had said 'No flowers by request' but did not state whose request. Her own wreath, a large cross of red carnations, was conspicuous on the coffin lid. As Dobson had directed, she followed the coffin in, walking slowly, her head bowed, her legs hidden by a black velvet evening skirt that crawled like a snake on the ground behind her. Her corsage revealed to advantage her broad, heavily powdered shoulders and full bosom.

Guy, his face taut with distaste, whispered: 'If she were a better actress, she'd manage to squeeze out a tear.'

Angela remained calm until the cortège reached her then, looking askance, seeing the coffin a few inches from her, she broke into agonized sobs that could be heard beneath the thumping and grinding of the organ. There was some furtive glancing back by the distinguished guests in the front row. Aware of nothing but her own grief, Angela sank down to her seat and buried her face in her hands, abandoning herself to heart-broken weeping that went on throughout the service.

The service over, Mona left the cathedral in front of the coffin, her head now raised to denote a ceremony completed. As the seats emptied, Guy and Harriet remained with Angela, making no move until it seemed likely that the hearse would have set out for the English cemetery. But Mona was in no hurry to curtail her advantage as hostess. When Guy supported Angela out to the porch, the hearse still stood by the kerb while Mona moved about among her select guests. She had found no one to escort her behind the coffin but there were several prepared to companion her for an evening's drinking. She gave a quick, elated glance at Angela's bedraggled hat and defeated figure, then she seized Guy by the arm: 'You're coming to Mahdi, aren't you?'

Guy excused himself, saying he had an appointment at the Institute.

She still held to him: 'You know there's to be an evening reception, don't you? I've arranged for a tent to be put up behind Suleiman Pasha. I thought we'd get our first at the Britannia Bar then move on to Groppi's and the George V, and reach the reception about six o'clock. You can pick us up somewhere, can't you?'

Though Harriet and Angela were standing on either side of him, Mona made it clear that the invitation was for Guy alone. He muttered discouragingly: 'I'll come if I can.'

The hearse was an old Rolls-Royce decorated with black ostrich plumes and black cherubs holding aloft black candles. Angela kept her eyes on the coffin with its great carnation wreath and as the equipage moved off, stared after it as though by staring she could bring Castlebar back alive.

Watching the string of cars that took Mona and her guests away, Harriet said: 'She's spending a lot of money, isn't she?'

Guy told her: 'It's all on the university. She's not only getting her widow's pension but a large grant from funds. She's had to put up some sort of show, and she thinks Bill would have wanted it.'

Guy conducted the women to the Semiramis and left them there. Harriet sat in the shuttered gloom of the Royal Suite, keeping watch over Angela, imagining she had no consciousness of time, but at exactly six o'clock, she sat up: 'Let's go and look at the reception tent.'

Still in her black dress but without a hat, Angela held to Harriet's hand as they went in a gharry through the crowded streets. The fog of heat still hung in the air. The faded pink of the evening sky was streaked with violet. It was the time when windows, unnoticed during the day, were lighted up, revealing a world of mysterious life behind the dusty, gimcrack façades of buildings. For Angela none of this existed. There were no crowds, no sky, no windows, no life of any kind. She sat limp, waiting to see the tent, the last vestige of the lover she had lost.

The tent was not easy to find. There were a number of small midans behind Suleiman Pasha and the gharry wandered around, up one lane and down another, until at last they came on it: a very large, square, canvas tent appliquéd all over with geometrical designs and flowers cut from coloured cloth. The flap was tied back to catch what air there was and the two women could see something of the interior. Carpets overlapped each other on the ground and there were a great many small gilt chairs. The scene was lit by the greenish glow of butane gas. The guests were near the open flap. There were not many of them and those that Harriet recognized were the hardened remnants of Mona's drinking acquaintances. She could see Cookson with his hangers-on Tootsie and Taupin. Then, to her surprise, an unlikely figure moved into sight.

'Look who's there – Jake Jackman!'

Angela did not care who was there. She stared at the tent and beyond the tent into emptiness, her face a mask of hopeless longing.

When Mona came near the entrance, her black hem still snaking after her, Harriet felt they had better go. They drove back to the hotel where Angela refused to eat but, worn out by despair, went willingly to bed.

Harriet, walking home, met Major Cookson and Tootsie. Cookson was in a nervous state and very eager to talk: 'My dear, the funeral! It began so well but ended, I fear, on an unpleasant note.' He told her that Mona, finding she was entertaining not the select few but Jake Jackman and others like him, became bored and resentful. She allowed them a couple of drinks each then told them if they wanted any more, they would have to pay for them.

'Dear me!' said Cookson. 'What a scene! Just imagine how Jake reacted to such an announcement! I am afraid there was a bit of a fracas. Tootsie and I felt it better to leave.'

'What was Jake Jackman doing there? Is he back for good?'

'Well, no. To tell you the truth, he's being sent to England under open arrest. He's to go on the next troopship.'

'What do you think will happen to him there?'

'I don't know. Probably nothing very much.'

Returning to the Royal Suite next morning, Harriet found

Angela surrounded by all her sumptuous luggage and clothing. She was attempting to pack and said: 'I can't stand this room a moment longer. It's so . . . so vacant. I haven't slept all night. The place depresses me. I really hate it. Look at that beastly view. I'm sick of the sight of it.'

'Where will you go?'

'God knows. Nobody needs me now.'

'Angela, I need you.'

Angela shook her head, not believing her, and Harriet said: 'Come back to Garden City with me. Your room is just as you left it. There's only Guy and Dobson now and if you don't come, I'll be alone most evenings. So, you see, I need you. Will you come?'

'Would Dobson have me back?'

'You know he would. Will you come?'

Angela dropped the clothes she was holding and sighed. Like a lost and trusting child, she put out her hand, 'Yes, if you want me. You know, this is the end of my life. No one will ever love me again.'

'I love you.' Feeling that enough had been said, Harriet stuffed the clothes into the gilt-bound crocodile and pigskin cases then rang down to the porter and ordered two gharries. When Angela first arrived in Garden City she had brought two gharries, one to take her excess luggage, and she would return with two gharries.

Awad spent the morning piling the cases under the window in Angela's old room that looked out on the great, round head of a mango tree. The air was very hot and filled with the scent of drying grass.

'Home again,' Harriet said.

Angela smiled and, putting her head down on the pillow she had so often shared with Castlebar, she said: 'I think I can sleep now,' and closed her eyes and slept.

Twenty-two

It was some days before Guy, wrapped up in his many interests, realized that Angela had become a permanent inmate of the flat. He had seen her at mealtimes and had imagined she was seeking the consolation of company: then he met her coming out of the bathroom wrapped up in a towel and it occurred to him to ask Harriet: 'Is that crazy woman back here for good?'

'If you mean Angela – yes, she is.'

'How did she manage that? I'm sure you didn't encourage her?'

'I did encourage her. In fact, I persuaded her to come.'

'Then you must be as mad as she is. She took poor Bill Castlebar away and finished him off. Heaven knows what she will do to you.'

Guy was angry but Harriet was not affected by his anger. She said firmly: 'Angela helped me when I needed help; now, if I can, I'll help her. So don't try and influence me against her. You have your friends; let me have mine.'

Guy was startled by her tone and she remembered how Angela had advised her to box his ears. And that, in a sense, was what she had done. After his first surprise, he was clearly uncertain how to deal with the situation. Harriet was moving out from under his influence. She had gone away once and had, apparently, managed very well on her own. He was unnerved by the possibility she might go away again. Even more unnerving was the possibility that Angela, who had taken Castlebar from him, should now attempt to steal Harriet.

He said: 'Apart from anything else, Angela is rich. She's used to a completely different way of life. It would be a mistake to put too much trust in a woman like that. Sooner or later, she'll go off as she did last time.'

Guy waited for Harriet to relinquish her independent attitude

189

and agree with him, but she did not agree. She said nothing and Guy, taking hold of her hands, felt it best to be generous: 'I know you are lonely sometimes and if you're fond of Angela and feel she's a friend, well and good. But don't forget our life will change when the war ends. It will all be different then. I'll have much more free time and we'll do everything together.'

'Will we?' Harriet doubtfully asked.

'Of course we will.' Lifting her hands to his lips, he murmured: 'Little monkey's paws!' Then remembering some pressing business elsewhere, he put them down, saying: 'I have to go but don't worry; I won't be late.'

Twenty-three

It was mid-September before Simon was declared fit for active service. Impatient and eager for action, he went straight from the MO's office to his ward and started to put his belongings together. He wanted to leave the hospital at once but would have to stay until he was posted somewhere.

Greening, who had been waiting for him, said: 'We'll be sorry to see you go, sir,' but Simon was too excited to regret his separation from Greening or anyone else.

Laughing, he said: 'This time next week, I'll be in the thick of it.'

'I wouldn't bank on that, sir. The MO recommends you take it easy for a bit. They'll find you a nice, cushy office job, I expect.'

'Not for me. "Active service" means "active service" and that's what I want. I've been pampered long enough.'

'Don't forget we had to remake you – that takes time.'

'I'll tell them I've been remade good as new. I need a fresh start. Fresh country. I've had enough of Egypt.'

The country Simon had in mind was Italy. Recently Allied forces had landed near Reggio, taking the precaution to come ashore in the middle of the night. It proved unnecessary for the Italians were only waiting to surrender. As a result the Germans occupied Rome, sank their battleship, the *Roma*, and sent the whole Italian fleet full speed for Malta.

Italy was where things were happening. It was the place for Simon. Ordered to Movement Control, he said gleefully to Greening: 'I know a chap there who'll wangle anything for me.'

The chap was Perry, a fat, jovial major, smelling of whisky, to whom Simon had had to report the day after Tobruk fell. Impressed by his youth and eager desire to reach the front, Perry had promised to send him into the desert 'at the double'.

The promise had been kept. Perry would see to it that Simon was properly fixed up.

But times had changed. Army personnel had been cut to a minimum and many offices had closed. Movement Control, once at Helwan, was now in Abbasia Barracks again and Simon found that Major Perry had been posted to Bari. The middle-aged captain who interviewed him was far from jovial. He stared a long time at the medical report and said: 'I see you're down for an office job, Mr Boulderstone.'

'Well, sir, I'd much rather see some action. I'm no good at office work and I'm perfectly fit. I want to be back in the fight.'

The captain, not unsympathetic, gave him a glance: 'You look all right to me, but we've got to fall in with the MO's advice. We've arranged for you to go to Ordnance. Stationery Office. You won't find it too bad.'

'How long will I have to stay there, sir?'

'Not long. It's just a token job. Anyway, we'll all be out of here soon.'

Appeased, Simon asked for accommodation in the barracks and was given a room identical with that he had occupied on his first night in Egypt: bare, with three camp beds and reeking of fumigating smoke. The sense of life repeating itself made him the more determined to get away.

Simon was now drawn to the Garden City flat, no longer in hope of seeing Edwina, but because it was the only place he could call a home.

Guy and Harriet had taken over Edwina's room at the end of the corridor, which for months remained redolent of Edwina's gardenia scent, and Harriet suggested that Simon move into their old room. He said: 'It's not worth the bother. I'll be off any day now.'

She knew what he meant for they all felt themselves transient, living on expectations though not knowing what to expect. The events that occurred about them no longer related to them. Like the captain at Abbasia Barracks, they all believed they would be 'out of here soon'.

Edwina came only once to the flat after her marriage. Finding Dobson and Harriet in the living-room, she confided to them that

Tony was a bore with no sense of fun and, giggling ruefully, she said she was already pregnant. After she left, Dobson shook his head sadly: 'I suppose that accounts for the hasty marriage! Poor girl! To think that men once waved guns about and threatened to kill for her sake, and here she is stuck with a dull dog like Tony Brody!'

'I don't imagine she'll be stuck for very long,' Harriet said. 'I bet, once the baby's born, she'll find another major; one with a more highly developed sense of fun. But *did* men threaten to kill for her sake?'

'I believe someone waved a gun about once, but it was a long time ago, when she was eighteen and quite exquisite.'

Dobson stared unseeing, distracted by the memory, and Harriet marvelled that beneath his ironical sufferance of Edwina's foibles, he had kept hidden this knowledge of her dramatic past.

Simon's job, that he described as 'stamp licking', did not last long. Early in October he was ordered to Alexandria to take charge of two hundred men bound for an unnamed destination. So far as Simon was concerned there could be only one possible destination. He would be off to Italy at last.

Guy, who went to the station with him, said: 'I envy you going to Alex at this time of the year,' but Simon, all prepared to fight his way up to Rome, had no interest in Alex. He was now a full lieutenant, rising into authority, but to Guy he was still a charge and one he did not want to lose.

'How long are you likely to be in Alex?'

'I don't know. Probably a week.'

'We might come up and see you.'

'Yes, do come.'

As the whistle blew, Guy put his hand on Simon's arm and Simon, covering it with his own hand, said: 'Thanks for everything.' It was a detached valediction – he felt as remote from Guy as he had from Greening – but to Guy it was gratitude enough. The visit to Alexandria, posed as a vague possibility, now became an imperative and as soon as he saw Harriet, he asked her to come with him. He was surprised that she did not immediately agree.

'You want to go, don't you?'

'I've wanted to go to a good many places since we married, but you've never had time to go with me.'

'Oh, darling, this is different. Don't be unreasonable. We may never see Simon again.'

They set out on the following Saturday, starting early when the light, now fading into the cool topaz of winter, gave a particular delicacy to the delta. Looking out at the belt of green cut into sections by glistening water channels, Harriet thought of their arrival in Egypt and said: 'Do you remember our first camel?'

Guy, intent on the *Egyptian Mail*, murmured 'Yes' and Harriet watched for a camel. One appeared, led by a boy on a very long rope. It moved slowly, planting leisurely feet into the dust beside the railway track, and slowed down when the rope was jerked, holding its head back, refusing to be hurried.

'Guy, look!'

Guy, coming out from behind the paper, adjusted his glasses and tried to see what she was showing him: 'You said something about our first camel – what did you mean?'

'Don't you remember? After we left the ship at Alex, when we were on the train, we saw a camel. Our first camel. It could have been the very same camel.' After a pause, she said: 'Egypt is beautiful,' and she felt sorry that they must one day part from it.

Guy laughed and went back to his paper and Harriet realized he could not see what was beyond the window. Beneath his confident belief in himself, beneath his certainty that he was loved and wanted wherever he went, he was deprived. She saw the world as a reality and he did not. She put her hand on his knee and he patted it and let it lie there, keeping his gaze on the lines of newsprint. Deprived or not, he was content; but was she content?

She was free to think her own thoughts. She could develop her own mind. Could she, after all, have borne with some possessive, interfering, jealous fellow who would have wanted her to account for every breath she breathed?

Not for long.

In an imperfect world, marriage was a matter of making do with what one had chosen. As this thought came into her head, she pressed Guy's knee and he patted her hand again.

Alexandria, when they arrived, was nothing like the city Harriet had visited during the 'flap'. Then, with the Afrika Korps one day's drive away, people were on edge, speaking German yet buying up food against a probable occupation, or else piling goods on cars, ready for a getaway. It had been a grey city under a grey sky, the shore deserted beside the grey, plashy sea. Now in the breezy, sparkling October air, people looked carefree, the most carefree being the young naval men still in their summer uniforms of white duck.

'I'm glad we came.'

Guy answered with serene certainty: 'I knew you would be.'

They were to meet Simon in the bar of the Cecil and they found him already there, a lone khaki figure among the naval crowd. He did his best to greet them cheerfully but they saw his spirits were low. Something, no doubt to do with his transfer, had disappointed him, but he was not free to speak of it and they were not free to question him. Though they might never see him again, there was nothing to talk about but the war and the Italian surrender.

To relieve the atmosphere of dejection, Harriet said: 'I think things will go our way in future.'

Simon asked: 'What makes you think that?'

'The Italians wouldn't have changed sides if they weren't pretty certain we'd win. Won't it be wonderful when the war ends? We'll be able to go wherever we like. Think of seeing Greece again!'

Struck by the mention of Greece, Simon said: 'You lived there, didn't you? What was it like?'

'We loved it.' Harriet turned to Guy: 'Do you remember how we climbed Pendeli on the day the Italians declared war?'

'Will I ever forget it?'

'Or those two old tramp steamers, the *Erebus* and *Nox*, that took us from the Piraeus? You sat on the deck singing: "If your engine cuts out over Hellfire Pass, you can stick your twin Browning guns right up your arse." Did you really think we'd make it?'

'Yes. I knew we'd make it somehow or other. We always do.'

Guy and Harriet smiled at each other, aware that they were joined by these shared memories and the memories would never be lost. Then Harriet looked at Simon for he, too, was part of their memories and they of his. She said: 'When we climbed the pyramid, the war was at its worst. Now it's turned round.'

'Yes, you're right. Things *are* going our way.' He laughed and for a moment he looked like the very young man of a year ago who, newly off a troopship, said of the desert: 'I don't know what it's like out there' and next day was sent to find out.

Then, giving his watch a glance, he sobered and stood up. 'I've got to rush. Sorry to leave you so soon, but we'll meet when it's all over.'

'Yes, when it's all over,' Guy and Harriet both agreed.

They watched him go. A shadow of anxiety had come down on his face and as he passed between the tables, he seemed older than the white-clad naval officers who might never have had a care in the world.

He went out through the door and the Pringles were left looking at the room's faded cream and gold, and its war-weary fawn carpet.

Guy dropped his gaze and sighed. There was another friend gone. As he called for the bill, he said: 'We might as well take the next train back to Cairo.'

Outside, where the light was deepening, they walked along the Corniche, watching the silver kidney shapes of the barrage balloons rising into position above the docks.

Putting his arm through Harriet's, Guy said: 'You'll never leave me again, will you?'

'Don't know. Can't promise.' Harriet laughed and squeezed his arm: 'Probably not.'

That morning, Simon had been briefed about his impending move. He was not, after all, conducting his men to Italy. They were bound for an island in the Aegean called Leros where they might never hear a shot fired.

Noting his downcast expression, the commanding officer said: 'This is an important assignment, Boulderstone. You'll be accompanied by a military mission with orders to put heart into the chaps on Leros.'

'I'd been hoping for a bit of a barney, sir.'

'You may well get it. The island is to be defended at all costs.'

Simon assented: 'Sir,' but he was not impressed. He was to be

196

marooned in the Aegean and likely to be left there till the war ended.

After his luncheon with the Pringles, he spent the rest of the day organizing his men and their equipment on to the destroyer. Told where they were going, the men grinned and one of them said: 'Piece of cake, sir.'

Remembering how Harriet had said of Greece, 'We loved it,' he began to think that Leros might not be so bad after all. The convoy that was taking provisions to the Leros garrison sailed at midnight. Standing at the rail of the destroyer, Simon watched the glimmer of the blacked-out shore, the last of Egypt. He felt he had left his youth behind and was taking with him nothing but his memory of Hugo; and even that was sinking back in his mind like a face disappearing under water.

'Not a lucky place,' he said aloud, then, tired from the day's activity, he took himself to his bunk.

Coda

Two more years were to pass before the war ended. Then, at last, peace, precarious peace, came down upon the world and the survivors could go home. Like the stray figures left on the stage at the end of a great tragedy, they had now to tidy up the ruins of war and in their hearts bury the noble dead.

Olivia Manning

Olivia Manning's *Balkan Trilogy* and *Levant Trilogy* form a single narrative entitled *Fortunes of War*, which Anthony Burgess described in the *Sunday Times* as 'the finest fictional record of the war produced by a British writer. Her gallery of personages is huge, her scene painting superb, her pathos controlled, her humour quiet and civilized. Guy Pringle is certainly one of the major characters in modern fiction.'

THE BALKAN TRILOGY:

THE GREAT FORTUNE
THE SPOILT CITY
FRIENDS AND HEROES

THE LEVANT TRILOGY:

THE DANGER TREE
THE BATTLE LOST AND WON
THE SUM OF THINGS

Also published in Penguins

SCHOOL FOR LOVE

In wartime children have to grow up quickly. One small boy, waiting to return to England, finds himself in Jerusalem in the care of Miss Bohun whose house offers a refuge to others washed up by the freak tides of destruction. There he can watch the unaccountable, wayward progress of the feeling called love – and there his real education in life can begin.

'Through the clear light of Miss Manning's sympathy ... we feel for this horror [Miss Bohun] some of that emotion, part amusement, part revulsion, part admiration for a triumphant assertion of life, that we feel for other comic horrors in literature, Tartuffe, Squeers, Mrs Proudie' – C. P. Snow in the *Sunday Times*

A Choice of Penguin Fiction

HOW FAR CAN YOU GO?
David Lodge

Winner of the Whitbread Book of the Year Award

How far could they go? On one hand there was the traditional Catholic Church, on the other the siren call of the permissive society. And with the advent of COC (Catholics for an Open Church), the social lubrication of the Pill and the disappearance of Hell, it was difficult for Polly, Dennis, Angela and the others not to rupture their spiritual virginity on the way to the seventies.

'Hilarious ... a magnificent book' – Graham Greene

OTHER PEOPLE: A MYSTERY STORY
Martin Amis

Huge acclaim for this sensational new novel by the author of *The Rachel Papers* and *Success* –

'Powerful and obsessive ... *Other People* is a metaphysical thriller, Kafka reshot in the style of *Psycho* ... a remarkable achievement' – J. G. Ballard in the *Tatler*

'Very funny ... It had me purring with pleasure' – *The Times*

'Without doubt Martin Amis's best' – William Boyd

CANNIBALS AND MISSIONARIES
Mary McCarthy

An Iran-bound Boeing is hijacked by terrorists. Their target is a group of prominent liberals, including a US senator, on their way to investigate human rights under the Shah. But 'the meringue on the pie' is the party of art-dealers in first class, millionaires embarking on a tour of Iran's galleries and museums.

As hostages and captors begin to collaborate in the struggle for survival, Mary McCarthy unleases a brilliant debate on our modern morality, the logic of violence, art values – and the value of art.

'A compelling read' – Martyn Goff in the *Daily Telegraph*

A Choice of Penguin Fiction

THE HEAT OF THE DAY
Elizabeth Bowen

Wartime London: and Stella's lover, Robert, is suspected of selling information to the enemy. Harrison, shadowing Robert, is nonetheless prepared to bargain, and the price is Stella.

Elizabeth Bowen writes of three people, estranged from the past and reluctant to trust in the future, with the psychological insight and delicate restraint that have earned her a position among the most distinguished novelists of the century.

A MONTH IN THE COUNTRY
J. L. Carr

Winner of the *Guardian* Fiction Prize

In the summer of 1920 two men meet in the quiet English countryside. One is a war survivor, living in the church, intent upon uncovering and restoring a historical wall-painting. The other, too, is a war survivor, camping in the next field in search of a lost grave. And out of their physical meeting comes a deeper communion, with the landscape, with history, and a catching-up of the old primeval rhythms of life – past and present – so cruelly disorientated by the Great War.

A PAINTED DEVIL
Rachel Billington

In this stark, chilling book, Rachel Billington explores the complexities of creative egotism and its power first to enchant its victims, and then to destroy them.

Edward is a painter. With the selfishness of a dedicated artist, he feeds upon the sufferings of others, unaware of the destruction and despair that crash around him.

And Florence in winter provides a setting for this story of two men and one woman, bound together in a strange love affair.

Also published in Penguins

THE SHOOTING PARTY
Isabel Colgate

Winner of the W. H. Smith Award

A group of men and women gather at Sir Randolph Nettleby's estate for a shooting party. Opulent, adulterous, moving assuredly through the rituals of feasting and slaughter, they are a dazzlingly obtuse and brilliantly decorative finale of an era. For it is 1913, and already change and violence have invaded the Elysian uplands of Edwardian England.

'Stylish, funny and infinitely subtle, it is as vivid and brilliant as a painting on glass' – *Daily Telegraph*

MOTHER'S HELPER
Maureen Freely

The Pyle-Carpenter household comes complete with three children who can do what they like as long as they have Thought It Through, an intercom that never turns off, with Weekly Family Councils and with the television padlocked into a bag. Like Kay Carpenter herself, it was a totally liberated, principled, caring, warm, nurturing nucleus ... And at first, Laura was completely fooled.

'A winner' – *The Times Literary Supplement*

'A novel to weep over or laugh with. Whichever will stop you going mad' – *Literary Review*

and, published in King Penguin

THE TRANSIT OF VENUS
Shirley Hazzard

Two sisters, Grace and Caro Bell, emigrate to England from Australia in the 1950s in search of their lives. Within the larger world of ideological clashes and social hunger, the sisters make their individual journeys towards middle age. For Caro, whose destiny is to love and be loved, the price includes betrayal. For, Grace, who risks less, knowledge tempered with anguish comes too late.

'An extraordinary book' – *Observer*

'Sumptuous ... impeccable' – *The Times*

THE WHITE HOTEL
D. M. Thomas

'This novel is a reminder that fiction can amaze' – *Time*

Interlacing history, lush sexuality, fantasy, psychological truth and the craving for brutality, *The White Hotel* explores the case-history of Lisa Erdman, a patient of Freud.

'A major artist has once more appeared ... the prose remains calm and precise but achieves ... such dreadful intensity that I could hardly bring myself to read it to the end' – *Spectator*

THE INFERNAL DESIRE MACHINES OF DOCTOR HOFFMAN
Angela Carter

Diabolic Doctor Hoffman wanted to demolish the structures of reason and liberate people from the chains of the reality principle for ever. He had chosen the human mind and the human heart for his battleground – and it was left to Desiderio to stop him.

'Combines exquisite craft with an apparently boundless reach' – Ian McEwan

CHRIST STOPPED AT EBOLI
The Story of a Year
Carlo Levi

'We're not Christians, Christ stopped short of here, at Eboli.' Exiled to a remote and barren corner of Italy for his opposition to Mussolini, Carlo Levi entered a world cut off from History and the State, hedged in by custom and sorrow. There, eternally patient, the peasants live in an age-old stillness and in the presence of death – for Christ did stop at Eboli.

'In turn a diary, an album of sketches, a novelette, a sociological study and a political essay ... a beautiful book' – *The New York Times Book Review*